Florine Thayer McCray, Esther Louise Smith

Wheels and Whims

An Etching

Florine Thayer McCray, Esther Louise Smith

Wheels and Whims
An Etching

ISBN/EAN: 9783337003036

Printed in Europe, USA, Canada, Australia, Japan

Cover: Foto ©Andreas Hilbeck / pixelio.de

More available books at **www.hansebooks.com**

WHEELS AND WHIMS.

An Etching.

BOSTON:

CUPPLES, UPHAM & COMPANY,

Old Corner Bookstore.

1884.

PRESS OF THE CASE, LOCKWOOD & BRAINARD CO.,
HARTFORD, CONN.

To American Girls;
who are distinguished
throughout the world
for their Beauty,
vivacity and Intelligence;
with the hope that they may
add to their charms the
invaluable possession of
perfect Health;
this book is affectinately
Dedicated.

"The abject people, gazing on thy face
  With envious looks,   *   *   *
  That erst did follow thy proud chariot wheels, .
  When thou didst ride in triumph through the streets."

(2d) KING HENRY VI.

In a word to the reader, it may be said that this book is not an attempt at belles-lettres. In it will be found no psychological perceptions, no impression effects, and no flowers of rhetoric—being simply an unadorned narrative of a tricycle trip by four young women, with its experiences, incidental, accidental, and adventurous.

If it will influence to out-of-door activity, and incite an escape from listless lounging in sunless rooms and the artificial heat and vitiated atmosphere of modern houses, to vigorous exercise in sunshine and open air, and to freer association with all nature's beauty, its object will have been accomplished.

PUTOUT.—"Thy tale thou didst well etch."

TELLPOOL.—"Etch! Wherefore? Thou art witty."

PUT.—"No, it is thou who art witty."

TELL.—"And why?"

PUT.—"Why? Because on Nature's metallic plate, the acts, the facts, the smiles, the tears, the light, the shade, do mark themselves with equal strength. 'Tis thy wit and thine intelligence doth bite and eat the impress with vigor that doth show the reprint with striking force. We do exclaim, 'Tis well done!"

TELL.—"Then am I clever!"

PUT.—"Ha! ha! Not so. Not as clever as yonder furry feline. Thou canst not scale that fir."

FROM STURM'S "LIFE'S COMEDY."

CHAPTER I.

Margery.

'T WAS the evening of Tuesday.
'T was Tuesday the ninth of October.
'T was October of '83.

It was with slow, weary steps, at a late hour, that Margery Prescott mounted the winding stairs to her room. Entering, she turned the key.

Touching the electric chain attached to the chandelier, the instantaneous flood of light illumined her pale face; a paleness of which she felt conscious, for she stepped quickly to the long mirror which stood between the gas-jets. Turning on their full blaze, she looked closely at her image in the glass. Then, straightening up, tall and defiant, she said in a strained voice, "Now tell the tale if you dare!"

For the first time in her young life, she felt a sore pain in her heart, which brought this pallor to her cheek.

"Yes, this comes from a heart-ache. I have hitherto experienced but one phase of love. Here comes the other. Pleasure, pain—joy, grief—inevitable, they say; but I had

(7)

not believed it. It shall not be so with me." She closed
her lips firmly together and still gazed at herself, almost
wondering at the hard look she saw in her own face.
"Those lines around my mouth—how hard they look, and
drawn and old—they are tell-tales, too, of pain within.
They shall not be." Here she forced a smile. "Have I
a frown, also? No, thank heaven! the brow is fair and
clear. No lines shall show there."

She pushed back the waves of her heavy brown hair,
and gave a proud toss of her head. She rubbed, with her
cold finger-tips, the glow again to her cheek, and bit her
lip a little, to give again its coral hue. A little laugh
came to show the pearly teeth, as she unfastened the lace
at her throat.

"Beautiful as ever! so it shall remain," she cried. "I
will not suffer, and pine, and droop. Indeed, he shall not
break my hopes of life; my heart shall not be torn by his
fickleness; I despise him for it! Man-flirt! How I hate
him! Shameful enough in silly girls—but a man-flirt is
detestable."

She loosened her long tresses; the brilliants in her ears
were unclasped; the diamond on her finger hastily drawn
off and dropped into the jewel-case without a glance at
them. Mechanically, she lowered the gas and sank into a
fauteuil by the window. 'T was midnight hour; the full
moon shone on all around. Cold and sad it streamed in
on her, as she raised her dark eyes to meet its rays with
burning glance. It was the fire in her soul that lent the
fervor to her gaze, for to all outward things she was
oblivious.

She pressed her hand to her beating brow. She buried her face in her hands. She arose and paced the floor.

"What—what shall I do?" she said. "Something! Somewhere! Where can I go? What must I do? I shall never see him again, never."

The hour was passing. Still she sat turning over in her mind the situation—the new and strange position of herself towards one other—to her, the one other of all the world. But now she was to give him up. What beside did the world contain for her? her heart cried, but she pressed it down with both her hands, and her proud lips replied, "The world is large. I have papa. For my own little world, he should be enough." But her heart would undertone, as it heavily beat, "What's the world to me? What's life, now?"

"Yes, what is it all for?" she moaned; "and I have so long to live." But now pride, which was the strong underlying quality of her nature, came to lift her out of this despair.

"It can be what I will make it," she exclaimed, and walking firmly to the glass, she saw a new courage in her eyes.

"It shall be grand, and good, and joyous, as any life may be; it shall not be a failure because—because—oh dear!" she sighed, drooping again. "If I had never known him at all! No! I do not wish that—I have found out what to expect. I have had my experience."

She stood erect and faced the black clouds which had obscured the light of the moon and dimmed all around. She drew the curtain and turned again to the lighted

mirror.   This time a brave, glowing face showed its reflection.   "No, I will not be a failure because of him!"   She
gave a trembling, upward glance.   A tear fell down her
burning cheek.   She gave a scornful turn of the lip, and
brushed it quickly away.   "I'll not shed tears for him,
however much it hurts me," she said.   "They may be
beautiful in the shedding, but their after traces tell poor
tales."

As she looked at the little bronze clock on the mantel
her eye fell upon a letter, which had before escaped her
notice.   Opening it, she rapidly took in its contents.
"Why, here is dear, good Mike," she cried, joyfully clasping her hands.   "Join her?   To be sure I will!   What a
god-send this is."   She re-read the missive.   "Just the
thing, exactly.   Papa will never object—he is such a
darling!   I fear I shall not sleep a wink ; but I must, for
he will see in a twinkling if aught is amiss with his pet.
Oh! what would I do without papa?   How glad I am that
Newport and Watch Hill are done with.   No more of that.
But what glorious times we did have, though!   But I hate
the very thought of them now—and of him," she said,
biting her trembling lip for an instant.   "What a novelty
it will be to go off with Mike and her aunt, Mrs. Mather,
too," she exclaimed, consulting the note once more.   "It
will be just delightful!   I am so glad papa had my wheels
put in perfect order.   They are all ready.   We can start
at a day's notice.   But I must get to sleep."

While she sleeps, we will look over the previous few
hours and learn what had so turned the tide in the affairs
of this lovely girl.   As the betrothed of Felix Plummer,

she had passed a year of uninterrupted happiness. Fine
fellow that he really was, he was wonderfully wound about
with the silken cords of her love, As the immediate cause
of her disquietude, we look to the events of the previous
evening. Margery had planned an informal party. Full
of gay anticipations of the occasion, she had, of course,
confided to Felix an account of all her arrangements.
He was as usual *en rapport* with all her plans, and promised to be early in attendance; even proposed himself to
assist in the reception of her guests. A sudden shower,
which came up just at nightfall, deterred a few delicate
ones from the scene, but only served to give greater zest
to the enjoyment of those who were assembled. Each, in
lively repartee and answering laugh, rivaled the other in
merriment, lest the disappointment might spoil the enjoyment of the hostess whom they all loved.

But Felix did not come. In spite of her regard for the
pleasure of her guests, she could scarcely conceal her
uneasiness at his unaccountable absence. Once she laid
her hand on her heart as she overheard George Fuller say
to Young White: "Pretty grass widow — considerably
struck — they do say." Impossible! Unkind! She
would not believe it; so she tried to smile, and finally
Felix appeared. He wore a deprecating air (as it seemed
to her now jealous eyes), and said, as she gave him a cold
hand, "So sorry to be late, Margie, dear." Aside: "Met
Mrs. Bangtry, without an umbrella, of course; could do
no less than protect her from the rain. So far, too. And
my watch had stopped, so I did not realize it was so past
the hour. Would have called a cab, had I known."

"Ah!" Margery felt a tremor of indignation thrill her frame. She drew her hand from his, nor would even meet his gaze. Felix was astonished.

"Margery," he said, "you surely do not —"

She had turned away from him and was talking with great animation to Alex. White, who was only too glad of a chat with her, having once been quite hopeful of more than passing favor in her eyes. Margery gave Felix Plummer no chance for further conversation during the evening She succeeded in avoiding him, and, finally, as the party broke up, offered him as escort to a limp, timid, young girl, whom she knew to be his special aversion, thus effectually dashing his hopes of an explanation of her coolness. An indifferent "good night" was all she conceded as he left the door, and such was the savage air with which he offered his arm to poor, bashful Miss Brown that she knew not whether to be most amazed or angry.

CHAPTER II.

Felix.

" NOW what in the name of all that's outrageous and unreasonable, did Margery mean by treating me in such a manner this evening?"

Mr. Felix Plummer, cashier of the Fourth National Bank, a muscular, blonde, and cheery specimen of humanity, had come in a few minutes before, in a state of surliness, which was a painful surprise to the black and silky Gordon setter, whom he loved and usually petted with the tenderness which all great hearts feel for kind and intelligent animals. But to-night, as the beautiful dog sprang up at his entrance, welcoming him with soft cries and licking his hand, he shouted: "Get out! Lie down! I'm busy." But then, as the sensitive creature sank at his feet with a piteous sigh and looked up in such mute surprise at this unwonted treatment, he softened a little, and said, stooping to pat her sleek head, "Never mind, Lady, I did not mean it. Good dog!"

Then he fell into a chair and glowered at the knob on the bedpost for some minutes. At last he arose with a

jerk, and, going to a little closet in the corner, commenced
to rummage among the things therein.

"Confound her meddling! I wish that green chamber-
maid, who isn't so particular about sweeping in the corners,
would let my traps be where I put them. That's the
curse of living in hired rooms," muttered he, tossing over
papers, diaries, books of trout flies, a reel of unwound and
tangled line, some cigars, a silk cap, some paper shells
ready loaded for his shot-gun, a few pairs of gloves, and a
silk band worked with his initials, for the inside of his
hat, which he would never wear, rather scorning the small
elegancies affected by modern dudism. "Well, where
under heavens did that knife come from? I have looked
high and low for it. Oh! here's the pipe, after all, on this
little ledge where I always keep it. I have been thinking," mused he, as he filled the capacious bowl of the
well-blackened pipe, "that I should have a home" (he
struck a match), "with a loving wife to take care of me
(puff, puff). But the way things have gone to-night (puff,
puff, puff), there don't seem to be much prospect (puff) of
it, for if she thinks," said he, raising his voice and addressing the wood-basket, "that I am going to stand much of
this kind of nonsense, she is mistaken, that's all."

Here Lady, aroused by his fierce tones, came softly
through the dim gaslight and licked the clenched fist with
which he had struck the arm of his chair.

"But perhaps it is just as well," he said, as he drew a
deep sigh. "Jim Osborn tells me that his wife is always
cleaning house (puff, puff), and when he has things
arranged to his mind and thrown carefully under the bed,

she will fish them out and say things. . . . . She gets his shoes and rubbers together and makes a row clear across the room, and whenever he speaks of getting a new pair, she goes and fetches out some of the old ones he is saving for fishing and throws them in his face — that is, metaphorically, I suppose. . . . . But what on earth ailed Margery to-night, passes my understanding ; the way she poked that slimpsy Brown girl on to me, and kept herself on an unapproachable pinnacle of dignity when I was near, and set to work, systematically, to bewitch Alex. White, is not to be borne by a man of any self-respect. I'll let her know I am not little Brown, to be smiled upon or scorned, as her ladyship chooses ! No, sir ! I shall teach her a lesson to-morrow that she will remember ! . . . . I am sure she loves me ! . . . . What can it be ? "

Here Lady, failing to attract any attention by her gentle caresses, began to shove her black nose under his elbow and to raise it up several times in quick, repeated knocks. Then her master, taking his fireless pipe from his mouth, laid his flushed cheek down upon her smooth head, saying, " Poor· Lady ; good girl," with a moisture in his blue eyes, that told he was much more grieved than angered, but, man like, was trying to disguise it, even to himself, by a show of righteous indignation and high words.

"Can it be," he ruminated, getting cooler, "that the evident preference that the little grass widow has for my society can have made her jealous ? "

Quite flattered by this idea, he raised his handsome head, and leaving the chair in which he had sat so long, he walked to the window and stood with his hands clasped behind him, looking out on the quiet street and at the shadows in the moonlight. As he cogitated, he smiled a little, and pulling and twisting his fair moustache, he said, "No, she would not be so foolish." A pause, another smile and lighting of the eyes. "If that is the trouble," he says, "she must know at once that a decent-looking fellow cannot prevent women from going for him." Then, unconsciously settling his neck-tie, "I vow, I believe that is it! Why, she ought to know that while a man cannot help being polite, and even a little sweet, to a festive little female like the Bangtry, he would never think of marrying her. . . . . I shall tell her to-morrow that my Margery need fear no rival in such a person, or anywhere. My rare, fair Margaret! How different she is from this other woman, whom she compliments enough to be jealous of!" He threw back his head. "Ha! ha! Well! well! That is too much! I'll go and see her now. Hum—I think I won't. It is past midnight. Poor dear! I know how glad she will be to see me! I will run up before ten in the morning. She will be freezing at first, of course (with a happy laugh), but I shall make her listen to me, and she shall give me a kiss before I leave, or my name is not Felix Plummer."

And so, sending Lady to her rug in the corner, he went straightway to bed, where he was snoring peacefully in less than five minutes, a combination of good nature, soft-heartedness, and self-complacency destined to be considerably disturbed by the events of the morrow.

The next morning Felix Plummer came to himself and started to get out of bed, but, oh! dear! how dizzy he was! His eyes ached and everything looked double. So he was glad to close them again; and, ugh! how sick and faint! His back and limbs ached in a dull and constant grind, and to lie still or to move was an equal agony. In a word, our friend had a slight bilious attack, and, being a man, he felt sure that he should die in a short time. Rapping on the wall to call his adjoining neighbor, whom he heard whistling as he squeaked about the room in new shoes, he managed to stagger to the door and admit his friend. As he sunk into a chair and rested his poor, snapping head on his feverish hands, he said in a woe-begone voice:

"Smith, I'm sick. I don't know what is the matter with me. Will you be kind enough to send Dr. Goodhardt up here when you go down town? No, no, don't bother yourself, I couldn't look at breakfast! Oh! dear! I have got something that I guess will kill me. Smith, didn't poor Brainard's sickness begin like this? Oh! Lord! how my head feels!"

Smith, who was a friendly little fellow, ran down stairs and out to the doctor's office and had the medical man in poor Felix's room in a trice. But the sick man ungratefully growled, "I thought you'd never get back," and "Doctor, I never was so sick in my life."

He had taken a small mirror, and squinting and shading his weak eyes with his hand, was looking at his tongue and at his sickly face.

"What's the matter, my boy?" said the genial doctor

as he entered the room, bringing an atmosphere of health and good cheer with him. "Lobster salad? Got a sick headache?"

"Oh! worse than that. I am afraid I am in for a tough time. Do you think you can stop the disease now, doctor? Oh! my back and legs!" groaned Felix.

"Oh! my lungs and liver! What do you want! Oh! goroo! goroo!" added the doctor, laughing heartily. "Really, Plummer, your exclamations remind me of the old ogre who frightened poor little Copperfield nearly to death. Well, well, to assume the gravity which your very serious case demands, I rather think you are pretty bilious. Been getting angry or uncomfortably excited? Nothing like that to stir up the bile. Does your business plague you?"

"No, nothing plagues me," answered Felix, gloomily, "except my head and stomach, and all my bones. Great heavens! Now these bed-clothes are out at the foot again, and my feet are out of doors, and these pillows are hot, and this cussed sheet is all of a wrinkle!"

Dr. Goodhardt shook and smoothed the pillows, pinned the edges of the sheet under the mattress so the uneasy patient could not rumple them again, and tucked the blankets in firmly at the foot of the bed.

Somewhat comforted, but still despondent, the demoralized individual who would hardly have been recognized as the *debonnaire* cashier of the Fourth National Bank, spoke again feebly.

"Doctor," he said in a trembling voice, "do not disguise it from me. Is my disease anything like poor Brainard's?"

"Disease! Ha! ha!" roared the doctor. "Plummer, my boy, you have a slight bilious attack; nothing more, as far as I discover, and you are so cross, I think you will be out to-morrow. Here, take this corrective; give your stomach a rest for a few days, and you will be all right. By the way, where did you go for your vacation?"

"Nowhere," said the young man. "Only run down to Watch Hill once or twice over Sunday."

"Take it this month, then," ordered the physician. "You cannot afford to neglect to give yourself a change and rest from the routine of business. You may find you have nerves, if you stick too close to the bank. This is the finest season of the year, and you must leave your work right where it is. Remember what I tell you."

The doctor departed. The morning grew to noon. Our very unheroic hero had slept again, and awakened feeling somewhat better. There came a knock at the door, and in response to his doleful "Come in," a lady walked briskly into the room, saying, "Hello, Felix! Dr. Goodhardt stopped at our door awhile ago to tell me that you were sick this morning, and so I came right down. Dear me! how yellow you look," she said in a very sisterly fashion. "Hair, eyes, and skin, all the same color. 'Whiskers reether redder than I could wish,' but shade in very well. Bub, you are a perfect symphony in old gold and copper, and the white pillows bring you out beautifully."

Felix smiled a little at this badinage, which he was so accustomed to hear from his lively, married sister.

"Kupfer und gold," he said musingly. "That's what

they used to call my chum Farnham and me at Yale. He
was a royal good fellow, with reddish hair, and we were
inseparable. But I say, Sis, don't throw any more Dickens.
at me. This is the second dose I have got this morning.
I believe Dr. Goodhardt would quote it if everybody was
dying," he continued, a little resentfully.

"Except himself," added his sister. "Yes, I believe he
would. By the way, Felix," she said abruptly, "where's
Margery gone?"

His fretful languor vanished, and a rush of crimson
blood colored his face.

"I stopped at the house as I came along, to tell her to
come down and see you after I had got you fixed up a
little," pursued his sister, "but Betsy said she had gone
away, and would be out of town several weeks."

"Gone away!" gasped the dismayed lover. "Bosh,
impossible! She was home late last night. The girl is a
fool! Gone several weeks," he repeated incredulously.
"I know better! But why did you not ask where she had
gone?" he demanded querulously.

"I did, and she said she did not know where."

Felix answered nothing, but buried his face in his
pillow, until his sister said, gently resting her cool hand
on his hot head, "Brother, is there any trouble between
you and Margie?" I should regret such a thing exceedingly, because I love and respect her already as a dear
sister, and I should fear that you were in some way to
blame."

"I am not at all to blame," protested the young man,
quickly turning to face her. "I don't even know what
it's about."

"Then there is trouble," said the lady, sadly.

"Yes, there is, Sis," responded her brother; "and if you, another woman, can tell me wherein I have done anything to offend her, or give any explanation of such unnatural capriciousness, I will thank you to do it."

He then rehearsed the events of the previous day and evening, and cried at last, with an air of abused virtue, "Now tell me what I have done! She is getting fickle, like other girls. They are all changeable as the wind. I thought Margery was an exception, but I have been a fond fool! They can't appreciate true love! They are too full of flirtation and vanity!"

Apparently not much relieved by this sweeping tirade, poor Felix sat disconsolately up in bed and reached out for a glass of water which the doctor had left on the stand by its side. His sister quickly arose and handed him the glass, but said nothing until she had returned it to the little table.

"Felix," she said in a low voice, but looking him straight in the face, "you were late at Margery's party last evening, because you went to see Mrs. Bangtry home."

"Yes, but what of that? Can't a man be decently polite to —"

"Are you aware that you have been classed as one of this lady's admirers?"

A flush rose to his sallow cheek and he opened his mouth to speak, but she continued:

"It has happened that you have been walking with her often, and at times when every one was on the street; you have, once, at least, taken her into your buggy; you have carried books to her house; and —"

"Stop! I can explain all those! I—"

"Very likely, Felix; but explain them to Margery, not to me," said his sister, raising her hand. "To put the thing in a nutshell, Mrs. Bangtry has flattered you. You have been pleased by her attentions, and your better judgment dulled. I may as well tell you, furthermore, that people are saying that Margery is getting left. She has doubtless heard something of this, and you can see that it needed only the last little drop, of last evening's happening, to overrun her cup of indignation."

"Could it have been such a thing, and Margery never spoke of it to me?" wondered the now somewhat conscience-stricken young man.

"I am convinced of it," rejoined his sister. "A woman of her pride and strength of character, Felix, is not likely to upbraid a man for preferring some one else to her."

"I have never preferred any one to Margery, and she ought to have faith enough in me not to notice the dastardly insinuations of contemptible busy-bodies. You know how it is, Sis; a man cannot treat any lady unkindly—"

"Yes, I know just how it is, Felix. Every man with any claims to good looks—and you have some of the family beauty," said she, eyeing him quizzically, "is insufferably conceited. Let him meet any woman like this gay widow-by-grace, and if she looks trustingly in his eyes a few times, asks information upon money matters, and seeks his opinions upon literature or art, tells him how she admires large men (or light, or dark, or anything to fit the case), confides a secret to his honorable keeping,

occasionally passes very near to him during an interesting interview, gives him the breath of her perfumed hair, and brushes the *frou-frou* of her silken skirts across his tingling feet —"

"Sis, you are too bad! Get a man sick in bed and abuse him like this! You know I would never dream of making love to her!" indignantly remonstrated Felix.

"I know it; but for such a woman's society a man will neglect his artless *fiancée*, draw disparaging comparisons between his sister's style of hair, and her more theatrical get-up —"

"I knew you'd never forgive me that!"

"Don't interrupt me! Snub his brother-in-law who ventures a warning word, get himself on the list of her lovers, and think it is all right, if he only assures his friends that he *would never think of marrying her!*" Felix winced. "Why, Bub, she would never think of marrying you! If her husband does not reappear, she will marry old Brown. A golden mustache looks well beside her dark eyes on the street, but ducats, my dear, gold dollars, are what she will marry. Now, if you consider your present position (in society, I mean) dignified, why, continue it, though your family will regret it. If not, find Margery, and be a sensible fellow once more."

Felix sat in bed with his knees drawn up, his hands clasped around them, resting his chin upon them, as he regarded his sister while she spoke. When she had ceased, he bowed his tousled head and said not a word for some time.

Mrs. Burton arose and busied herself in replacing and

packing up some books. Felix raised his head at last, and, speaking in a pitifully dejected manner, he said : " Sis, do you think — if I have been such an ass, such a villain, as you make me out, that Margery will ever forget it ? She may forgive me, but will she forget it ? Won't she tell me of it all my life ? I could never bear that ! "

" His sister smiled, consciously, "she might" she said, " if you were ever likely to repeat the experience."

The humbled suitor sought his loved one's door the next day, only to receive in answer to his inquiry for Margery, " She's gone away, sir."

Where ? " I don't know, sir."

Then, well-nigh bursting with surprise, rage, and grief, but trying to preserve his usual equanimity, he went to the office of Mr. Prescott and found, " He had just gone to New York, sir."

CHAPTER III.

The Plan.

SCENE.—The Prescott's breakfast room.
Margery, more than usually excited and brilliant.
Her father, tender, thoughtful, and complacent.

MARGERY kissed her father warmly, as she entered the breakfast-room the morning after the party. She hovered caressingly around him, as if to charm him by her magnetism into acquiesence with all her plans. She had just mentally framed a very nice way of telling him of her desire to leave him alone for a short time, a few days — a week or ten days — it might be a fortnight — and of her plans, which were all formed, between the fitful slumbers of the previous night. But she waited. He seemed about to speak. He laid his hand upon some letters by his side —freshly-opened letters from the morning mail. He gazed abstractedly at her a moment, and the current of his thoughts turned from his business to her.

"What is it, pet? Your eyes and cheeks are as bright as the sunshine! You have some scheme on hand that your mind is full of, I'll warrant."

"Yes, papa dear. I want to go off on a little excursion with Mahala Wright. I received a note from her yesterday.

(29)

She talked of the plan the other day when she called, but
I did not give it much attention, as I was thinking of
other things. We want to go on our wheels a little trip
down the river."

"What! You two alone? or is Felix—"

"Oh no!" interrupted Margery, "not we two alone,
Mrs. Mather and Miss St. John are to be of the party, four
of us."

"Well, I thought Mahala rather wild to take care of
you," said her father, "and you surely are too young to
chaperone her!"

"You understand, papa, that her aunt, Miss St. John, is
in the habit of going off on her tricycle on sketching trips.
She is going again this week. So, it is a capital chance
for a novel jaunt for us all. Now papa, you know nearly
every one down the river, and with letters from you, we
would get along splendidly! Mike writes that Joe wants
to go too. You know he goes everywhere with her.
Such a devoted brother! But we don't want any gentlemen along. It would spoil half our fun. We want just
ourselves. I have always taken care of myself, papa, and
never had any trouble."

"Yes, my dear. I sometimes wish you had a sister, and
were not so much alone," responded he, thoughtfully,
"But won't Felix—"

"Felix need have nothing to say about it, if you agree,
papa." A slight color came to her face as she said this.

"Well," slowly spoke her father, "it may be the best
thing, for I have letters here, which will necessitate my
leaving you, for perhaps even a longer period than you

propose being absent. I do not like leaving you here alone with Betsy and John. Very safe, but not very enlivening companions."

Margery quickly answered, "Oh, if you want to stay longer, papa, and think I had better not be here" (a fortunate idea, she thought), "Mahala will let me stay with her till you return. Mrs. Wright is always so kind in urging me to go there. She says no one can keep Mike in order so well as Margery Prescott."

"But how will you manage about clothing, my girl? You cannot live three weeks in a wheel-suit. Though," he added, "I never saw you in a more becoming rig than that last new gray."

"Yes, is it not neat?" said Margery, much pleased to see her father appreciate a creation that had given her some anxiety. "Mike and I put our heads together over those suits. The others are just like mine. In fact, we expect this style will be adopted by the club. I am so glad you like it, papa. Oh, we shall get along nicely with one large trunk," continued she. "Express it to any point where we wish to stay a day or two. We shall not want to ride all the time, you know. Now, papa, you make us a list of the best stopping places and points of interest; those old farm-houses of which you are always telling, and country taverns where we can stop for dinner. If you write them out we will make no mistake."

Betsy now laid the steaming breakfast upon the table. Margery proceeded to pour the coffee for her father, who declared again that no cup was ever quite as delicious as hers.

Mr. Prescott had drawn out a little plan of the river towns. Giving it a few more touches and taking the cup of fragrant coffee from her hand, he said, "Here is a list of the places you'd better make your points of rest. I will telegraph to three — the three underscored — so there will be no trouble about your reception. You, yourself, have been with me at several of these places. There you of course will be known. Miss St. John visits in Cromwell, and Mrs. Mather has relatives in Essex. They will not be at a loss, I am sure, to make up any deficiencies in this list, both having friends and acquaintances along the river. But, daughter," said he, as he cracked an eggshell, "when you are ready to return, had you not better take the boat and come directly home? To retrace one's way is often tedious. And probably you will by that time have had quite enough of wheeling."

"You are right, papa, as you always are. I am glad you suggested that idea. So then we can ride as far as we like without a thought of the coming home. I will tell the girls about it."

"Well, now, my dear, how long will it take you to get ready?"

"How long? Why?"

"Because, Margie, I must leave you before noon. If you can be ready in an hour—think you can?—John can drive you to Judge Wright's, with your trunk. The 'cycle can be taken to you this evening, and you will be ready if the rest are, for your trip at once."

"Yes, we can be off to-morrow, I am sure," exclaimed Margery, excitedly, "because they are only waiting for me. Then, papa, I will write you—at what point?"

"At New York, to-night. Give your letter to John, to post on the midnight train, so I will get it before starting west. Telegraph to this address in Chicago"—he took out a card and wrote on it—"in case of any accident. If all goes well you can write me there, and it will be forwarded to me. Now eat your breakfast, dear; you have scarcely swallowed a morsel."

"Oh! I have eaten a great deal. I have finished now," said the girl, swallowing her coffee in haste. "I will be ready in half an hour, you see if I am not," and she ran nervously out of the room. The packing was soon dispatched, the gray suit laid carefully on top to be worn for the first time on the morrow. Her hands trembled in her haste, especially when she took out her box of jewelry and she saw the discarded ring glitter in the darkness. But she would not think. "I must hand this to papa for the safe," she said. She pulled out, folded up, and tucked away, in unfaltering determination. She pressed the disk which rang the bell for her maid, in whose care she left the room for re-arrangement. She gave the girl permission to go to her home during her absence. Only Betsy and John need stay to care for the house. Margery evaded any direct reply to the girl's questions, merely saying she might be gone two or three weeks. "I will send you word, Susan, when I return. Take care of yourself and have a good time, while I am away." "Well, indeed, Miss Margery, I'd rather you stayed at home, inself," answered the faithful creature.

Margery snatched her gloves and sped down stairs as she heard the carriage coming around. She was flying from him! Faithless! Trifling! She must get away.

In tight embrace her father kissed her, once and again. She was all to him—all he had left. She seemed a little tremulous and nervous, but she was tired with her party and these hurried preparations. This trip would do her good.

Mr. Prescott put her into the carriage, telling John to return for him as quickly as possible.

An hour later, while Mr. Prescott was arranging business to take the fast train for the metropolis, Margery sat in Mahala Wright's sitting-room, hearing of all the plans for the anticipated trip. She produced her father's directions, which she had placed in her little satchel, and read them excitedly to her friend.

CHAPTER IV.

Rules and Regulations.

SCENE.—Evening in Mrs. Wright's well-lighted reception-room.

Mahala poses, with both elbows on center-table. She complacently regards her friends.

Mrs. Julie Mather stands near, embraced by Margery.

Aunt Dude (otherwise Miss Lucy St. John), coming across the room, essays to get a peep at the folio which lies before her niece.

Mahala instantly covers it with both hands, and makes an impudent face at her aunt.

MAHALA. "Now, everybody sit down." They take chairs. "I say, these rules have to be implicitly obeyed; or the party is *non est*."

AUNT DUDE "Go on."

MAHALA. "Rule first, then, received with no objection?" looking with questioning air at each individual.

"Rule second. Each member of this party shall consider herself for the time being as belonging solely and exclusively to this party. No outside interest shall rival that of this party, which compels the exclusive devotion of each and every individual to the amusement and diversion of the party collectively. Sworn?"

ALL. "No objections. All right."

(35)

MAHALA. "Rule third. On meeting with other parties or individuals *en route*, no communication whatever must be made."

JULIE. "But, Mike—"

MAHALA. "No interruptions." Reading again. "On occasion, each member shall simulate deafness, by raising the right hand to the right ear, and inclining the body. If chaperone number one or number two judge best to ask 'what?' then all three shall repeat 'what?' in a louder tone. If chaperone chooses after that to hold further conversation, it will be allowed."

Great laughter and cries of "Oh! Mike! what an idea!" and so forth.

MAHALA. Stamping her foot. "Swear!"

THE TRIO. "Well, sworn!"

MAHALA. "Rule fifth. Each member shall carry blue eye-glasses (already provided by Miss Wright) which, under any embarrassing circumstances shall be immediately placed upon the bridge of the nose."

ALL. "Sworn!"

MAHALA. "Rule sixth. One good pistol—"

MRS. MATHER. "Yes, I have one."

MAHALA. "Silence! That one good pistol shall be carried by chaperone number one. Also that three large toy pistols, unloaded (already provided by Miss Wright), shall be visible upon three other members. Any objections?"

ALL. "None—no" Laughter.

MAHALA. "Rule seventh. One tin horn, small size, to be carried by Mahala Wright concealed in the folds of her dress.　Small ivory whistles (also provided) to be worn by other members for convenience in calling the party together in case of any separation."

MARGERY.　"For instance, when the artist stops for an impression, or Mike pursues a specimen."

MAHALA.　"Rule eighth.　At hotels and farm-houses, no one will be allowed to form any acquaintance, except that of host or family of host."

ALL.　"Agreed."

MAHALA.　"Rule ninth.　Letters to be written on Sundays only.　No posting except on Mondays."

Demurs from Mrs. Mather, who turns appealingly to Margery.　Margery flushed and looked away.

MAHALA.　Coming down with great suddenness from her administrative tone.　"Oh! Yes! I know how it will be! Just how it will be! When I want some fun and entertainment, you and Margery will be scribbling to your devoted highnesses' devoted lover and husband.　I've been there before! 'Now don't—now, please keep quiet —I want to write,' etc., etc.　Letters on Sundays only! Swear one and all.　I insist upon it!"

"Sworn!"

A wicked twinkle comes into Mrs. Mather's eye.　She gives Margery's hand a little squeeze.

"I guess we shall get along," she whispers.

MAHALA.　"Nine rules! Now give me your hands on this, and we'll be off to-morrow at eight o'clock!"

TABLEAU.　All stand around the centre-table.　Hands clasped.

Good night.

CHAPTER V.

———•———

𝔗𝔥𝔢 𝔖𝔱𝔞𝔯𝔱.

THE meeting of the quartette the following morning, at Judge Wright's door, was, according to agreement, at an early hour. At eight o'clock, after much preliminary activity on the part of the four friends, which we will leave to the imagination of those who have undertaken similar excursions. the party was ready to start. They wore the gray cloth suits tastefully trimmed with black braid which edged the plaitings around the full skirts, adorned the collar, cuffs, and flaps of the jaunty postilion basques, and met in frogs across the front of the perfect-fitting waists; black poke hats, the severity of which was relieved by various short, curling feathers, which were massed on one side toward the front; and black kid gloves drawn up over the close wrists of the sleeves.

Their blue glasses, which were not without practical utility in an out-of-door life of whole days in the dazzling sunshine, were attached to a black cord which encircled the neck.

The butts of four pistols peeped out of small pockets on the hips, and which one carried the real, defensive weapon,

(38)

and who the toy imitations, it would have been difficult to decide.

Small silk umbrellas, folded in smooth cases, were fastened to the handle on the left side of the tricycles.

Judge and Mrs. Wright and the boys were interested assistants in the preparations, and interspersed their consultations with advice, cautions, and injunctions, which the wheelers did well to remember on subsequent occasions.

Miss St. John was diligently engaged in strapping her sketching apparatus on behind the saddle of her machine. Her artistic traveling outfit comprised a light camp-stool, a box of water colors, a case of pencils and brushes, and a pad of paper.

These would be sufficient to enable her to catch any choice bit by the way. Her oils, canvas, folding easel, etc. she had placed in the trunk. She could only use these to advantage when she had time to work out an idea.

Margery had several paper-covered books of light fiction attached in a roll to her saddle, and stood, tall and fair, chatting gracefully with Judge Wright, as she drew on her gloves. Mahala, closely superintended by her older brother, made ready a box for butterflies, and tied a net on to her tricycle.

"Now do be careful, Mike, if you get anything nice, not to break its wings. Remember to look for a lunar moth on the trunk of some tree in the woods. It is getting late for all moths and butterflies, so secure all you can before the first frost comes. This bottle of cyanide you must be careful about, as it is deadly poison. Tell them all about it," said her good brother Joe.

"Yes," spoke up Frank, who was standing on the curb-stone with his hands in his pockets, looking on enviously at the busy scene; "if you don't, they may be putting it on to their faces for lily white!"

"What do you know about lily white?" retorted Mahala. "Boys of fourteen should be seen and not heard. Don't you wish you could go, Bubby, dear?" she said tantalizingly, giving his nose an exasperating little tweak. "But it must stay at home, 'cause it's too little," and she ran briskly into the house.

"Humph!" he called after her; "I can travel right around you on my bicycle! I would not go on such a slow trip, anyhow!"

"Well, I would," said Joe, "if they would let me. I am only provoked that we fellows had not thought of it first."

"There is no copyright on the idea, Joe," said Margery, smiling at him.

Mahala ran down the steps. "I came very near forgetting those insect-pins, Joe," she said, as she opened the box and placed the paper and the wide-nosed bottle within.

"I say, Mike" (again Frank), "don't those thick boots make your feet look awfully big?" Her particular pride was a dainty foot, and he knew it.

"Do they, Joe? Mamma! Are these boots very clumsy? I was afraid they were, when I got them, but—"

"No; they are very neat and sensible, dear. Don't mind him," quickly answered Joe.

"Frank, be quiet," said his mother.

"Let her call me 'Bubby,' then, that's all," and the

young gentleman grinned and gave his head a threatening shake.

Meanwhile, a portly, middle-aged gentleman was holding the hands of Mrs. Mather, and talking earnestly.

"Be very careful and not take cold, Julie; and if you see the least cause to fear any tramp, use your pistol. Don't hesitate a moment. Shoot one as you would a mad dog, if he offers to molest you. I am almost sorry that I consented to your going. If anything should befall you—"

"I would not think of going, Fred, if you were not to be away," answered his wife; "but this trip will serve to pass away the time until your return. I will write you at every possible point."

"Do, dear; and be sure to send to the post-office at all your stopping-places."

"Do you think you need to tell me that?" said Julie, archly.

Mr. Mather raised his hat to the other ladies as they mounted their tricycles, and turned again to kiss his wife. She looked sadly back at his retreating figure as she laid her hand on her wheel, and waved a farewell with her handkerchief, as he stopped to look back. Then she quickly took her seat.

"Well, girls, are we away?" she said in her cheery voice, looking around.

"All away!" they answered, and she pressed the treadles and sped along the street. A confusion of cries followed them as they left.

"Good-by, good-by."

"Be careful, Mahala, dear."

"Get some nice pictures, Dude!"

"Good-by, Miss Margery."

"Look out and not make a mistake about that face-powder, now!"

Mrs. Mather turned once again to catch another glimpse of her husband just as they turned the corner, and the flutter of her bright handkerchief was the last thing he saw.

In a short time they were well through the town and coming to the hill which rises to the colleges. Here occurred the first annoyance, which, indeed, they scarcely minded, being used to various expressions of surprise at their comparatively new mode of locomotion. Passers by the way, who saw the tricycles for the first time, often gave expression to their ideas about them in more or less complimentary language. As they ran smoothly along the macadamized streets, laughing and talking blithely,

full of pleasant anticipations, and enjoying to the utmost every moment in the invigorating air and genial sunshine, they scarcely noticed a company of boys, who, "with shining morning faces," and straps of books dangling from their hands or slung over their shoulders, came noisily trudging to school, earnestly discussing the affairs of life which are so absorbing and important to them. They were all well-dressed, and most of them were at that age when they have passed their usefulness as pets, but have not yet grown into the innate sense of honor and generosity which ennobles most young men in their conduct towards ladies. Suddenly, one saw the riders approach. He gave the word to the others, and they all stopped to better realize the unusual sight.

"Oh, fellers!" cried he, "see the women's righters!"

"Oh-h! Oh!" chimed the party, in derision.

"Hullo, Susan Anthony!"

"How are you, Susan B.?"

"When are you going to vote? Sa-ay!"

While almost deafened by the din, the ladies could not keep from smiling, but Miss St. John was seen to exclaim (they could only see the working of her mouth) that she would like to teach them better manners. But all at once the jeering ceased — the stillness was almost painful. A natty little fellow of fifteen had made himself heard over all. He had to jam the hat of one of the more earnest vociferators down over his eyes with a crushing blow to secure his attention, and ordered: "Shut up! Stop your infernal noise, I say! That's Frank Wright's sister! Keep still, will you?" And having effectually quelled the riot, he raised his hat, with reddening cheeks, in response to a bright little bow from Mahala, who said, "Thank you, Harry," and cast such a look of pitying contempt at the insulting boys that they began to have business somewhere else at once. They became much interested in something over the fence, and passed on in haste.

While the tricycle party, having dismounted, were pushing their light machines up the hill, Miss St. John, who had been walking ahead for some time in silence, turned to her friends.

"What a bold and unbecoming thing it seems to be a 'woman's righter'!" she said, repeating the term used by the derisive juveniles. "How even the masculine youth resent the slightest innovation upon what they consider their exclusive rights!"

"Ah, but we have taken the right to dress sensibly, to walk, and skate, and row, and swim," said her niece, "and they will soon all get used to our using the tricycle."

"Yes, they will, of course," assented Miss St. John, "but how truly they sense the tendency of all these emancipations from indolence and inefficiency. Their very ire shows their selfish fear of the result of a healthier condition of mind and body in women."

Mrs. Mather said she did not believe boys gave the subject much thought.

"It is bred in their bones," retorted the lady, "and fostered from the first minute when they discover that Sister cannot do this and that because she is a girl. If so many girls were not spoiled in bringing up, one great obstacle to the coming era would be done away with."

"You mean—" began Mrs. Mather, hesitatingly.

"I mean the duties and privileges of full citizenship," declared the artist. "I do not often say this aloud, because it is at present rather unpopular, and especially so in an unmarried woman."

Mrs. Mather raised her eyebrows dubiously. "Women seem to be gaining admittance to the professions," she said. "They can select any work for themselves, and if they have a strong purpose and persevere, they can achieve a modicum of success which is due to their abilities and not in any way precluded by their sex. I really do not see that to vote is at all necessary to their happiness or advancement."

"It is not strange that you do not, who live and move and have your being in your husband's love. You are evidently so enervated by the balmy atmosphere of his protection that you do not care to trouble your contented heart with these problems."

"Well, really, Dude," answered the matron, "I do not quite know whether to consider that remark as complimentary or not."

"You must judge it from your own standpoint," said the other, laughing, "but is it not true?"

"Yes, it is," acknowledged the loving wife. "I try sometimes to brace up to it and to look discriminatingly into the question for the sake of other unfortunate and lonely women, but I cannot yet see how the franchise is to help them."

Mahala spoke up. "Suppose women could vote, and that a war was inevitable or necessary to preserve the interests of the Republic. Women are physically unable to back up, by their ability to fight for anything, the votes they may have cast for war."

"Ah, Mike," said her aunt, "You know that argument is good for nothing, although I doubt not you hear your father and other intelligent men advance it. In the first place, it is only very rarely, as in the case of our late war, that the masses rise to put down a great wrong. War is usually brought on by the differences of a few diplomats, who, mind you, do not do any of the fighting they have caused. Secondly, and this is an argument for allowing them to vote, no majority of women would ever vote for a war. They are essentially merciful and averse to blood-shedding. Supposing these questions and differences were all adjusted by arbitration, would the world be less Christian or in any respect hindered in its progress towards the right?"

"Oh! I surrender, aunty! Don't grind me to powder, to impalpable paste, I pray thee!"

Here Margery interposed. "It is an argument, you know, Miss St. John, against admitting women to the ballot, that you place a dangerous power in the hands of many vicious and ignorant ones at the same time that you extend the privilege to the purer and more intelligent portion of the sex, so that politics will not become purified, but only more complicated."

"Well, girls, I do not intend to spoil our pleasure on this perfect day by a lengthy argument on this question. I will only remind you that the fear of corruption in the bad ones, and the indifference of the pampered darlings," here she looked hard at Julie, who opened her lips in a reply, but thought it not worth while and said nothing, "has not the slightest bearing on the point of doing justice to one-half of humanity who are now without a voice in their own laws.　But my grand idea for the purification of politics, for the enlightenment of the masses, and an irresistible incentive to the education, industry, and frugality of every individual, is this.　It has been in my mind as a solution of many growing evils and abuses for a long time, but I have never given it utterance, realizing that it is so far in advance of the world's civilization that it is not yet available."

" Hear! hear!" cried Mahala, and all listened attentively for the exposition of the plan for the saving of the Republic.　The lady spoke impressively as she leaned against the saddle of her machine, and emphasized the portentous words with one finger on the palm of the other hand.

" I would have an educational and property test which should be applied to every candidate for the elective franchise, male or female.　No one should be allowed to vote who could not pass an examination upon a good common-school education.　No one should vote who had not a small property, say three or five hundred dollars' worth, unincumbered by debts.　Individuals who cared enough for the privileges of citizenship to educate themselves to this extent, and who, in saving this amount of taxable goods had gained also habits of industry, would not make careless voters.　They would not be led blindly by any demagogue who would stoop to do it, and they could not vote away money which they have never earned, as they now are so free to do.　Thus you would exclude the dense ignorance which is now permitted at the polls, the only passport at present needed being a certificate of masculinity. I also recommend it as a remedy for the disease known variously as Communism, Nihilism, Socialism, and so forth. But," resignedly, "I do not expect to live to see it."

"No, I am afraid not, aunty, unless you can stick by as long as Methuselah did," suggested her irreverent niece, dashing ahead in "a terrific burst of speed," as the race reporters would say.

"But, Dude," said the chaperone of the party, after a respectful silence of about two seconds, "politics are not becoming to you. If you only knew how much more lovable you look when you are sketching."

Miss St. John turned upon her friend with unconcealed exasperation, which was certainly justified by the irrelevancy of the remark, but her lips softened into an indulgent smile as Julia kissed her gloved finger-tips to her in her own ingenuous manner and rode ahead, laughing at the indignation she had provoked.

"This will take us over the lovely ridge-road," said Mrs. Mather, leading away to the left. When they came to the narrow single track which runs for some distance between the fence and a high bank, they rode in single file. Lest they should meet some vehicle in the narrow way and be forced to pull their wheels up the steep bank to let it pass, Mahala blew a lusty blast upon her tin horn to warn approaching travelers that some one was on the single road. She was considerably conceited over her forethought when, on emerging into the broader way, they met a heavily-loaded team which was waiting at the entrance for them to pass. Then along the beautiful road which, stretching by the side of the ridge, gave such a glorious view of the gorgeous world of woods and meadows to the left. They selected several building-spots for themselves, to be purchased when their ship should have come in and they be searching for an unsurpassed location for a summer villa.

They conciliated barking dogs, admired homely farmhouses, discovered a busy mother-cat hunting in the fields, and spatted their hands and trundled swiftly after a snorting and disapproving old horse who was wandering aimlessly in the road, until they were tired.

Even pale Margery was forgetful of everything but the beauty of the day, the merry jests of her companions, and the novelty of the excursion. They did not stop to consider anything as better than laughter on this day, and wheeled along the road — how light and noiseless! — at a rapid rate. At length they ran around the corner at Wethersfield, on the main road. They had made many a turn in and out from the highway, ever and anon catching glimpses of beautiful scenery which was too enticing, and they must get a nearer view. One " wee bit of the river," had to be jotted down in the sketch-book — "just one, for the first day," the artist pleaded, and the others graciously loitered. Mahala cast her eye about for entomological specimens ; but saw nothing save some plebeian beetles, which she said "Joe had a million of now."

They were at Wethersfield, their first stopping-place. "Yes, here we are at Aunt Phebe's," said Margery, as she alighted from her saddle. "Did you ever see grander trees ? "

"What a dear, old-fashioned house!" exclaimed Mrs. Mather, looking up to the gambrel roof and at the quaint little dormers.

"But the inside is full of interesting things," said Margery, as she shook her skirts to free them from all dust, "and when you see Aunt Phebe, you will love her at once. Just a kind, silver-haired woman, of sterling worth and sweetness. She will be so surprised to see us! But I am always sure of a welcome. Inconvenienced? No fear! She will be delighted. There she stands now!—out under that old back stoop. She has her basket full of — oh! ripe tomatoes," said Margery, stepping lightly through the open gate, to greet her aunt. The lady came forward with the hesitating air of a person whose sight does not serve as quickly as in younger days, and could not believe her eyes until she was fairly in the warm embrace of her favorite niece. The basket of tomatoes was still upon her arm.

"What, all four of you! came from Hartford — and on those things!" The lady had been shut up in the house, an invalid for more than two years. "Well, you will not need any oats for your horses!" she rejoined, smiling. "You would be welcome if you did. But you need rest and food for yourself and your friends. Bring them in, dear, and tell me who they are."

Margery beckoned smilingly to the party of tricyclers, who had remained modestly at the gate, and presented them.

"Thomas Wright's daughter! Oh my dear!" The pleasant eyes looked searchingly at Mahala as she held her off to get a clearer sight. The young girl had impulsively bestowed a kiss upon the kind face. "Why, your father —" she paused and felt for the glasses. They were not in their accustomed place. She wiped her eyes as if to clear the vision. "Your father and I were friends, years ago. Do they say you favor him?"

"They tell me I have his laugh and his eyes," answered the girl.

"Well, well, and so he has a daughter as old as you — you are the oldest?"

"I have one brother older, twenty-one."

"Twenty-one," repeated the lady, meditating. She put the basket down, still looking at Mahala.

"Yes, it must be thirty-eight years ago; we planted that tree together. 'Twas a happy day." Here the tomatoes began to fall, slowly bumping down the steps, the basket having toppled over from its insecure resting-place. Both stooped to catch them, but the quick movement of the older lady's hand was with her apron to her eyes; while Mahala caught and replaced the fruit.

"Yes, it is so," and she looked up at Mahala's lissom figure. "Then we — then he went away. He studied law, I heard. I never saw him again until after he was married. He came one day to see how the tree had grown. That was when you were in the Land of Nowhere, dear. I remember now your brother was a little thing; he told me of him and of his wife; and you are his daughter," she said, coming back to the present moment. "Well, I will love you, too," she said, with glistening eye resting on the interesting face glowing with youth and beauty, and she

laid her gray head beside Mahala's dark locks as she took
her into her arms.

Mahala had unfastened her hat and stood bare-headed
under the trees, accepting eagerly all the interest of the
occasion, and wondering if she had ever heard papa speak
of this winning lady.

The entertainments of the remaining afternoon and
evening were as enjoyable as the day's beginning.

To see all the antique belongings of this ante-revolu-
tionary mansion was a feast in itself. There were glimpses
in the dining-room of the delighted artist, making a study
of the big fire-place. One could sit inside its yawning
mouth in the corner in comfort, if the fire were not too hot.
There was an ancient piano with attenuated legs, a violin
of historical value, and interesting associations; little yellow
sheets of mournful music, marvelous wall-paper, scores of
things to keep the young visitors in enthusiastic expressions of admiration, and to further win the heart of their
owner by their manifest appreciation of her cherished
relics.

The friends were shown at night into a large room with
two beds in it. Their trunk, which had been brought to
the house by an expressman, stood awaiting them in a
corner.

"What a day this has been!" exclaimed Mahala, as she
sat down in a chair and stooped to unbutton a boot. She
yawned.

"It has certainly been most delightful in every respect,"
agreed Mrs. Mather, as she vigorously brushed her gray
waist at the window, and they congratulated themselves

on their hostess, and chatted of the home where they felt so sheltered. "The roads are in prime condition, too," said Margery, "and the weather absolutely perfect."

"Yes," answered Miss St. John, "and the foliage is beginning to take on just the coloring I want to study for my last picture."

She was carefully rinsing and wiping some brushes, and making ready for an early start on the morrow.

They were all weary and longing for rest. Each one was busily preparing for bed.

"Now, is n't it perfectly delightful," said Mahala, as she kicked off one boot, "to be able to take such a jaunt as this, without any men along to dictate, and bother, and spoon!" She put such vindictive force into the last word that a button flew off from the second shoe, which she was removing.

"Oh! dear! there goes a button, and the first day, too! Now I have got to sew it on. I tightened them all up, yesterday." And she got out her little work-box, and commenced to sew. "If there is anything that I perfectly abominate, it is untidy shoes. But," returning to the subject of special rejoicing, "is n't it jolly not to have any masculines with us?"

"Yes, indeed," quickly responded Aunt Dude, who was pasting her hair into montagues, and tying them down with a piece of white net.

"Of course it is nice, very nice, to go it alone, when no more difficulties are in the way than we have met to-day. I hope it will all be as smooth sailing," said Mrs. Mather, sighing faintly.

"Wheeling, you mean, little woman," added Mahala.

"Gracious! how lame my legs are!—or limbs, I suppose I should say. Twigs would be even more modest."

"I believe ladies are allowed to have legs in these days," said their diminutive chaperone, smiling at Mahala's undiminished flow of spirits.

"Well, they have got to have them to ride a tricycle, at all events," said the irrepressible hoyden. "Mine are sorer than they have been before, since Sim Blodgett first loaned me his wheels to try."

By this time all were in bed except Aunt Dude, who put out the light, and Miss Wright declared her intention of being asleep in less than a minute. But in ten seconds she burst out :

"Margery, what did Felix say to your taking this trip? He is so partial to clinging-vine women, that I should have expected him to be horror-stricken at the idea."

Poor Margery, under the cover of the darkness, was able to reply, quietly, "O, he made no objection; you know, I am still my own mistress."

"So am I," said the pert young miss, "and furthermore, I mean to remain so."

Another quiet spell, and a delicious drowsiness began to steal over the senses of the tired travelers, when the little wretch was heard to giggle convulsively.

"Goodness gracious!" exclaimed her aunt, getting out of patience, "why don't you go to sleep? I am sure we are all tired enough."

"I was just about to start my mill (knitting up the 'raveled sleeve of care,' you know) when I happened to think of how Sim proposed to us girls, and how we paid him. Let me tell you,—it won't take but a moment."

"Oh, Mike!" groaned Julie. "Keep it until to-morrow," begged Miss St. John, who well knew that conciliation was the best policy at such a time. But it failed in this instance, for Margery, who was not disposed to sleep, and was glad of anything to divert her thoughts from her lover and his supposed trifling, said, "Go on, Mike. Let her tell it, girls."

They all used the name which had been given to merry Mahala by her brothers, and accepted by her as a matter of course. Encouraged by Margery, she began. "Well, you all know just what kind of a fellow Sim is—dresses well, is attentive to all the girls, indispensable at every party and picnic, and can do everything, from leading a German to sewing on fancy work or making a salad. He's real nice" (generously), "but you'd never think of marrying him, never" (positively). "But Sim is getting old. He has let at least half a dozen sets go by him and sink into the insignificance of married life, and he has begun to think it is time he married some girl whose father will board him, and her, while his salary will just about pay for his clothes. You see, if she will furnish the bread, he will try and get the water."

"Don't elaborate, Mike, and on borrowed wit, too," said the voice of her aunt in the other bed. "Make it short."

"Well, it suddenly popped into my head that he was getting unusually sweet on me, and one evening, going home from Margie's house, he proposed to me. Of course I told him it was of no use; liked him as a friend, and all that, and furthermore that I meant to live and die entirely free and at my own sweet will."

"Don't be too positive, Mike. You are not very old yet," interjected Mrs. Mather.

"It was too good to keep, of course," continued Mahala, "and I had to tell Em. She commenced to laugh, and said, 'Poor Sim! he proposed to me, too.' 'No,' says I. 'Yes,' she says, 'and to Stella, too.'

"Well, you know, that was too much, so we rushed over to Stella's, and I fell up the steps and tore the ruffle off my new garnet silk. It was an awful tear; went zig-zaggy in every direction. Had to take it to the dress-maker's and have a piece taken out."

"Never mind the tear, tell us about Sim," said Margery, who was laughing in spite of herself.

"I was just going to, my dear, if you had not interrupted me," retorted Mahala, briskly. "So we put our heads together, not to make a plank walk" (this execrably stale joke was allowed to pass without remonstrance), "but to make a plan, and we wrote three notes, each one saying—in different language, of course—that we had changed our minds ; that if he still loved us we would accept his faithful and unswerving love, and asked him to wear a white rose-bud in his button-hole—Em. said a pink one, and Stella named daisies—as he went to church the next day. We mailed them at the same time, and of course he received them simultaneously. Sim has been perfectly demoralized ever since. Won't go to a party, or look at one of us on the street. They say, now, he is going to marry a wealthy girl in the country. Was n't it rich? Good night, girls. I am tired half to death and really must go to sleep. I have not—made this—as interesting as I could if I was n't so—slee—.'"

CHAPTER VI.

They go to Church.

IT is not the intention of the authors of this sketch to follow the tricycle-riders over every consecutive mile of their route along the banks of the Connecticut river, from the (nominal) head of navigation to its mouth. We shall content ourselves with an outline of the more interesting scenes and incidents among the great variety of events and experiences which befell our venturesome quartette.

Sunday morning found them all well and in the best of spirits (except, perhaps, Miss Prescott, whose pride however enabled her to effectually conceal the rankling hurt in her heart) at a home-like hotel in a pleasant town some miles below Wethersfield.

As they sat at breakfast, Mrs. Mather addressed the neat maid who waited upon them at table. "Maggie, I think there is a church in this place?" "Oh yes, ma'am," the girl answered in some surprise, "there's two or three."

"Yes, yes, I understand you, Maggie," said the lady, kindly, "but I refer to *The Church*—an Episcopal Church, of course."

"It is very evident that our little chaperone has con-

victions on some subjects, if not upon others," said Miss
St. John behind her hand to Margery.

"Thank you, Maggie," said the lady, graciously, "I was
informed there was a church here. It is such a comfort,"
she continued, turning to her friends, "to know that
wherever you are, at home or abroad, the doors of the
Church are always open to you. One needs no introduction or permission to enter; the universal God is everywhere. One fears encountering no personal diatribes from
the rector. The sermon is not a lecture with a religious
tendency, but an explanation and application of the Word,
as the great minds in Church office understand it. It is
such a rock in stability and strength! I suppose the service is at the usual hour, and we will find our way by
inquiries."

They were all glad to welcome the day of rest, and were
soon ready for church, as no change could be made in
their dress, except to put on clean collars, to carefully
brush their hats, and don better gloves and shoes than they
wore while traveling.

"There!" said Mrs. Mather, as she shook a fresh handkerchief out of its folds, "I feel quite like a respectable
member of society once more."

This caused Mahala to remark that she believed Julie
would be happy cast away upon a desert island, if she could
only have plenty of clean and pretty handkerchiefs.

Soon the bells began to ring, sending their urgent
resonance far over field and river, quickening the feet of
devout souls whose inclinations led them to worship, and
increasing the speed of family carriages which were

decorously wending their way from distant places, "a few to Church and more to *meeting*" Mrs. Mather said, sententiously.

The four companions walked along the pretty street with a directness and purpose which at once marked them as city women.

"It's a female seminary!" said a youth who, with others, was curiously watching the gray suits approach.

"I don't believe it. They are temperance workers!" said another.

"Not much!" asseverated the youth. "Humph! I guess not! They are too good looking!"

Here, one of the younger boys, who stood behind in the group of bystanders, gave the youth a vigorous push, so that he was violently projected into the path in front of Margery. She, passing swiftly, stepped on to his foot.

"Oh, sir! I beg your pardon!" she instantly cried, sensing the whole situation, "did I hurt your foot?"

"Oh, no! No, indeed! Not in the least; it was all my fault!" protested the crimson youth, and the low-voiced "sir" and her beautiful smile warmed his heart for many a day after.

The friends entered the church-door. Above it was the legend

This is a Free Church.

But Mrs. Mather, politely accosting a tall gentleman who stood in the vestibule, asked him to show them a seat. He replied, "This is a free church, madam. You can take any seat you like."

"Is it really so?" said Miss St. John quickly, looking up to him in her bright way with a glint of sarcasm in her gray eyes, "or shall we mortally offend some good pillar by occupying the pew which he has acquired by right of possession? Free seats in theory, is one thing ———"

"*This* is a free church in practice," answered the gentleman, with a pleasant smile, and a look of interest at the party.

"I congratulate you!" said the artist, as they passed inside.

It was, indeed, a blessed hour in the subdued light and stillness, which was broken only by the rich voice of the rector, as he recited the impressive words of the service, and the low responses of the kneeling congregation. A restful peace fell upon the troubled breast of proud and wounded Margery, and at the words : "Almighty God, unto whom all hearts are open, all desires known, and from whom no secrets are hid," the tears came unbidden to her eyes.

Mrs. Mather paid strict attention to every change in the service, entirely absorbed in the ceremonials so dear to her. Miss St. John allowed her thoughts to wander to a very tasteful window, which she observed with an artist's eye for color ; and Mahala sat quiet and attentive, unconsciously raising a disturbance in the cardiac region of a young physician who sat in the pew behind. He assiduously found the hymns for her, and leaned over the back of the seat in passing her his own book to get a look at her eyes. Conspicuous in gilt letters upon the flexible cover of his hymnal was the name Dr. Launceolot Cutter.

"He ought to be a good surgeon," breathed Mahala to Margery, without moving her lips, as she looked demurely at the stamp. She cast a bewitching glance of gratitude toward the young Æsculapius as she returned the book, which he understood to be full of meaning and rapturous possibilities—and never thought of him again.

The strangers all joined in the singing, and Mahala's bird-like soprano rose sweet and clear, so that several staid worshipers turned about to see where the new voice was, and were considerably distracted from the remainder of the service thereby.

As the visitors filed out with the slow-moving congregation, they were met at the door by a beaming and cordial lady of perhaps forty years. She was rather stout, with large pleasant eyes, a funny little nose, which was inclined to be red, and a smiling and voluble mouth.

"I perceive that you are strangers here, ladies," she said in a most hearty tone, "and I am very happy to welcome you to our little church. I am Mrs. Moore, the wife of the rector."

"It is very pleasant to meet such a greeting, Mrs. Moore," said Mrs. Mather, with feeling, "when, except for the sheltering arms of the Church, we felt we were among strangers. These are my friends, Miss St. John, Miss Margery Prescott, and Miss Mahala Wright," said the chaperone, who was much touched, as indeed they all were, at this unexpected and, alas! unusual kindness.

"This is my daughter," said the good lady, presenting a young girl of sixteen, who was standing near and eagerly scanning the interesting group.

"I am so glad to know you," asserted the daughter, with a youthful reproduction of her mother's cordial manners. "I could hardly wait to get through the service," she said to Mahala. "I was so impatient to know if you were not the ladies who came here yesterday on tricycles."

"I suppose we are," answered Mahala, showing her dimples as she smiled pleasantly upon her new acquaintance.

"Oh! then, you will let me see them, won't you?" exclaimed the little Miss. "I am just crazy to ride one!"

"Fie, fie, Jennie! how wild you are!" her mother said, gently.

But Mahala gave her hand a little squeeze as they stood together, and Jennie understood her.

"Henry, dear!" Mrs. Moore exclaimed, as the rector, now divested of his robes, came out the green-baize door,

"here are some ladies whom you wish to know. This is
—" and she remembered every name. Then they saw
that it was the rector that they had spoken with on their
entrance.

"I met these ladies before service and felt sure you
would capture them, wife," replied the rector, who was a
tall man with grayish hair and beard, and a deep musical
voice. "Have you invited them to lunch? We shall take
you home with us this noon," he said, bending politely to
Mrs. Mather.

"Oh! really, sir—" she commenced.

"Yes, we shall," he insisted; "my wife always does so.
She purposely sits back, so that she may detect and way-
lay any unsuspecting visitors."

"Henry!" exclaimed the lady, laughing. "But you
will go, will you not?" she said earnestly to Miss St.
John. "We shall deem it a favor to us."

Mrs. Mather looked at Miss St. John an instant, in
pleasurable doubt.

Miss St. John nodded just a sixteen-thousandth part of
an inch.

"There is certainly every inducement for us to accept
your kindness, and no reason to refuse, except that we
hesitate to trespass so much upon your hospitality, Mrs.
Moore," said Mrs. Mather.

"Then you *shall* go!" said the young daughter, who
already had Mahala by the arm. She joyfully skipped
along by her side in fervent admiration of her new friend.
Her quick eye had taken every detail of the city girl's costume, from the stylish hat that sat so jauntily upon the

dark curls, to the ends of her daintily-clad hands and feet. "Oh, mamma," she begged an hour later at lunch, "can 't I have my new dress cut in Hartford? They," looking wistfully at the symmetrical gray waists, "they are so different from Miss Seamer's work."

Yes, reader, the strangers were actually taken home by this minister and his family. Mr. Moore walked attentively beside Margery and Mrs. Mather, while his wife chatted in a most agreeable manner to Miss St. John.

"To explain my husband's dreadful insinuations concerning my artful designs," she said, as she trotted along, "I do sit rather far back in church, with an idea of the better seeing and greeting our parishioners, and so I naturally meet all the strangers, and one can do no less than make them welcome," she said, in an almost apologetic way.

Miss St. John thought grimly, that *some* could do considerably less.

"Will some one kindly stick a pin into my arm, pull my hair, or in some way convince me that I am awake?" said Mahala, in a suppressed voice, and offering a plump elbow and a curly head, to her companions when they were left alone for a moment in the cosy sitting-room of the rectory. Mrs. Moore had bustled away with her daughter to prepare lunch, and the rector had stepped up stairs to procure a book he had been talking of. "Will no one accommodate me with a pinch?" she inquired again.

"S-sh! Mike, no nonsense now," whispered Mrs. Mather, shaking her head at the frolicsome member. "But is n't this too delightful for anything?" she said, as she looked around with glistening eyes.　She was highly appreciative of the kindness shown them, and proportionately affected by it.

"It passes belief."

"It is true Christian love and fellowship." chimed the artist and Margery.

A simple and satisfying lunch, pleasant conversation, during which all had become as old friends, exchanging information regarding themselves, expressing opinions, gaining ideas; and, after two hours, the traveling party, who had almost forgotten that they were pilgrims and comparative strangers, went back to the hotel, but not until they had promised to spend another hour or two the next morning at the rectory, and give Jennie a chance to try the fairy wheels before they went on their way.

CHAPTER VII.

On the Road.

MONDAY morning was fair, and after paying their small bill at the hotel—Mrs. Mather was purser, and paid all expenses from a common fund, keeping a strict cash account, as well as attending to the dispatching of the trunk — they called upon the Moores as agreed, much to the delight of the sprightly daughter, who, under Mahala's kind tuition, achieved her wild hopes and rode the tricycle up and down, round and around, for an hour. Then they bade good-by and God-speed, parting with mutual reluctance, and were once more upon the road.

They were within a mile of Middletown when.

"Girls! assume your glasses; here comes a man!"

Instantly, at the word of the chaperone, who rode in advance with Mahala by her side, the four pairs of eyes were covered with blue glass. The tricycles slowed up considerably as they came nearer to a team, which, by means of a sedate and thoughtful old horse, was making its way along the road. Attached to the sober animal was a rusty vehicle which had once been a nice affair, but its shining freshness was past long ago. On the middle of the high

seat sat, or rather perched, an individual in black clothes
with worn and fraying bindings.   A small clump of sparse
whiskers grew on his rather prominent chin.   This masculine adornment would naturally have been gray, but the
owner, evidently deluding himself with the idea that a
purple-black dye would conceal his age and add a general
festivity to his appearance, had used the deceitful fluid
upon them, but some days before, so that, as the beard
grew out and was unavoidably dampened by his daily ablu-
tions, it showed a quarter of an inch of dirty yellow next
the face which deepened through various shades of orange,
pale green, and greenish purple, into the deceptive and
fascinating black, which looked about as much like nature's
glossy jet as his faded satinet clothes resembled the fine
broadcloth of a fastidious gentleman.   A severely high
collar, surrounded by a wrinkled black neck-tie, held his
long neck as in a vise.   He wore a tall hat with a wide
weed, and black kid gloves, through the rips in which the
ends of his thumb and several fingers were seen.   The expression on his sallow countenance was an indescribably
funny mixture of priggish dignity and amazed curiosity, as
each party turned out for the other.

> "I know it is a sin
> For me to sit and grin
> At him here·"

Muttered Mahala;

> "But his shocking weedy hat,
> And his gloves, and all that,
> Are so queer."

"Be still, Mike," whispered her leader.   The man was

looking at tnem, and urging the indifferent beast into an imperceptibly faster walk. Seeing that he was about to speak to them, Mrs. Mather forestalled his intention by saying in a tragic tone, " Sir, please tell me, are we nearing Portland ? "

The shabby gloves pulled up the dejected steed, and the owner slowly surveyed the quartette and then replied, " Portland ? You are on the wrong side of the river, madam."

" What ? " quickly asked the stern woman, with her hand behind her ear.

" You are on the wrong side of the river," he repeated in a louder voice. " This is Middletown."

Four pairs of dense blue glasses remained leveled at his face, and no one said a word.

" Is the lady hard of hearing ? " inquired the stranger, turning to Miss Wright, who came next.

" What ? " ejaculated Mahala, raising her hand to her right ear, and sending the monosyllable with such force that the man fairly jumped.

He suddenly caught the ghost of a smile on the face of Miss St. John, who rode in the rear, and putting on a sickly smirk, intended to be attractive, he said to her, " Madam, your young ladies are playful. Nothing like merriment in the young. Oh! yes, let them laugh and joke while they may, for when they have passed through trials and bereavements " (an affecting sigh), "when they have lost a dear partner in life " (a sniff), "they will not feel so gay. May be, ma'am," said he, leaning over impressively towards the artist, "may be you, too, have suffered such a loss."

She put her hand behind her ear. " Wha–at ? " drawled she.

This was a poser.   He looked searchingly from face to face, and failing to perceive the truth, as no betraying eyes were to be seen, turned in doubt to Margery.

" Miss, I do not know whether an insult is intended or not. If your friends are really deaf, perhaps you can be ears for them.   I have a work here which I am introducing to the intelligent people of this community.   It is a very interesting and instructive book.   Deacon Smart of Middletown, whom perhaps you know, the Rev. Mr. Oliphant, Miss Sharp, the music-teacher, and many other distinguished names, are upon the list of my subscribers. Perhaps you would like to look at it," he said, encouraged by the interested expression Margery had wickedly assumed.   He leaned far out of the wagon and extended a large book towards her.   She turned her glasses upon it but made no move to take it from his hand.   He gave it a little twist and added, " It is the life of—"

" What?" said Margery, politely, and in her sweetest tones.

The man's eyes opened. His jaw fell, and after an instant of apparent petrifaction he picked up his lines in solemn wrath and drove away.

Mahala dashed along the road with her handkerchief stuffed into her mouth, and when the rusty team turned a bend in the street, with its driver still casting now and then a puzzled look to the rear, she tumbled off from her saddle, and sitting down on a stone by the way, held her hands to her sides and laughed till the tears ran down her cheeks.

"Oh! dear! dear!" she gasped. "How my sides ache! Was n't it too funny for any use? Ha! ha! ha-a-a! And when—he! he!—and when he discovered an affinity in Aunt Dude, I thought I should die."

"Pshaw! you silly girl," said Miss St. John, flushing a little while she laughed, "do not call upon your imagination in order to get a joke upon me."

"But, girls, I'll leave it to you, did n't he look too utterly sweet as he spoke to her, and threw his chin out sideways in such a captivating manner?"

Mrs. Mather and Margery wisely refrained from taking sides on this important question, and the young mischief-maker continued on her way, feeling that the plan for the battery of blue glasses and the baffling "what," which had been hatched in her fertile brain, had proved a brilliant success. As they rode on, she repeatedly broke out into one of her infectious chuckles, so that all were forced to join again in the enjoyment of the ludicrous scene just enacted.

At five o'clock, after a run of seven or eight miles, they came into a beautiful shaded high street in the little city of Middletown. "You remember, do you not, Mahala," said Mrs. Mather, "that Dickens refers to this town and this street with particular admiration in his 'American Notes?'"

"Oh! is this the street?" said Mahala, casting a look about them. "I knew he did praise one thing in America. I am glad to see it with my own eyes."

"He told us many distasteful truths, though, did n't he?" said Mrs. Mather, smiling, and they stopped at the house of a friend of Mr. Prescott's.

CHAPTER VIII.

Sane and Insane.

"YOU must certainly visit the Connecticut Hospital for Insane at Middletown," Mr. Prescott had said to Margery, and had given her a letter of introduction to an old friend of his, who held a position of trust at the institution.

Therefore, in pursuance of a part in the plan to which all had looked forward with interest, they started about ten in the morning to ride out to the hospital. It is beautifully situated a mile or more out of town, upon an eminence which commands an enchanting view of city and river.

They rode steadily out of the handsome streets, on to a low road, by some factories, across a bridge, and soon came to the hill. Here, as usual, they dismounted and pushed their machines, but as they reached a neat little lodge at the gate which opened into the extensive grounds, they took to their saddles again and rode rapidly up the well-kept drive, which ran in graceful curves to the main entrance of the building.

They remarked the slope of the green grass stretching away to the boundaries of the grounds, and saw several rustic arbors with seats for many people underneath their canopies. They noticed in the flower-plats, which were cut in many graceful designs, that a few brilliant blossoms remained untouched by the frost.

"I presume the more delicate plants have already been housed," said Margery, "for papa tells me that they have a perfect bower at the end of every ward where the patients are at all capable of appreciating them, although they are obliged to protect the plants from irresponsible hands by wire screens."

Having given their machines into the charge of a polite coachman, who met them as they drew up to the massive stone steps, they rang the large bell at the door, and were shown at once into a reception-room by a young lady. She took Margery's letter of introduction, accompanied by her card, to the office of the gentleman, who soon after entered the room.

He was known to all his associates in the building as "the major," and was seen to be a remarkably fine-looking gentleman of sixty or thereabouts, with a well-filled figure, which was clothed in garments of fashionable style and finest quality. His gray hair, which was receding from his already high forehead, grew thickly upon his temples, and was continued in a full mustache and side-whiskers, which he was prone to clasp and pull to their extreme points when discussing or considering a question. His manners were graceful, and held a flattering deference to all ladies.

"Is this Miss Prescott?" he said, as Margery arose and came a step forward at his entrance.

"It is."

"I am very glad to know your father's daughter," said
the major, "and wish to extend him my thanks for sending
you with your friends to call upon us here."

Margery now introduced her friends, and they spent a
few minutes in pleasant conversation.

Miss St. John had made up her mind about the major in
five minutes of a close scrutiny of his face and general
deportment.

"A perfect gentleman of the old school," she said aside
to Mrs. Mather, who sat near her, and this was much from
her, as she had a critical eye for the short comings of the
male sex.

"Now, let me see," said the major, rising and consulting
his watch, "you will wish to go about the building, of
course."

"Yes; if you please."

"I will go out, if you will excuse me, and see if Mrs.
Duncan has returned from her morning rounds. She is
the matron, and is an indefatigable worker, and just at
present has several quite sick patients upon her hands. So
perhaps — ah, here she is now!" he said, as they heard a
business-like voice in the hall. It was saying: "Yes, doctor, it seems to me that Miss Merton is now in a fair way
to recover. But Johanna is still a very sick girl. Don't
you think so?" and as they all waited, a low conference
ensued. "Did you want me, major?" she said at last, perceiving him in the doorway, as they heard the invisible
doctor walk away.

"Yes, if you are at leisure," he said, turning to present
her to the visitors who sat within the reception-room. She

was a lady of energetic action and of very attractive countenance. She carried several keys at her belt and had a small glass of some cordial in her hand. They all knew that she had been in charge of the women's wards since the hospital was instituted, and held a large responsibility, which she discharged with unvarying promptness and good judgment.

"We shall certainly be pleased to show you about the place," she said to them, "although it is not our regular visiting day."

"Oh, then, I am afraid we are giving you too much trouble," said Mrs. Mather.

"Not at all," was the reply. "I trust you will find things in comfortable order, although some of the patients who are scrupulous about their appearance may not have on their best dresses," she added, smiling. "Will you come with us through the north side, major?"

"Certainly, if the young ladies wish, and you will permit." As they started out he turned to the matron and said : "Perhaps I may as well tell you now, Mrs. Duncan, that Miss St. John, after presupposing that we have some dark and noisome dungeons down in the earth where howling maniacs lie in chains, on filthy straw, overrun with rats and smaller vermin —"

"Oh, sir!" said that lady, with some spirit, "did my small insinuation that you did not show all your wards to visitors convey such an exaggerated idea to your mind? I merely asked if we would be allowed to see the worst cases."

"That was what I was about to add, Miss St. John, and

was going to ask Mrs. Duncan to gratify your truly femi-nine desire; I will not term it curiosity," and he laughed in amusement, at her expense.

"It is only for you to elect," said the matron, "where you will go. Later, I will take you through one of the worst wards, and if you are not then satisfied, you can see more."

She was unlocking a door which opened into a sunny corridor which, having a strip of bright carpet running through it, was hung with pictures, and a large stand of green plants was seen at the wide window at the further end. The doors of the neat bedrooms opened into the hall, and the inmates sat or walked about on every side.

Just as the door swung to behind them, a tall woman with her front hair in curl-papers seized the major by the arm.

"You never delivered that note I gave you! I know you never did!" she cried, vehemently. "If you did, why don't he come to see me? You are trying your best to prevent him from marrying me, but he promised to do it, and will, if you do not break it up!" and her expression of angry impatience somewhat discomposed Mrs. Mather, who clung close to the matron.

"She is harmless," said Mrs. Duncan.

"Oh, now, Mrs. Small! don't scold me so. You know I am willing to help you all I can," said the major, taking her by the hand. She snatched it away.

"You are not! What do you want to tell that for? What have you got against me, anyhow?"

"Well," was his answer, "I really do not approve of

those thing-um-bobs in your hair. If you want to please the doctor you must take them down, you know."

She struck fiercely at his hand, but a gleam of amusement showed in her eye, although she tried to look as cross as she could.

"There now! you look much prettier already," said the major, in a bantering tone, "you will be much more likely to win him if you smile."

"Oh, go away!" was the sharp reply.

"She is not really sincere in that talk, is she?" said Mrs. Mather to the matron as they passed on.

"It is impossible to tell. She talks it every waking moment," answered Mrs. Duncan.

They looked into the neat rooms with their clean white beds, and saw old women lying quietly upon the couches, and touched their wrinkled hands with their young fresh palms, as the aged patients looked up with a degree of interest and pleasure in their feeling eyes. One pale, slender girl, whose thin hands and hopeless face stopped Mahala's feet, begged to be allowed to kiss her.

"She is very gentle," said the matron, and Mahala lent her round cheek to the wistful caress.

Some patients flung themselves around in impatient scorn of the visitors as they came in view, but many followed softly along with the party and gently touched their garments or their hands.

They looked into a large room where were cases filled with books, some lounges, work-tables, and a piano.

A girl with short hair and the usual emaciation which attends the "mind diseased" was playing an accompaniment which did not chord with an incoherent song she was singing, but which seemed to give great pleasure to the performer.

They remarked that there seemed to be no association among the inmates. Each patient was alone, with her own delusion or fantastic imaginings. Those who sat near seldom spoke to each other, and when one was in any way refractory, the others merely stood around and laughed wildly at the scene or paid no attention to it.

"They do not associate or sympathize," said the lady who was in charge. "It is this fact which makes it safe and possible for two attendants alone to manage a whole ward."

Up stairs and down stairs, unlocking doors, speaking with attendants, and looking with pitying eyes upon scores of demented human beings, they went, until almost bewildered with a repetition of the same sad scene.

Once they met a beautiful lady with gray puffs at the side of her face, who came with a graceful walk into the hall. She was attired in a handsome calling costume.

"Good morning, Mrs. Duncan. Ah, major, I am glad to see you within our precincts once more," she said, with a perfectly possessed air and the general style of a well-bred lady. She was introduced to the visitors as Mrs. Clapham ; and greeting them in a queenly manner, invited them to come to her room, and rest when they were tired.

"I have just been over to town, to the dentist. A most unpleasant ordeal, I think we all find it, but nevertheless an act of prudence. I shall be ready to receive at any time ; until then, good-by," and she sailed away down the hall.

"She is doubtless some official, or the wife of some of the doctors," Mrs. Mather had whispered to Margery.

"The lady we just met is —" Miss St. John began, inquiringly.

"Is a patient."

"Not insane!"

"Yes, and sometimes very troublesome. But again, as to-day, she has lucid intervals, when she can be allowed to go to town, but with always some watchful eyes upon her," and Mrs. Duncan smiled at the surprise of the unsophisticated visitors.

"Would you like to visit a bad ward now?" she said, turning, key in hand, before a door. "You will perhaps not feel like speaking to any here, as they are sometimes excitable. Shall we go in?"

"Yes," said Miss St. John.

"Yes," echoed her niece, more faintly.

"Shall we?" said Mrs. Mather to Margery, who did not seem very anxious to do so.

"O, I do not know; well, yes, if all wish it," said Margery, gathering up her courage with a long breath; and they went in.

The ward was perfectly neat and clean, with, however, no superfluous ornamentation. "Nothing that will smash or tear," the major said, quietly. "You will have observed," he continued, "that we have no patients under any fixed restraint. We profess to live up to the most intelligent and humane ideas in the care of the insane in this institution, and you will see that the superintendent carries the principle of non-restraint into the wards where are

w. & w.—6

the most violent sufferers. The restraining hands of attendants are always ready to prevent injury to themselves or others, but we use no gyves or fetters."

"Yes," said the matron, "in this liberation of the violent ones, we consider that the Connecticut stands ahead of other State hospitals."

"Is Maggie out of her room to-day, Mrs. Duncan?" said the major.

"O, yes, she is here, and quite enjoying herself."

They looked, and there upon a bench sat a woman with a shock of brick-red hair, a face covered with large freckles and spotted with a hectic flush. Her light eyes glanced continuously from one thing to another, seeing nothing, and as she drew up and straightened out her bare legs they saw that she wore a dress of heavy sailcloth which hung in shreds around the bottom and came just below her knees. From the short sleeves protruded thin and cordy arms, and in her claw-like hand she held a piece of thick canvas. This she was biting and tearing with her jagged yellow teeth, and occasionally emitted a wild shriek.

"She is comparatively quiet to-day, so we brought her out of her room," said the woman in attendance to the matron.

Miss St. John thought, "What a subject for a painter!"

Mahala had taken refuge behind the form of the major, who assured her that the maniac was under the watchful eye of her attendant, although not in any way restrained by straps or straight-jacket.

"O! Julie's fainting," said Mahala, suddenly.

"No, I am not," said the little lady, "but I am sick;

shocked to the core. Let us get out of here! O, that there are such possibilities as that for any of us." She shuddered and buried her face in her hands.

Margery clasped her friend's waist and they shortly emerged into the center, or officer's department, "which is where ostensibly sane people reside," said the major, smiling.

They sat resting for a few minutes in the pleasant parlor set apart for Mrs. Duncan; and the major, who had previously excused himself at the door, came back with a young physician, whom he introduced, and asked to accompany them to the south side.

"I am sorry," said this officer, "that our superintendent is at present away and that so poor a representative as myself is left to do the honors of the institution. I trust, however, that you will receive every attention. I am glad to do all in my power to make your visit a pleasant one."

Mrs. Mather replied politely to the seeming cordiality of the doctor, as they proceeded on their way; but he was evidently not able to devote much time to the entertainment of the ladies, and when they met an assistant physician in the halls, he excused himself, delegating his office to Doctor Manly, who made the other's place good and accompanied them with respectful kindness through the south side, or men's department.

They found that the acumen of strangers was sadly tried in passing among this motley crowd. They shrank back from a young man whose eyes, "in fine frenzy rolling," evidently meant mischief, and were introduced to a gentlemanly attendant. They engaged in a pleasant talk with an elegant gentleman who told them astonishing things about the institution, and were laughingly requested by the major not to waste any more time on that lunatic.   They had commented freely on the beauty of a certain young lady on the north side, and were somewhat confused when she smiled very sanely and informed them that she was in charge of some patients, and did not need their pity.

A noticeable object among the men was Mr. Murphy. He stood out in the hall, his spare form animated by the music which was thrumming in the parlor, and his feet trotting out every note.   His small skull was covered by a thin parchment-like skin drawn tightly over it.   A sparse growth of white hair covered his cranium, and his fleshless face was adorned with one blind eye.   His nose and chin were becoming near neighbors over his shrunken lips, which, parting, disclosed two teeth only upon the lower jaw.   His natural charms were enhanced by a red silk handkerchief which he wore under a much-prized straw hat, the corners of which hung down beside his amiable countenance in the most jaunty manner.   His politeness upon introduction was extreme, and he thought he saw a resemblance in Margery to her father, whom he considered a handsome man.   This gave rise to sad memories, and he wept.   "As for me," said he, in a broken voice, "I resemble my poor mother."   They were sorry the old lady was dead, but were willing to forego a vision of like feminine beauty.

That some of these unaccountable creatures like fun and even perpetrate a pun upon occasions was seen.   A powerful man, playfully called "Old Cobby," upon introduction,

opened conversation by saying to Mrs. Mather, "I am going to hammer you." The Major, appreciating his little
joke, squared off as if to defend her, and gave him a little
tap on the nose, whereupon he pretended to be dreadfully
frightened, said he did not mean it, and begged pardon.

The doctor, assisting the fun, pointed to a little eruption
on his cheek and asked, "Is that where he hit you, Cobby?"
when he quickly rejoined, "O, no! that's where I boiled
over a little." Then becoming suddenly dignified, he
made a courtly bow to Miss St. John, and said, "Could
you favor me with a chew of tobacco, madam?"

At the hour of noon they were enabled, through the
kindness of the doctor, to see some of the patients at table.
The insane men behaved generally with great propriety at
dinner. One, who labored under the impression that he
was the King of Ireland, was very polite, assisting all
around him to whatever they wished, and carried himself
with princely condescension and kindness. This was entirely unexpected, as he was usually anything but urbane
in manner. It had been his habit to thrust his head under
a faucet of running water many times a day, and visitors
felt inclined to shrink behind a corner as he came down
through the hall, his wild eyes rolling and his hair dripping
with water, as he fiercely asserted his claims to the throne.
A most venerable old man, whose resemblance to William
Cullen Bryant was remarkable, sat at the end of a table,
accepting the viands offered him with a quiet grace.

"Red Patsy" was an attractive individual, who had
gorged himself to repletion, and sat lazily contemplating
the world over his ponderous body. He certainly weighed

three hundred pounds. His Henry the Eighth head and face bristled with short red hair, and his skin was of the same brilliant hue. They were told by Dr. Manly that Patsy was formerly a great fighter, sending terror to all hearts when angry; but he is now settled into imbecility, knowing just enough to eat.

One man confided to Margery that he had eaten one hundred and fourteen potatoes. He said he sometimes composed poetry, and proceeded to repeat some which was certainly remarkable.

"But," said he, "it's an awful hard job to be deranged the year around."

They visited the Annex, where insane convicts are confined. They peeped into the laundry and sewing-rooms. They wondered at the enormous kitchen and larder, and confessed themselves tired and their minds full of interesting remembrances.

After a lunch, which was hospitably tendered them by Mrs. Duncan, they went to the South Hospital, where incurable patients are kept. There they met Doctor Dempster, who has this department in charge, and after a short look about this new building, with all its modern improvements, of which the doctor is justly proud, they rested in the cosy sitting-room belonging to the physician and his wife. They were surfeited with pitiful sights, and glad of the change to agreeable and intelligent conversation. Their entertainer here was a very fluent talker, and the flood of anecdotes, quotations, comparisons, and original conclusions that fell from his lips served to partially dissipate the sense of horror that hung over at least two of the visitors.

"What is it? What makes them crazy," Mrs. Mather had said to him. "It must be overtaxing the brain. And yet they told us many of them were servants, cooks, ditch-diggers. I cannot understand it."

"Ah, madam," said the doctor, gallantly, "if we could understand it, we might hope to prevent much of the misery which the friends of the demented undergo."

"The friends?" repeated the lady in some surprise. "Do not the poor victims of such a malady suffer beyond all endurance?"

"Probably not," said the physician. "They rarely, I might say never, shed tears, and are often happy in their delusions. These are usually of an exalted character, and, as far as we can judge, they are happier than most sane people."

"Oh, Doctor!" said the soft-hearted little chaperone, "you surely would not tell me that the poor man was happy who met us at one door of a hall, and, as we entered, tried so hard and yet in such a hopeless way to get out. He had on a shawl, and his hat was in his hand, and he said 'I want to go home. Why can't I go home?' with such a wretched voice and look of misery—" the lady's eyes filled with tears. "They tell me he never leaves the door, in the vain hope of returning again to his loved ones at home."

"Yes, I know," said the doctor, respectfully; "that is old Whitney. I allowed myself to be considerably troubled over his ungratified longing for home until I learned that when he had been let out for a short time that he pounded his wife and children, and became the terror of the neigh-borhood, so that they begged us to take him back here."

"Oh, how incomprehensible!" sighed Mrs. Mather.

"Very!" said the doctor. "Crazy people are apt to be."

"But are they mostly made so by overwork, brain-work, and a whirl of excitement, the madness of Wall-street speculation, or strenuous efforts to win a high place in the world?"

"I am truly sorry, my dear Mrs. Mather, to be obliged to answer you to the contrary, but I will take a catalogue (this one is a year old, I see, but it will serve our purpose as well as another), and read you some facts. I am not a Gradgrind, but facts *are* stubborn things."

"Girls, you must all hear this," said the lady; "we are going to find out from statistics what makes people insane."

"While not willing to say that I can answer so intricate and baffling a question," said the doctor, with a deprecating smile, "I merely intend to show that it is frequently monotony that kills the intellect. That it is not those who are pleasantly occupied with a pursuit which is interesting and varied, even though it may be somewhat exciting, who oftenest lose their reason."

"Pardon me, Doctor!" interposed Miss St. John, in her crisp way; "can you judge the whole subject by the patients who come to you here? In the first place, Connecticut has no hurrying, scurrying, tearing, and nerve-destroying metropolis. Our small cities are steady-going places. Secondly, is it not a fact that you do not receive the wealthier class of patients? Are they not in private asylums?"

"Miss St. John," said the doctor, "your points are well taken. I can only say that I think you will not find any great difference between the occupations of the patients in other State asylums and those of ours. As to the men of brains, of professional callings, and busy lives, you are perhaps right in supposing that their friends are apt to place them in some smaller and more expensive hospital, feeling a repulsion to sending them to a hospital in part supported by the State. Still, as their cases prove obstinate or of long duration, they are very generally sent here. But even allowing for a large percentage of unknown brain- workers who have gone 'daft,' the showing is a surprisingly large majority of people who have mentally stagnated. It is no doubt a surprise to most people to see, upon a study of these tables, that it is not those who lead lives of business, distracted by the turmoil and excitement of the world, who lose their reason, but rather those who rust out; those who are crushed by the hopeless monotony and ceaseless grind of uninteresting work. Out of the two thousand three hundred and thirty-three patients admitted from the beginning up to the time this catalogue was made, six hundred and ninety-nine are housewives and domestics."

"Of course, the majority of female patients are entered under these two heads," spoke up Miss St. John.

"But, here are two hundred and sixty-two farmers; of day-laborers, two hundred and twenty-six; of factory employees, one hundred and twenty-six. Consider these figures as against one broker, three engineers, two lawyers, five physicians, and three telegraph operators. Saloon-keepers, it seems, are kept bright and sane by an occasional fight, or a visit from a customer's irate wife; here are only four. Landlords meet with a constant variety in the different excuses as to delinquent rent, in the unexpected departure of a tenant whose money was due, in inventing plausible reasons for not doing repairs, saying, 'Why, the house does not carry itself now, sir.' Only one landlord has been wrecked in the storm of life. Seriously, it is monotony, routine, that destroys the mental faculties. See again, thirty-nine seamstresses have gone crazy, stitching on

> " 'Band and gusset and seam,
> Seam and gusset and band,
> Till the heart is sick and the brain benumbed,
> As well as the weary hand.'

"Yet only two milliners. They can pin on a knot of ribbon and a bunch of plumes and tell Miss McFlimsy that 'it's a little beauty, modeled after a Paris hat, and *so* cheap at twenty-five dollars.' "

Mahala was a little doubtful if the doctor was not running on in this light manner to relieve their minds of any unpleasant impressions which might remain from the pitiable objects they had seen lying and sitting about in the wards by scores.

Miss St. John considered it a very attractive way of putting hard facts. They thanked the genial doctor who had done so much for their entertainment and instruction, and returned to the entrance of the main building, where they had left their wheels. He insisted upon seeing them off and walked over with the major to see them mount and run their curious vehicles.

"I shall fear going crazy constantly," said Margery, "after this day."

"I shall not," declared Mahala, "I never was so sure of my sanity in my life."

CHAPTER IX.

The Rainy Day.

MAHALA looked out of the window.
"Now this looks, as Joe would say, 'rather jubious.' What is to be done? Here we are, miserable prisoners in this town, which yesterday seemed so beautiful. All because of the rain. Say! who has rubbers — any one? We have our umbrellas, if we had only thought of rubbers!

"I have mine," said Miss St. John, with a superior air, "and will lend them. For my part, I think a rainy day not much loss. There is a lovely old highboy in the kitchen and a quaint side-board in the dining-room of which I shall make a sketch."

"Of course," merrily rang out Mrs. Mather's voice, "there is always something an artist can take hold of for diversion. Mike, where do you suppose I found your industrious aunt this morning before breakfast? At work on some old barrels in the door-yard there, one tub half full of water, and a quantity of other wet truck that she said were delightful bits for light and reflections; and really they did look so, after she had caught the effect with her pen and ink. I don't see how she does it! and the way she works while I sit idly gazing is a marvel to me.

She has that sketch-book three-quarters full now, and here we are only a week out."

Miss St. John smiled at this effusion, but was too intent upon her work on an old tumbledown mill which could be seen from the window, to give any expression to her thoughts.

The raindrops fell from the eaves with steady plash and patter upon the line of pebbles below. The wet wood was delicious in its darkness, and as the moist herbage stood erect and dripping with the rain, the vines surging to and fro in the wind, loosened here and there in swinging ends from their support, it was in some respects more satisfying to sit and idly gaze than to make even an attempt to depict the beauty one could not but feel.

"Come, Margie, you and I can venture out. Let Aunt Dude and the *devoted wife* meditate and work at their pleasure. We will have some fun, if it can be found in this stupid —"

" Now, Mahala, don't call this place any bad names ! It is just charming here, and I think this is almost the best day yet. This rain will soon cease and we may get a gray day, by way of variety. These autumn colors do come out so forcibly against a gray sky. I never half realize the gorgeousness of this turning foliage till I see it in contrast with the grayness about and above. Do come and see it, Mike."

"Yes, aunty sweet, I know it all. I am just getting on my boots, though, and hunting out your rubbers from the family trunk, so please forgive me if I only turn my mental eyes to the appreciation of your divine scenery. My material optics are turned to my bodily needs at present."

Here she dragged the long-sought-for rubber shoes from their tight pack near the bottom of the trunk.

"Say, girls! what do you think about peanuts? Let's have some, and some molasses candy! I wouldn't talk so much if I had something to chew on occasionally. Caramels, for instance. Caramels! Fifteen cents a quarter!" sang out Mahala, as she skipped across the room, swinging Margery around in a *deux temps* till they both lost balance and came plump against Mrs. Mather, nearly upsetting her in the mad whirl.

"*Ah, Madame Julie, pardon! pardon, Je vous prie,*" cried Mahala, and, in turn, she caught that little lady and performed a similar escapade.

"Come, come, Mike," endeavored Margery, in persuasion. "Let us be off, or the rain will be over, and we shall have not half so much sport as to go with umbrellas and waterproofs."

"I am all ready now," said Mahala, and the two sallied forth.

"Dude, do you think I might try to make that tree? Lend me one of your pencils. I have some paper."

"Surely, you may try, Julie," said the artist, who was always ready and pleased to encourage any attempts in her friends to catch a reflection of the face of nature. "That is an admirable subject for a trial."

Mrs. Mather made a few traces resembling a tree and then her pencil glided off into something like this:

"MY DEAREST OLD FRED:— If that door would only open and you would walk your dear self through it, I should be in the seventh heaven of ecstatic bliss; *i. e.,* I should be in your arms in a twinkling. Those girls are just off for a frolic, and I shall get a chance to drop this little note (if they remain long enough, it may be extended to a letter) in the mail to-night. I thought of trying to telephone you yesterday, I did so want to know if you had returned from your hunting expedition all right and well. But Miss St. John will be wanting to look at my tree, which I began, so I will wait now till she has approved of my sketch, and I haply find her in a more absorbed state in regard to her own work."

The girls went down the street, through and around innumerable puddles, passing under the dripping trees, which showered them from the tips of their wet leaves as the wind soughed through their heavy branches, and stepped gingerly across the little rivulets that ran across the path. A procession of waddling ducks was coming up from an adjacent pond, quack-quacking as they marched in irregular single file. They squawked and spattered along in loud consternation, making little dives and dips with their broad bills as the strangers drove them before.

Proceeding further the two unabashed misses stopped a milk-wagon, and each took a pint of fresh milk from the top of the can, paying double price for the detention of the cart. But whether the extra bit, or Mahala's enlivening remarks upon the occasion, most pleased the astonished driver of the steady establishment, it is not for us to say.

"Now, will you please direct us to the drug store?" said Margery, in a manner so sweet that the young man said he would carry them there if they wished. It was quite a walk in a stormy day.

"Oh, but that is too much trouble for you. We could not think of taking your time for that," said Margery.

"Not at all! not at all, miss. I was just going down that way myself." A curious fact, considering the direction of the horse's head.

Mahala nudged Margery. "Let's!" said she, in undertone.

"Well, we certainly would be glad of the ride," said Margery, "if you are surely going that way. Thank you!"

They were soon handed down at the drug store, much to the excitement of those rainy-day loungers who seem to be indigenous to country stores. The milkman was fully rewarded for his part, by the interest and evident curiosity which was displayed by the heads at the glass in the door. They plainly could not explain the advent of such pretty faces, in such weather, and with Silas Bound!

Your real country lady has a fixed antipathy to going out of doors in the rain.

The idlers within the store speedily dispersed, only one or two of the more courageous remaining to see what the young ladies came to buy, and to ascertain, if possible, where they came from. One of these took refuge behind the well-thumbed morning paper, and another picked his teeth meditatively with a pine sliver as he stared at the rows of jars upon the top shelf.

MAHALA — "Do you keep peanuts, sir?"

DRUGGIST — "No, miss. You will find them next door.

MAHALA — "Any caramels?"

DRUGGIST — "Those you will also find at the store above here."

MAHALA — " Peppermints ? "

DRUGGIST (promptly)—"Oh, yes, we have all the medicinal confectionery. One-quarter of a pound, did you say?"

MAHALA (laying down the change)—"Any lime drops?"

DRUGGIST (with increasing alacrity)—"Very fine fresh ones, miss. One-quarter of a pound? Thank you !"

" Hello-o!" came in stentorian tones from the back part of the store.

The girls jumped as if struck.

"Do not be startled, ladies," said the polite apothecary, "it's only the telephone and the new clerk."

" Who is it ? "   A pause.

" Well, who is it ? "

" Stop buzzing so, or I can't hear a blamed word."

"Stop your own noise and listen, boy," quietly commanded the patient pharmacist. "Listen !"

" Yes, who? Collinses? Yes ! How much baggage?"

"Oh ! Four packages. All right. Two colic plasters. Colored lasting?"   "Well, I thought not." Mahala snickered.   Margery passed her handkerchief over her mouth.

" All right ! What ? Two dudes ? "

Mahala laughed outright.

Poor clerk, with a very red face,—"Wait a minute. I'll get a piece of paper and take it down."

" Hello ! Go on ! "

"Who are you talking with? It's me, Mr. Opdyke." He straightened himself up as he threw a glance over at the young ladies and stroked his smooth jaw. Another anxious time of listening at the tube.

" He wants you, Mr. Smythe," and that gentleman relieved him at the telephone, while Opdyke, a little crest-fallen, presented himself behind the counter to receive further orders from the customers. They had, however, completed their purchases, and with suppressed mirth were making their way out as fast as possible.

"Where now," said Margery, as they stood upon the sidewalk. "Suppose we go to the dry goods store. I want to get something pretty, to fix over Mrs. Furness's bonnet. It is altogether *too* shabby for the poor thing. It will delight her to somewhat approximate present fashions. She is so overcome with *our style*, as she calls it."

"Very well. Perhaps we will see a little more of — of the natives, you know. Find some specimens for instance. There go four ladies, or waterproofs, anyway."

"Let's follow."

They fell in the rear of the four ladies, who entered the only dry goods store in the place. They saw a small, wiry, thin-nosed person in advance of the others, and were just in time to hear her say to the girl behind the counter : "Have you any v-very—v-very nice purple gros-grained ribbon ?"

The girl looked inquiringly.

"Something uv-very, uv-very fine, you know. Purple gros-grain. About so wide." She measured the width upon the forefinger of her much-worn but carefully-mended glove, with the black kid forefinger of the other hand. "Best quality. About so-o wide "

The box of ribbons was handed down.

"Is that the width you wished," said the clerk, as she took up a roll, glancing at the same time at three others, who awaited in suspense the words of the speaker.

W. & W.—7

"Do you think so, Mrs. Plum?"

"Ye-es, the width is right, I believe, but is it nice, Mrs. Joy, you know!"

Mrs. Joy took it in her hand, and after fingering it carefully, held it to the light.

"Well," she said, with the deliberation befitting so important a question, "I think a great deal of color. Yes, this is good color. Royal purple. Will wear well, I judge. You know we want it to wear well. What do you think, Mrs. Bliss?"

"O, it is all right if you think so, Mrs. Joy. You are such a good judge."

"Perhaps," assented the other, modestly; "but you have had actual experience." Then sympathetically, "I know that Mr. Bliss handled the others twelve years."

"Yes, true," sighed Mrs. Bliss, and looked around with a sense of her large responsibility in the matter.

"What did you say was the price?" asked the first speaker, with a little sharpness.

"One dollar and a half a yard."

"A dollar and a half?" the thin little lady repeated. She looked inquiringly at the faces of the other three, who had gathered near.

"Did I understand you to say a dollar and a half a yard?"

"Yes, ma'am."

"It is too much!"

"Not for this ribbon," answered the girl; "it is the best."

"Yes, certainly it must be the best," came in chorus.

Then the first speaker leaned confidingly over the counter towards the girl. "Well, you see," she said in an impressive voice, "it is for religious purposes. Do you think, if we could see Mr. King, that he would throw a little off for us?"

Every one of the committee bent eagerly forward to catch each word of the reply, and as the girl went towards the desk to speak to the proprietor, each lady advanced two steps in that direction.

They all earnestly scanned the features of the store-keeper as he came forward to deal with them.

"Mr. King," said one, in undertones which were distinctly heard by the interested bystanders, "you see we want to buy new book-marks for our church pulpit. We all feel a deep interest in getting a good thing. And generally, you know—for religious purposes—money being raised in small levyings upon each member—it is advisable to make a good bargain." Here the lady smiled and looked fascinating. Each other lady simultaneously smiled and murmured, "As good a bargain as we can."

"You feel the importance of this, Mr. King. You yourself are a church member. Baptist, I believe."

Mr. King assented with a nod.

"Could you not do better with us than—"

"A dollar and a half?" put in the first speaker, aching with impatience through the long sentences of the other, and feeling she must speak now.

Mr. King debated a moment as he bit the end of his pencil. "Profit's little enough, any way," he murmured, "but to accommodate customers—"

"Yes," quickly exclaimed one of the ladies, thinking this was a point not to be lost, "church custom is considerable, of course," and the three cast glances of approval and admiration upon the able diplomatist for her perspicacity.

The store-keeper drew a piece of wrapping-paper towards him and made a few figures upon it.

"I suppose I might call it—dollar thirty-seven and a half, if you wanted any quantity." He looked at the end of the roll. "I don't think I have more than five yards, of that width. You can have what is here at that price," and he sighed slightly.

The four women gathered in close conference.

"You know we shall divide the old ones up for our silk bed-quilts. Each one can have a strip, if she likes," said the one called Mrs. Bliss.

Mahala had drawn near, apparently looking at the things in the show-case, while Margery made her purchase from the clerk.

The first speaker then said audibly, "Those marks that we are now reluctantly discarding, have been placed by holy hands since 1810. Four divines lived and died under them. Does Mr. King know this? It may be so with these, if we buy them of him." She cast her eyes to the ceiling with a religious glow upon her face. "So comforting! Isn't it?"

But Mrs. Joy now had Mr. King's ear. "We do not want so much as five yards," she said, "but if we can have the quantity we want at that price, we will take it, Mr. King."

Now all four ladies edged the counter.

"Two yards is a great deal for three marks."

" It needs three, doesn't it, Mrs. Bliss?"

"Three are desirable.   One for the hymns you know."

" Yes, one for the hymns," in chorus.

" Well then, that will make—"

" Could you measure off five-eighths, Mr. King?   Well, thank you ; giving you a great deal of trouble, we fear. Now, three times five-eighths—"

They all looked inquiringly at the merchant.

"One yard and seven-eighths," he answered, after penciling on the edge of some paper.

" Well, now, that is just it! " said the wiry little woman, who seemed to stand eminent as a financier.   " Call it one yard and three-quarters, and you'll have us !   Isn't that so, ladies?" said she, turning to the others, with a keen light in her eye.

All assented, with an anxious glance at Mr. King, who was by this time pretty well worried into acquiescence with anything.

"Mamma—ma!   Just look here a moment."   Mrs. Joy went over to where stood her daughter, who had gone into the store a short time after the ladies.

"Ain't this handkerchief lovely? and so cheap!   It's only two dollars!   It is just the shade I have hunted and hunted for.   Couldn't find it in Hartford last week."

" This lot came in only yesterday," said the clerk.

" Can't I have it, mamma?   It would look so sweet with my blue velvet.   Just that shade, Rob says, is all the rage.   Something between a peanut-skin red and an orange.   Neither one nor the other!"

"Buy it if you wish, my dear. I am just now very busy. Get it charged," said Mrs. Joy, as she turned back to the ribbon counter.

"Well, Mr. King," she resumed, "if all are agreed, you may please cut off a yard and seven-eighths. Here is just the money for it," counting it out. "One penny short, by mistake. Mrs. Bliss, have you another cent?"

"Let it go," said the man, with anything but a religious expression of countenance. Then the women, all chatting together, left the store.

Margery had found something very pretty for an old lady's hat. The rain was now over, and they made their way home as fast as possible, hoping for another start on wheels by afternoon.

CHAPTER X.

Whys and Other Whys.

THE artist was seated in view of a barn interior. Mrs. Mather and Mahala were searching for amusement.

"Behold her!" exclaimed Mahala, with a theatrical pose, as they came upon Miss St. John, who, after spending an hour in looking for a study, finally put her camp-stool down under an old apple-tree and was taking "an interior" of the most rustic order.

"True genius is a fellow who has an idea, and works with all his might to carry it out. I say, Aunt Dude, how long is that remarkable creature to consume? I am pleased to announce that the man has brought around our tricycles in splendid order, although I, as the most cautious member of this party, was very much afraid to trust them to him. We ought to make a good run in the next two hours. I feel 'like a bird let loose,'" she sang, in a sweet voice.

"Will you please not sing around her, Mike? See, she is a fine old model, that bossy. Just look at her beautiful eyes! they are so steadily fixed on me. If you will only move quietly on now, you may tease as much as you like when I am through this."

"O, yes, in the 'sweet bye and bye.'   Well, let us take
ourselves into the 'beautiful beyond,' Julie.   But mind,
aunty, if you don't hurry up I will be here again soon and
assist, or my name is not Mike Mahala Wright.   Come
Julie," whispered she, as she tried to please her aunt and
go quietly away, "there's that rustic drawing water with
the old oaken bucket; let's interview him!   Don't he look
dudey this morning; actually got a neck-tie on.   He has
evidently been regarding himself in the mirror.   Do come
and award him a smile of appreciation.   I am frightfully
thirsty; let's quaff from the old bucket.   'Touch thy light
finger to its metal rim, burnished gold it becomes to him.
On its rough brim rest thy ruby lip; 'twill remain there
forever, when he goes for a dip.'   That last line is rather
superfluous, considering the meter, but absolutely essential
to the rhyme, you see!   Now, isn't he a real specimen?
Genus homo, species rustico.   What a pity he is a little too
large for my cyanide bottle."   And Mahala ran on in this
nonsensical strain, as if she never had a serious thought.

She had been dreamily walking under some apple-trees
a day or two before, when her eyes suddenly caught a
glimpse of something clinging to one of the tender twigs
which was not a leaf, although its body-color was almost
imperceptible against the green tree.   It was a large worm,
with a brilliant head.   The red knobs which protruded
from its back had arrested her quick eye, and seizing a
pole which was in the yard she eagerly bent down the
limb and soon had in her hand the little branch which held
her prize.   She ran to her friends, holding out her latest
acquisition, and cried in delight, "O, girls, see what a

lovely thing I have found! Joe will be so pleased. He has not found one this year."

"What is it?" said Margery, going to meet her. "Oh!" and she recoiled with a little cry of disgust. "A horrible worm! What can you want of that? Throw it away! Please don't put it near me, Mike; I shall die if you do."

Mahala looked at her with a pretense of scorn.

"No, I don't think I will trust it near you. Likely as not you would burn it up, or some such thing! The poor thing can't live much longer, anyway, and he shall have a nice nest and plenty to eat;" the girl stroked his hideous form with her taper forefinger.

"Why, my dear," said Mrs. Mather, coming up, "what will you do with this crawling monster? If you gently suffocate him as you do your beetles, you have no way to preserve such a fluid body. It will soon decay."

"Well!" said the naturalist's sister, addressing an imaginary audience in the vicinity of the well-curb; "I must say that the shameless ignorance of some people who pretend to a fair amount of intelligence is positively astonishing. Do you suppose I would poison this gorgeous creature? Not for the world! Look at those lovely scarlet knobs with the little black prickers which crown him right royally! See those little spots of blue enamel, which bead his neck so beautifully against his light-green skin! Where can you find another such exquisite combination of seemingly conflicting colors? Aunty will appreciate that. But you certainly must respect the spike on the end of his tail.

"Yes, we do!" shuddered Margery.

"But you need not fear; he is tired with living.   It is getting chilly, and after he has eaten a little more he will go into his winter's sleep.   Poor fellow!   How short and apparently useless has your little day been, and how soon do you give it all up."

"What a strange combination that girl is," said Margery, as Mahala walked away, tenderly shielding and talking to the sluggish creature that clung with his great feet to the branch.   "Her alternations from boisterous mirth to the tenderest solicitude for any beast, and sentimental soliloquies over objects that merely fill me with creeping chills, are a constant surprise to me."

"Mahala is indeed a very interesting character, and not the least of her charms to me is her innate all-pervading love of nature," responded Mrs. Mather.   "She has a spontaneous interest in and love for everything that God has made.   A crawling worm, that we shrink away from, she finds a fascinating study.   A lonely child or a sick mother will elicit a flow of sympathy from her that no society queen can command."

"Yes, it is so, Julie."

On the morning of which we write, the artist at her work and the two others, who were making preparations to depart, were startled by Mahala, who came running to them with a cracked fruit-jar in her hand.   "O, girls, my beautiful worm is dying!   It's very accommodating in him, certainly, to assume this portable form, so I can send him home in a box.   You know I have kept him supplied with leaves, but yesterday he stopped eating and in the night he commenced to spin his cocoon.   See!   He is weaving his own shroud of finest silk. If I only could have seen him at work! But he has taken his last look at earth and now is almost hidden from sight. You can just see the red spots on his head down in this enveloping case How he seems to have shrunk and dwindled away. O, the wonder of it! To make these preparations to preserve his chrysalis for another life in the spring time. His little day is ended. What was that existence for? Why should it have to be given up and a long oblivion ensue before coming out into the beautiful winged floating existence in the future? I wonder if it is painful, this change; or is he so weary and chilled that he is glad to wrap this mantle around him and lay him down to rest?"

"Mahala, child," said her practical aunt, "do not trouble your young head with these vain conjectures. It is after all but a poor worm undergoing a change which is inevitable in the order of things. It is a natural transition from the worm to the chrysalis, to the moth, and again the egg, which hatches the worm. And so we go, round and round, life after life; and so we wax and wane. Leave weakening reflections, and do what we can as we go, I say."

" But, Dude," gently said Mrs. Mather, "this, being an emblem of human life, and death, and immortality, it must and does appeal most powerfully to a thoughtful mind."

" True, Julie! I merely make a general objection to the constant turning over and over in the mind of these questions, which will never be answered in this world. As we do not know, and cannot possibly find out what this existence is all for, let us *do* what we can. Accomplish something in this life, and then accept its termination as trustingly as we did its beginning. We shall be equally helpless and ignorant of the future."

Meantime Miss St. John had finished her sketch, and gotten together the paraphernalia necessary to her work. She now went to assist Margery, who, with her little housewifely ways, was always picking up and settling things so as to make the progress of their journey easy and comfortable. Impatient calls were heard from Mahala, and soon the friends were assembled at the gate, ready for departure. With many kind wishes from all at the farm house; and promises from the travelers to return some future day, they took their leave. Even the old watch-dog gave a friendly wag of the tail and turned sad eyes after them as the party rolled off and were soon lost to sight. The day was fresh and bright, and the wheeling good. The glow of cheeks and the flow of spirits showed this to have been a most exhilarating jaunt. Nothing had occurred to mar their vivid enjoyment of the road, the scenery, the people. They were now prepared with pocket-luncheon for a good eight hours' pleasure, with hopes to rest at nightfall at Haddam.

"Friends," said Miss St. John, "you must let me halt at my first call. When I get a glimpse of a lane — an overgrown, weed-covered, untraveled, long, winding lane, vines running over the side-fences, tumbled-down stones, little standing pools of water made by cattle hoofs, low bushes, and all that — a lane such as one where my childish feet used to wander, while I, picking berries or flowers by the wayside, felt that I could go on and on forever (for I never reached the end), when I come on just such a perspective, leading out from the roadside, I shall call a halt and you may take a rest.

Here Mahala cried "Oyez—Oyez—Oyez!" and waving her hand not ungracefully, as if addressing an audience. "When, lying before me in dim uncertainty amid the green grass, I behold a hopper of unusual size, I halt to further examine the creature, if I cry out 'A specimen, a specimen!' then let this body of riders gather itself in a circle around the animal while I make a capture. If aunty is allowed at every view to check the onward moving of this procession, and for so simple a thing as an 'impression,' I too shall crave your leniency. A 'specimen' is what I am in search of, and having thus far found little worth sending to my expectant brother, who, we all know, is to be the future naturalist of Connecticut, this day I shall devote myself to an earnest and continued search till I meet with success."

"We make no objections to your artistic or naturalistic departures, I am sure," quietly said Margery. "At the Junction the other day I came across that new story we were talking of. As the book-boy stepped off the train I caught sight of him, and as he had just the one I called for, the book was mine in a trice. Here in my belt-satchel it was lain, awaiting just such an hour. We can enjoy it by ourselves, Julie, under some quiet shade, while you, our artist, impress your lane, and Mike makes a capture."

"But won't you assist?" asked Mahala.

"No, no."

"How can I catch a vile creature without some help? I should—"

"Now don't say 'smile.' 'Tis too stale for anything," put in Julie.

"Scream, probably, then," continued Mahala. "Suppose it should not be a grasshopper at all? Suppose it a green snake or a great lizard."

"Lizards are small."

"Or a horn-beetle."

"Or a butterfly," suggested Margery.

"Or a *bear*," growled Mahala, making great eyes at them.

Onward they rode.

The sun shone on the darkly-green grass. Golden-rod and purple asters blossomed on every side. Merry little chirpers sprang up from the roadside and hid themselves again a second afterwards. Crickets chirruped in the warm hedge-rows, and occasionally a songless bird flittered through the clear air above. After a time the tricyclers came into some cool woods. Overhanging trees shaded either side.

"Really," said Mahala, taking off her hat and throwing back the curls from her moist forehead, "this shade is delicious! The sun is almost as fierce as in June. To-day seems like a return of summer. Hark! Was not that the notes of a wood-thrush?"

"No, Mahala; it is too late in the season," said her aunt, as she measured the proportion of a graceful tree with her eye.

"Well, it was a wood-thrush, just the same; I am sure I am not mistaken—there!"

It came again; the clear flute-notes echoing through the distant trees :—

"How sweet in the dear little thing to greet us so!" said Margery, as they stopped their wheels and listened. But he sang no more.

"I'll write Joe about that," said Mahala, delighted, as she reluctantly started her pedals. "How the lusty fellow did pipe it up! He is not going to hump up and look forlorn, although winter is coming. He is glad to have one more such perfect day, and when the cold pinches his toes, I'll wager he will not complain, but make the best of it. He is a kind of Mark Tapley among birds, and I like him!"

Refreshed by the change from the almost oppressive sunshine to the umbrageous coolness of the woody air, on and on they went. Each moment in their swift transit new beauties sprang into life at their gaze. As they neared again the open country, devotional stillness seemed to have fallen on our party, as if the "splendor of the grass, the glory of the flower" were all too glorious, too beautiful for expression. Each soul was glad with an innocent delight—joy so filled their hearts, and beauty so gladdened their sight. Now they came out to a view of the picturesque village. Midday light shone on the homes as they lay snugged in below the hills; the farms, the winding roads, the glistening stream, busy life, lay all before them. Church and school-house stood in relief in the landscape.

" Please tell me," said Mrs. Mather, as she rode beside Miss St. John, "why is it there is always a certain unquestionable beauty in a spire? Is it really beauty of form that always excites pleasurable emotions? Is it really that two lines simply meeting do enclose a form of beauty. Almost any other angularity seems objectionable."

The artist, after a little thought, said, "I believe it is not in the lines; not in the thing itself."

" Be that as it may, is not everything earthly, however beautiful in itself, enhanced or spiritualized as it approaches a heavenly nature?"

" You think, then," said the artist, "that the view of a spire, tapering as it does insensibly to the heaven above us, awakens in us all the secret associations of that heaven, even though we ourselves may be unconscious of the mental process."

"Aha!" derisively shouted Mahala, checking her wheels and falling back into line with the others, "so much for impressionism. I can do better than that :

'If eyes were made for seeing,
    Then beauty is its own excuse for being.' "

" Original, of course! Suppose nobody knows Emerson but Miss Wright," quickly retorted Mrs. Mather.

" Well, we must put a stop to sentimentality," imperiously declared Mahala, as she rode forward again. " Now tell me, Aunt Dude," she continued, as she stopped in the road and waited for the more steady riders to approach, "why, of all things in earthly (or heavenly, if you will) creation, does a spider affect you with such shivers of horror, that you feel each individual hair creep and stand upright inside your new poke? Why are you thrown in a malarial condition at the sight of this harmless creature? Why do your hands grow cold? Why does sweat appear in beads upon your artistic brow and come dripping down your pale cheeks? O, say."

"You little goose! if you don't let us have a little common sense once in a while," exclaimed her aunt, laughing, you will demoralize the whole quartette before we get home. You just march ahead and keep Margery company."

"Very well, if you and Julie cannot answer civil questions I will return to my more congenial companion." But she continued in distinct tones, turning her face half way around so that they might hear, "Margery, *why* do alligators usually inspire me with an awful feeling of respect; and *why* in their tracks do even wise men fear to tread?"

"Because—because," began Margery, laughing and hesitating, "of the inequality of the line of their backs, I guess; or a certain regularity in the shape of their teeth, perhaps."

"And why does a snake, even though his line is a curved one, and frequently even spiral (especially when coiled for a spring), *not* inspire one with that sense of beauty which would ordinarily move one in other beautiful curves? And why, unconscious though one may be of the mental process, is one affected to a rapid withdrawal from the scene?"

A general laugh ensued. Whistles were blown as signal for rest and lunch.

CHAPTER XI.

—•—

Confessions and Confusions.

IT was one of October's perfect days. The sun shone
brilliantly across the landscape, now resplendent with
the gorgeous hues that only a New England climate pro-
duces on the dying leaves. Masses of color in a thousand
hues, from the deep maroon of the oaks, through the
countless shades of crimson to fiery scarlet and orange in
the maples, to the pale yellow of the walnuts, dazzled the
senses with a flood of delicious tints. Ferns in the open
field showed a combination of browns in every shade, from
chocolate to a woody yellow, and even to a pale white in
the bleached fronds, which stood like pure spirits of departed friends among the dying ones. The deep green of
firs and the bright emerald of the grassy fields gave a perfect background, and on the more distant hills there lay a
purple haze softening the whole view into a dreamy
beauty. The air was so soft and thin that distant sounds
came to the ear, faint, yet clear; the lowing of kine in '
far-away places, the tolling of bells, or the call of a child,
came floating over the land, musical and almost unearthly
in effect.

"It is near here," said Miss St. John, whose artistic soul was full of joy in the beautiful day, "that I made that little study last year. Now if you girls can amuse yourselves for an hour, I can get just the effect in this autumnal haze that I want. Yes, here are the bars where we went in before."

"Very well, Dude," said Mrs. Mather, "we certainly can find enough to enjoy anywhere to-day. You go ahead with your traps and begin work, and we will take care of your tricycle."

The artist disappeared, all intent on her beloved work, and as soon as the trio had pulled their wheels inside the wall and walked over the knoll, they found her already hard at it. An umbrella, fixed on a stick, which was thrust firmly into the ground, her folding easel in position, her green bag of paints and brushes lying on the ground by her side, she sat on her camp-stool, working rapidly.

"There, now she is using her diminishing glass, and see what a wrapt and ecstatic expression she wears, as she replaces it in her little watch-pocket," said Mahala, as they approached the absorbed artist. "Now see her draw down the outside corners of her eyes and squint at the innocent river. I always know something is going to be done when she does that."

"Well, dear, we won't disturb her," said Margery, with a smile. "Suppose we sit down on this old tree-trunk."

"You can, if you wish. I am going to explore this region a little. Good-by."

"Don't fall into the water, Mike, and don't go too far away; remember, there may be tramps about," cautioned her chaperone and loving friend, as she sprang away over stumps and knarled roots down towards the water, which ran in a limpid stream around the knoll.

" No fear!" answered the volatile miss, as she ran across a teetering log on to the sward beyond.

Margery was very quiet as they sat together on the log, breaking up the bits of sticks and throwing them listlessly into the water, and Julie, who it will be remembered had been prompt in swearing to keep all of Mahala's rules before starting, was taking a few notes, as she said to Margery. She wrote:

"MY DARLING OLD BOY:—I am having a charming trip, of course. If you were only along! But then it would not be a feminine excursion, and I quite enjoy it daytimes, and have many funny little things to tell you; but when it comes night how wretchedly homesick I am! Then I vow I will never, *never*, NEVER, NEVER leave you so long again."

Here Margery, who had been lost in reverie, with her eyes fixed upon the rippling water, turned suddenly towards her friend, who smiled guiltily and blushed a little as she thrust her pencil and the scrap of paper into her pocket.

"Julie!" said she, reproachfully, "you are writing to your husband!—and you promised not to."

"Sh-h, sh-h!" said the faithless one, "do not let them hear us! Margie, I will say to you in confidence, that no loving wife ever promises anything without a mental reservation in favor of her good man. When any one says 'You must not tell a soul!' I say 'Oh, no; certainly not (except Fred);' and when another assures me that she would not for the world have any one but me know, I say, 'My dear, it shall be a sacred trust to me (and Fred) alone.'"

"Oh, Julie!" exclaimed Margery, somewhat shocked at this confession of duplicity in her friend, "then it is not safe to tell a married woman anything you do not wish her husband to know!"

"Not as a rule, my dear," answered the intrepid lady. "If a woman loves her husband she is pretty sure to make him the repository of all her thoughts and feelings, and if he is worthy the confidence, his opinions and views, from a masculine standpoint, are often of the greatest assistance to her in advising her unmarried friends.   But keep it in mind that a married woman is only one-half of a composite being.   It is not at all unsafe to confide in the wife of an honorable man, Margie, but beware of others; for they, nearly all, will tell their other half everything they know.   Perhaps you consider this acknowledgment damaging to the veracity of the sex, but it is true nevertheless. Still," said the artful little woman, "you who are the promised wife of a noble man, too, Margie, should not wonder at the near and dear companionship which supersedes all girlish intimacies, and shares even the most trivial idea as sympathetically as the most important concerns of life."

Margery turned her face away toward the babbling river, which here rippled over a stony shallow; her eyes followed a fleck of foam as it rose and fell upon the miniature billows and whirled about and sailed smoothly on as it reached the deeper water further down the stream.

Her friend, who had seen that something, an indefinable shadow of sadness and occasionally an unnatural and surprising bitterness was clouding the crystal purity and refined brilliancy of Margery's mind, would fain have inquired into its cause, but dared not.   She leaned forward now to look into the proud face, and pressing the hand which lay listlessly in her lap, she said, "Margery?" and conveyed at once an affectionate sympathy and a tender inquiry in her tone.

"Julie," said the girl, suddenly turning her face to the other, "I wish I might ever again have the faith in a good man that you have in your husband. But I find that one whom I loved the best in the world, thinking him all that was noble, chivalrous, loving, and generous, is not above petty flirtations, trifling love-makings, which are an insult to me, his affianced wife! This has come to my ears from various sources, and at first dismissed with incredulity and contempt for the friendly warning voice; but the disgraceful thing has been corroborated by his own lips, and I *refuse* to remain any longer an object of the sneering pity of my own associates! Felix Plummer is *at liberty* to play lover to all the grass widows on earth if he chooses!"

The rapidity and force with which the indignant and wounded Margery poured forth her grievance, and the tragic emphasis laid upon "refuse" and "at liberty," as well as the proud gesture with which she rose to her feet and swept her clenched hand with now spreading fingers out into a swift circle as if to cast her faithless lover to the four winds, was a stunning surprise to Mrs. Mather, who, while loving her elegant and self-contained companion, had sometimes said to Fred that she thought she lacked force and depth of feeling. But now, as Margery sank trembling and weeping and resting her graceful head upon the little wife's lap, she felt an admiration for the sobbing girl she had never before experienced. She rose to the occasion, and a flood of gladness came over her affectionate heart that the trouble she vaguely suspected was out at last, and that she, as she felt sure, could bring about a reconciliation between the estranged lovers. She smoothed the soft hair of the bowed head and said, "Tell me all about it, my poor child. Possibly you do Felix wrong."

The proud lips unclosed upon the humiliating theme, and gave the facts as we have already become acquainted with them, only adding that Mrs. Bangtry had been indecent enough to boast that she could take Felix Plummer away from his cold and stately fiancee if she desired, "and it seems she could," cried the mortified young lady, in ending.

"Fie, fie! Margery!   Be a woman!   Think," said her friend; "do you know of cause enough on the part of your lover, so that you are warranted in not giving him one chance to defend himself?   Things are wretchedly perverted and magnified in coming through the mouths of one or two mischief-makers.   No girl is right to throw away her happiness on mere hearsay, and without a word of explanation!   Why, Margie, I am surprised that your pride should have so run away with your common sense. Oh! if people would only talk more!   Why not speak of any wrong as soon as it is felt?   One need not descend to fretful fault-finding, but trifles, which would melt into thin air at one reasonable word, grow into mountains of sorrow in an atmosphere of silence and distrust.   Promise me, Margery, that you will write to him at once (Mike's inflexible rule, notwithstanding).   I am sure you have been unjust to him, and, also, that when you are his precious wife, for you will be, dear—" Margery was shaking her head.   "O yes, you will be, sure as you both live—promise me that you will speak of anything that hurts you, as there will be many times, of course, men not understanding such a proud, sensitive, *wicked, cruel* nature as yours—"

Julie had the now faintly smiling face by the chin, and

while talking to it in this incoherent and thoroughly womanly manner, was giving the fair cheek a little pinch as she added the last adjectives, when there came a piercing shriek from the woods across the river.

"Hark!"

"Oh! oh! oh! Help, girls! Ah-o-o-o! Hurry! e-e! Help, quick."

"Mike's drowning!" gasped Margery.

"Or being murdered," said Mrs. Mather, in a low voice with clenched teeth, and she started on a run down the woody slope to the bank of the stream.

"Margery!" she panted as they ran, "have your pistol ready! You took it this morning; cock it in your pocket! I can use this club! Run! Faster! Yes, yes, Mike, we are coming!" she screamed.

Margery fell to the ground. "Oh! Julie! I have broken my ankle! I am going to faint!"

"No, you are not," said the plucky little woman, fiercely, "you shall not! Come on! Mike is being killed!" and she dragged Margery to her feet and sped away across the log bridge into the pasture beyond, with the strength that fear lends. Margery followed as fast as her sprained ankle would permit.

That Mahala was still alive was evident by the screams, which apparently issued from a patch of white birches across the open field. As the two friends came in haste to the spot whence the cries seemed to come, their terror increased, for, in the woods or along the river they could see nothing of the girl, when, "Up here! Up here! Put something under me! I can't hold on a minute longer!

Can't you get hold of
the tip and pull this
tree down? Or climb another tree
and pull this one up so I can get my
feet on something. Do something
quick. I've been hanging here an eternity now!"

Mrs. Mather saw at a glance that there was no way to straighten up the tree or pull it farther down, as they could not touch the ends of her toes as she clung to the willowy birch, kicking and writhing in the vain attempt to swing back to a hold upon its slender trunk. Her hat was on the ground, the dark curls hung in hopeless confusion over her frightened eyes, and her distressed face was red and distorted in agony.

"Mike," said Mrs. Mather, decisively, "the only thing for you to do is to drop. We will catch you and break your fall as much as possible."

"But I shall kill you!"

"No, you will not. Now drop."

They held up their arms and Mahala let go of the birch, which quickly rose to a perpendicular, while the three young women came in a heap to the ground with tremendous force.

"I know I have killed you both!" exclaimed Mahala, jumping up. "Julie, have I hurt you? Tell me, Margie, dear, aren't you terribly bruised?"

"N-no," said Mrs. Mather, who had now regained her feet, "I guess I am all right, except my elbow; I think that is barked," she said, as she felt of it, "but the sleeve is so tight I shall not know until bed-time."

Margery now leaned forward and spat out a mouthful of blood. Mahala began to weep hysterically at sight of it.

"Oh! dear Margie!" she cried, "you have some internal injury, and I—I am to blame."

"Oh, no, Mike! I only bit my tongue as my chin came down on something hard. It will stop bleeding soon, I think."

Mahala began to rub her head thoughtfully, and a gratified expression came over her face as she said, "I do believe it was my head. There's a great lump on my bump of cautiousness. Oh! but it is sore. I am so glad! I was so ashamed when I thought I was not hurt at all."

"Well, Mike," said Margery, who could not forego this mild retort, "if this occurrence will in any way help to fill out that organ, which is naturally a cavity, it will be a relief to your friends, and they will bear their wounds with cheerfulness."

Mahala looked at Margery reflectively for a moment, and then stooping picked up her hat and put it on her subdued head. Julie tightened up her disheveled hair, and with Margery limping a little and occasionally stopping to discharge more blood from her mouth, they took their disheartened way back across the field. Nothing was said for some time as they walked slowly toward the river. At last Mrs. Mather remarked, "It may be proper now to inquire, Mahala, how under heavens you came to be in the awkward, not to say dangerous predicament in which we found you?"

"Why, I was only swinging on the birches, as I have done thousands of times before with the boys," she answered, in an injured tone. "It's glorious fun!" added the giddy thing, brightening a little

"So it seemed," interpolated Margery, coolly.

"Well, it is, when you do it right! You climb the tree by the little branches and when you get to the top where it is too limber to go higher, you just jump right out into the air, and over you go, flying to the ground like a bird."

"Yes," said Mrs. Mather, laughing a little in recollection of the recent scene, "you looked like a bird, but it was a stork with red legs!"

Not apparently noticing this thrust, which keenly wounded her pride, for reasons best known to herself, Mahala continued, "But you must not get an old tree that will break with you, nor one that is too large and stiff. That was what was the matter with the last one. I had swung twenty times, I think, and it was just lovely! I was just going to have one more and then return to you," she added, ruefully.

"Well, my dear," said Mrs. Mather, good-naturedly, "like many another harum-scarum, you dared your fate just once too many times. However, it is not as bad as it might have been, so we will think no more about it, if Margie's ankle does not prove troublesome." Suddenly, "Why, where is Dude all this time? Can it be possible that she has heard nothing of all this?"

"Of course," said her saucy niece, "give Aunt Dude some trees, a bit of water, and a rock or two, and she would not hear the sky fall! There she sits," said Mahala, as they drew near the spot, "oblivious of the rest of the earth." Here she tittered. "She would not be holding her head on one side in such a satisfied manner, if she knew that cow was looking over her shoulder! Cattle are the only things in the world that she is afraid of."

"Well, girls," said the unconscious lady, rising as they neared, "have you got tired of waiting for me? I have succeeded in catching a most charming glimpse of—ugh! a horrid cow." She had turned slightly to get a diffⅰrent light on her canvas, and caught sight of the great face of the animal which was sniffing at her shoulder. She threw herself forward away from the dreadful monster, and upset her easel, throwing the picture to the earth. Green bag and basket, umbrella and stick, camp-stool and canvas, were scattered broadcast at the mercy of the gentle cow, who evidently was wondering in a dreamy, bovine way, what the melee was all about. Mahala took her by the horn, and patting her brown neck, turned her away and led her to a distance. "Did it fall on the buttered side?" she said, returning again.

"No, for a wonder," answered the disconcerted lady, who was picking up her picture, "but thanks to you, Mahala, that the creature did not step upon it." She was gathering up her artistic paraphernalia and engaged in packing it into a surprisingly small space and making a compact parcel. "But where have you been so long?" she queried, and then they told her.

They continued their ride. As soon as Mahala could get an opportunity to speak to Mrs. Mather aside, she said, "Julie."

"What?"

"Did I make a shocking appearance, up there, hanging to the tree?"

"Why, without doubt, there was considerable braided underskirt mixed up with some very lively red stockings," answered Mrs. Mather, smiling.

"Of course," rejoined Mahala, shortly, "you could see that, being right under me; but could any one, I mean could you, see more than my feet, across the field?"

"Why, I did not give it a thought, I was so frightened. I really do not remember. But why should you care? No one was near to see you."

"That's just it," said poor Mahala, choking a little and swallowing hard, "I am sure there was some one in the woods, and I am afraid it was—a man," winking back tears of vexation, "for just as we fell I heard a crash through the brush, and when I got to my feet, his back was just going down behind the fence, and it was a great broad back, and I know he saw me, and I ha-ate him!"

Her voice broke a little, and she furtively wiped a tear from her eye. "I despise creatures who are always poking around when they are not wanted!"

Mrs. Mather, who could not feel that it was any serious catastrophe if some farmer had perchance been cutting rails in the adjoining woods and so become a witness to their adventure, dismissed the subject from their conversation and said to them all, that they had better get back to the hotel as soon as convenient and take a rest.

Margery's wrenched ankle, which had been the only severe hurt in this chapter of accidents, was found to be only slightly injured, much to the relief of the whole party, who had feared a dentetion on her account.

W. & W.—9

CHAPTER XII.

The Bodges.

A BRIGHT morning after a rain, and our party of happy wheelers bade good Farmer Bodge and his wife good-by and started away down the winding road, which had been plashed and packed firm and smooth by the rain-drops which had fallen during the night.

Mrs. Bodge had acknowledged to them, as they were chatting and oiling up their machines, which were safe on the barn floor, that she had not been clear in her mind about them when they arrived. "I see," said she, as she took a seat upon a cart-tongue, "that Jerry was jest be-witched, when he come a runnin' acrost the barn-lot with his cheeks as red as Balding apples and his eyes a shinin', and he bu'st into the wood-shed, where I was (I had stepped out for a handful of kindlin's; my fire had got low and bis-cuits must be done quick or they ain't fit to eat), and says he, 'Mother, there's four ladies a-comin' up the road and they're all a-ridin' on machines which they call tricycles. You know Uncle Ben told us about how he saw them in England. They are all in gray dresses,' says he, 'with snipperdings on the front of the waist and little coat-tails

(130)

behind, and they can just spin over the ground faster'n
old Dick can trot.'　Says I, 'Jeremiah Bodge, stop your
puffin' an' blowin'.　Set down in the chair and tell me what
you mean!"

"'Wal, mother,' says he, 'father and I were down in
the further pastur', mowin' brush, so as to plow it to-mor-

rer, when father looked up, and says he, 'Jerusalem crickets!'　I looked up and I tell yer ther' wan't no more
mowin'.　Whiz!　They come along just as smooth and
pretty with them spider-web wheels, and their hats all
covered with feathers, and they were all singing something

like peek-a-boo, peek-a-boo! Wal, father leant on his
scythe, and couldn't say a word, but I knew in a minute
they was city girls from the way their waists set, and when
they came nearer, such pretty shoes!' Says I, 'Jeremiah,
they're bad women. They must be some of those circus
creeturs like what enticed Sam Burnet away to New York.
Come into the house,' says I, 'and I'll lock the door.
Come right in and we'll peek through the front-room
blinds, and see 'em pass!' 'No, no,' says he, 'they're
comin' here!' 'Comin' here,' says I; 'wal, I guess not!
If your father can be made a fool of, I can't, and I can tell
him no such truck shall darken my doors! I'd sooner—'
'But hold on, mother,' hollered Jerry, as I started to bolt
the doors, 'they are nice ladies! Yes, they are, real ladies.
One of 'em is a daughter of Mr. Prescott, who was here
huntin' partridge last year! Wait till I tell you, before
you fly off the handle!' I am a little touchy about bein'
at all familiar with strange women. If everything ain't
jest right, I suspicion it right away; but the minute he
mentioned your father's name, I cooled right down, and
settin' down to the churn, let the boy run on. I
was dreadful late about my churnin' yesterday morn-
in'. I don't know whether it got chilled or what
was to pay, but that cream would not come. I had
about made up my mind to give it up when he come in;
but I guess I put extra venom into the handle after he
scart me so, for it come all of a sudden. I hadn't got it
out of the churn when you rode up. But he told me how
you stopped at the bars and asked him how far it was to
Mr. Bodge's house, and father, says he, 'I am Mr. Bodge,'

and how sweet and genteel one jumped off her machine
and come into the lot and gave him a letter introducing
you, and then Jerry run acrost lots to tell me. Jerry said
you was all perfect ladies, but the one with her hair cut
short in front and parted on the side with little curls all

around her face and behind the ears, with her dimples and
white teeth, which she showed all the time because she
was always laughing, was enough to make a man strike his
grandmother if she asked him to!"

Mahala blushed. "O, dear, Mrs. Bodge, I would not
ask any one to do such a wicked thing."

"Of course you would n't!" said the matron, rolling her bare arms up in her apron preparatory to a run for the house, "that's only his exaggerative way of speakin'. I hate to have him use such language, but his father is awful on by-words too!"

"I'm darned sorry to have you go," said Farmer Bodge, as the tricycle travelers made their last preparations for starting away from the comfortable place that had sheltered them for a day.

"By John Holland!" he continued earnestly, in his slow and heavy way, "when I see you four comin' down the road yesterday, I was beat. I'd heard of them machines, but never expected to see ladies on 'em. But it must be good for you, judging by the looks of these rosy cheeks and shinin' eyes."

Farmer Bodge felt a little dashed at his own gallantry as displayed in this last remark, and looked around quickly to see that "mother" was not near enough to hear him.

"Thunder and orcrow!" he exclaimed, "if there ain't Jerry ridin' on one of the things now, along with Miss Curlyhead! Jerry 'll be spiled for the neighbor girls now, sure. Haw! haw! Sarah Pease won't be nowhere!"

Jerry, who until these fatal days had not realized that his hands were coarse and his feet inelegantly shod, had begun to despise his own pleasant, though confessedly verdant personality. He had taken his father's razor the evening before, and by the light of two kerosene lamps had succeeded in scraping off the soft growth from his cheeks and chin. He carefully omitted to perform this operation on his upper lip, and, by dint of the least bit of

burnt cork on his finger-tip, had darkened the incipient
mustache until it was visible to the naked eye.   The lad
was almost handsome, as, with burning cheeks and a new
and strange expression in his eyes, he followed his merry
companion around the square.   Then, as they stood
together lowering the saddle again for Mrs. Mather's use,
as the travelers were soon to depart, his hands trembled.
He bit his lip, and looked down to where he was smooth-
ing his forefinger to and fro along the wire spokes.

"You have been very kind to us, Jerry," said the good-
hearted little flirt, "and when you come to Hartford I
hope you will call and make the acquaintance of my
brothers.   Jo has a wonderful entomological collection,
not to mention quantities of minerals and an aquarium."

"I would like to call and see—your brothers," wistfully
murmured the miserably-happy youth, "but you would
not want a countryman like me around," he added bitterly.
"Probably you have dozens of fine fellows in new style
hats and tailor's clothes, with white hands and all that.
No!" he shook his head, "unless I could be as elegant and
easy and—and—no!" he said again, vehemently, "I shall
never call upon you."

Mahala was confused, seeing that in her desire to be
kind to the young man she had innocently wounded his
pride.   She tried to think of some pleasant disclaimer to
his consciousness of his disadvantage in appearance beside
city-bred boys, but remained silent, distressed by his manifest feeling, which she could not truthfully controvert.

When they all shook hands in saying farewell to their
kind entertainers he made no reply to her bright "Good-by,

Jerry," but squeezing her little hand in his sinewy palm,
he turned and walked hastily away to the barn, and threw
himself face down upon the haymow, where we will leave
him with a pang in his boyish heart.   With this new and
painfully sweet experience, which no one can know as a
country lad who is fascinated, enthralled, by the unconscious graces, the hundred little aids and appurtenances of
toilet, the captivating self-possession, and the innocence
of her own charming ways, which are among the attributes
of a bright and lovable city girl.

CHAPTER XIII.

The Artist's Day.

A BY-PATH, woods in rear, school-house near.
"If there is n't Aunt Dude before that easel again!
I thought we stipulated for one day's respite," said Mahala,
always first to speak. "If she is not the most persistent
worker! Aunty, you make me feel tired!"

"I wish," retorted Miss St. John, "I could make you
feel tired of doing nothing, then you would go to work
and perhaps make something of your gift; I can't call it
talent, for that implies cultivation."

"But what should I have done, I wonder, without Julie
and Margie all the quiet days? A pretty scrape I would
have gotten into, if, according to your first proposition, I
had accompanied you alone on this expedition! You and
you only," she repeated, leaning over her aunt's chair and
touching her lips to her cheek. "A pretty scrape! I'd
been worn to a shadow from very pining and loneliness.
Was n't it a happy thought to get such a jolly, charming,
fascinating trio to make your trip complete? You ought
to be very grateful to us for coming, to make a variety for
you."

"It was, indeed," answered the artist, smiling, "but now, most jolly, fascinating, and charming trio, if just as agreeable to you, I will permit you to dispose of yourselves as you like. You may leave me to my work this morning; I have a great deal more before me than I can master. If you will kindly amuse yourselves under those lovely pines, your absence I shall not feel at all. Try that path leading down the ravine. If you follow it to the little bridge, you can cross the brook. Mount the opposite hillside; there you will find a charming view to the southward. If you find a scene to please you, Margie, mark the point of view. I will paint it for your wedding present," she added, casting a swift, searching glance at the young girl.

Margery made no answer—gave no sign.

Mahala had started off, at her aunt's first suggestion, Margery and Mrs. Mather following more slowly.

"Well, what is it, Margie?" said the latter, as, passing her arm through that of her friend, she gazed inquiringly up into her face.

Margery tried to smile, made a sorry failure, blushed hotly, and tears came into her eyes.

"Not be troubled about it?" she said, repeating her friend's kind words. "How can I help it, Julie?"

"You probably expected to receive an answer to your letter about this time," said Julie, in a low voice, "perhaps it may not yet have reached him," she suggested.

"Oh, it must have done so. There has been plenty of time for a reply too," returned Margery, in a choking voice.

"Yes, but he might be out of town. Not an improbable surmise, is it?"

"Oh, he is at home. Perhaps too angry to read it even. He may be more pleasantly engaged," she added with a curl of her lip, "than in reading letters from me."

"Pshaw! Margie, for shame! I tell you it is more likely he is disgusted with himself, for ever having looked

at Mrs. Bangtry.   The apparent flirtation was evidently
all on her side; a man's vanity is easily reached, and
upon reflection he may only blame himself for ever having
given cause for remarks, by his polite attention to her in-
vitations.   Almost every man (as well as most women),
sooner or later, has some experience in that line, only to
call himself a fool afterwards."

"Oh, Julie, how can you say that? I never should
have—"

"No, perhaps not. You probably never will, and I make
no confessions myself in that line. But I do not hold it a
bad thing to test the caliber of your lover now, before he
is tied."

"Tied!" repeated Margery, "I wonder what an engage-
ment means, if it is not a tie, as sacred, too, as marriage!
I felt I was bound to him, before all the world."

They had walked slowly, talking as they went, and now
they had stopped under an old tree.   Margery leaned up
against its gnarled trunk, and stood picking bits of bark
from its rough side, letting them fall unheeded to the
earth.   "My whole world was in him," she said, with
tears

Mrs. Mather rested on a broken limb, which had been
torn nearly off, and hung with its smaller branches upon
the ground.   She feigned to be interested in the tortuous
course of a tiny ant which was laboring up the limb,
dragging an insect of twice its size over the many obsta-
cles in its path.   She absently picked off a few scales of
dead bark to make a smoother way for the industrious little fellow.   Then she said quietly, "Some men there are,
real men, with true hearts and unswerving affections—"

"I thought him such," said Margery, with rising emphasis.

"Who do so love," continued Mrs. Mather, without noticing the interruption, "that it is impossible that they should give a thought beyond the one woman who absorbs their love, and there are women who are worthy such devotion, but," she added, hesitatingly, "the world is not crowded with such people. Felix, however, has had one lesson. A rather severe one, I think, considering his slight and very excusable fault. His proud maid is not to be trifled with in this way, and I presume it will not hurt him to find it out now; and perhaps," continued she, slowly, and smiling a little, "it is a lesson to you, too, to take to heart in another way, Margie."

"I did not need it," declared Margery; "I despise petty jealousy."

"Ah! so you think. But were you not very hasty? A few words from him would have doubtless assured you that there was no cause for your anger and sudden departure. I would have advised you by all means to have given him a chance to explain all those things. But don't worry now, dear, we have talked it all over; repetition can do no good; you have written to him, and the answer must surely come ere long."

"Do you believe so, really?" said Margery, leaving her place by the tree and brushing the bits of bark from her gray dress. She looked more cheerful and wiped a tear from her cheek as she spoke: "Julie, you are such a comfort to me. I am so anxious to believe that you are right that I almost feel it will be so."

"I am confident of it," said Mrs. Mather.

A cry from Mahala broke in upon this quiet interview. The bridge over which she had tripped consisted of two logs with short planks laid across them. In her usual haste, Mahala had attempted to spring over the gap to the opposite landing. She had not miscalculated the distance, nor her ability to leap it, but the ground was covered with pine needles dropped from the overhanging trees. It was thus too slippery to gain a secure footing, as the bank sloped steeply to the water. She fell and lay helpless upon her side, unable to regain her feet, and fearing to slip further down the bank if she made the attempt. "Oh, do come and help me," she cried. "Cross down on the stones below there. You can't come this way. You'll jump on me. Don't, don't," she persisted, while the two friends hastened down the stream to where the water was low. "I'm slipping—I can't get up—I've nothing to hold on to," she cried, trying to dig her fingers into the earth. "Oh, hurry, do, or I shall wet my feet. Call Aunt Dude. If she wasn't at that everlasting painting I'd get some help!"

"Well, hold on to silence, a minute," called Mrs. Mather, "you are three feet from water, and in no danger of getting wet, if you will only be quiet until we can get at you."

"Here we are, now," said Margery, giving her hand to the prostrate girl, who speedily crawled to her feet. "What's all this great cry about?" she continued, looking around. "Mike, you will have to have a special body-guard if you do not take better care of yourself. Julie and

I cannot have a moment's quiet talk, but, alas! a shriek from you. And you have never once used your whistle, according to programme; it is always a feminine squeal."

Margery had commenced her remarks with a little impatience, but was forced to smile at the impudent indifference with which her rebuke was received by the erratic individual whom she had so lately rescued.

"Now, please, Margie, don't be hard. I'm bruised enough already," rubbing her side. "Don't hurt *my feelin's* too; though probably they are not so tender as my flesh."

"It *is* slippery here, Mike. Take care, Julie—oh!" and as Mahala was now upon her feet, down went Miss Prescott, in the most undignified manner imaginable. Mahala was convulsed.

"Pshaw!" exclaimed Mrs. Mather, as she attempted to raise Margery to her feet. "It is very strange—" and down they both went together in great discomfiture. Mahala clapped her hands in irrepressible glee, and they all joined in the laugh.

"What is all this cry about? And it is certainly very strange that you people cannot stand upon your feet! Oh, that the artist were on the spot now!" cried Mahala. "But they never are around when needed. They always come in when it is all over, and make up the picture from imagination. That is why their work is seldom really touching."

Meanwhile, the artist was far from all these disturbing influences. She quietly lived in her dream of nature and its mystery. An hour had passed in uninterrupted work,

when she heard approaching footsteps.   Supposing her
companions to be near, without even glancing up from the
canvas, she gave expression to her thoughts in measured
sentences something like the following: "They baffle me,
those changing shadows upon the hills.   I put them in, I
put them out.   Each fleeting effect seems more beautiful
than the last, and so I try to catch it.   If I could only keep
to the one idea, when once recorded, keep it, the same
effect often returns and—"

"Wal, I dunno," said a deep voice, in a sort of grunt,
behind her.

The artist started violently, nearly upsetting her easel.

"Wal, I dunno," it said, and a horny hand came forward
over her shoulder to save her picture from falling, imprint-
ing a big thumb in the sky in one corner.   Not at all
aware of the fright he had caused, or of any harm done to
the sketch, the honest man continued: "It beats all fire,
how you can do it," and a burly figure came round to her
side and scanned the picture closely.   "I 'spect it pays,
though.   I've heerd how they get big prices for them kind.
Ile paintin', ain't it?"

"Yes," said the artist.

"Wal, I vow.   Do tell how much you expect to get for
that!   It's terrible real now, ain't it?"   He looked at it
from one side and then from the other.   "That blue sky
now, and them hills; I tell ye, it can't be beat!   I say,
how much 'll you git 'f it sells?"

"I always wait for a purchaser.   It will be time enough
then to set a price," answered the lady, smiling.

"I don't suppose now I could buy it.   Squire Jim had

his place took, barn and all. 'T wa'n't colored, you know; took by a photographer, and he spent nigh onto two dollars for 't. I'd give that 'f I could have it all colored; but probable you ain't a-takin' it for money," said he, half-ashamed of his offer, and looking at her a little sheepishly.

"Not just now, but if your farm is near, and I could get there easily, I might find some good cattle, or a favorite horse or cow, to sketch for you."

"Oh, now, would you? That would be kind. Could you paint my Jersey cow? Registered stock,—pretty creetur as I ever milked. Gentle, too, as a kitten."

"Very well. To-morrow, if you will come and show me the way," said Miss St. John. "I would like right well to see her. I am fond of cows—at a picturesque distance. We are at Widow Ryerson's, down by the post-office."

The good man was heartily pleased, and with some further complimentary remarks upon her skill he walked away, saying he would "hitch up and take her over in the morning," and the artist fell busily to work again.

After a time she heard approaching footsteps again, and turned to face the intruder this time.

"Ain't it pretty?" It was a small, weak-looking woman, who, however, showed a lively interest in the strange lady and her picture.

"That's them trees off there, ain't it?" she said, looking entirely in the wrong direction. "Oh," with a nod, as she was righted in the view by the artist. "It's first-rate, any how; I couldn't begin to do it so well myself," and she passed on, wrapping a faded shawl tighter about her slight form.

The school now had its recess.   The children, catching
sight of the umbrella and easel, made a rush for the stand
and soon surrounded the artist, not quite to her pleasure.
She made no sign of consciousness of their presence.
They in turn fell into a sudden silence.   Little whisper-
ings went from one to the other.

" See how she dips in all them colors ! "

" What great long brushes ! "

"And what a lot of 'em,—one, three, four, seven,—ten
all together ! "

" See that umbrella; how funny it sets on the stick."

They were all so quiet, nudging, and whispering, and
treading their little feet on the turf, that Miss St. John was
amazed on turning to find some twenty or more boys and
girls staring at her work.

One little boy and his sister had climbed up on the fence.
Their relationship was apparent in the two tip-tilted noses,
which bore a striking resemblance to each other.   The boy
sat on the top rail holding on to the bar with his hands
between his knees.   The little girl stood upon the lower
rail and resting her elbows upon the top of the fence, supported her fat cheeks upon her tiny fists.   The artist engaged the others in conversation until she had made a
rapid sketch of these two, and then said :   "Now, the one
that wants his picture put in just here," pointing to her
canvas in the fore-ground, " may run off there and take
that stick and hunt for chestnuts in the leaves.   Now,
when I call stop, then he must stand quite still for five
minutes."

A dozen eager ones ran for the stick, but one quiet little

fellow caught it, and also the idea, for when the word stop came he was able to pose in a very satisfactory manner. His fair-haired little sister stood behind, eagerly watching the progress of the study, calling out to him from time to time: "Keep still a little longer, Eddie,—one minute more!" in the proud supposition that she was lending material aid to the artist.

Soon a modest young woman appeared at the school-house door and rang a bell, and the children ran reluctantly back to their books, not without first stopping to see how the little boy was put upon the canvas.

"Jest as if he stood there, ain't it?" and all scampered away in haste.

Miss St. John was left in quietude again. The shadows

were lessening. The artist's hour was passing. Under the advancing noonday sun, Miss St. John was giving the last touches to her picture, when a surly-looking old man made his appear-ance, coming over the neighboring hill.

"Say," he accost-ed the lady, in a rude tone; his hat was pushed down upon his head with a determined air; "say, if you think you can set down here, and paint around my place, and then send in your bill, as they did last year for Deacon Wells's house, you 'll be mistaken. Mis' Gleason, what's jest been here, told me you was here to work, and I want ter tell you beforehand that I ain't a-goin' to pay no such bills. I ain't no objections to your settin' and your paintin', but I warn you now that I ain't doin' no payin'."

" Here is a queer individual," thought the lady, "I think I will be deaf, just now."

Instantly she glanced at his moving lips with a dazed expression, though inwardly much amused, and applied her hand to her ear.

"Deef, eh ! "

She inclined a little more toward him as he stood before her, with a basket of potatoes in his hand. She still expressed no understanding of the situation. He repeated, in a louder tone: "I hain't no objections to a lady settin'—"

She arose as if to hear more distinctly; she seemed so very deaf.

"And paintin'!" he screamed. Still she did not hear. "Thunder!" he muttered, "I'd ruther pay her bill than to set them school-children at me with this hollerin'. Little torments, they 'll pester a fellow about anything. They are jest like hornets. It don't make no odds if they ain't very big; I don't want 'em to git set on to me ag'in, as they did t 'other day when I got mad cause they 'd broke down my bars," and casting an uneasy glance at the windows of the school-house, he started back over the way he had come, talking to himself. "I wonder if she makes her livin' at that blasted nonsense. Humph! Wal, my farm's pertaters, and they bring an honest livin'. I don't suppose she makes enough at that tom-foolery, a-settin' and a-paintin' on that paper stuff, to put salt on 'em. I reckon they don't git much outer me with their pictures. If she heared or didn't hear, she's been warned, and if she brings in a bill, I won't pay a darned turnup for the trash.

That's all there is about it.   I don't like the looks of the creeturs around.   I don't hanker after 'em gittin' into my diggin's.   Now, if Betsy Ann was to set eyes on sech doin's, she would soon be sp'ilt for the fryin'-pan and the wash-tub.   I have seen it before.   I have had trouble enough with the boys, a-learnin' city goin's on and turnin' away from the lights of their parents.   I don't calkerlate to see Betsy sp'iled too," and he strode over the fence into the adjoining lot.   "But I've warned the creetur!"   He turned and saw the quiet worker picking up her things for removal.

As she watched his retreating steps, she saw a rough, uncanny man, with a pack on his back, meet him, and after a moment's wrangling, he came on towards the woods, shaking his black and curly head and pounding his thick staff into the ground at every step.   He was evidently angry at what he considered interference with his trade, and consequently not likely to be very agreeable to any defenseless woman.

"Oh, dear," sighed the artist, "here is another.   I wish I were out of this.   I do not like his looks.   I do wish the girls would come."

She dared not blow her whistle, lest she might attract his attention, when possibly he might pass on without noticing her.   But, no; he saw her, and, turning aside from his way, he made rapid strides in her direction.   She affected not to see him, but kept busily at her picking up.

"Penting, hey?" he said, with a hideous grin, and he stood looking at her as he leaned upon his stick.   Then he let down the pack which he carried from his back.

"Vell, uf you'd ghoost step 'ere und look at my laces—"
Hereupon he was proceeding to open a case and to hold

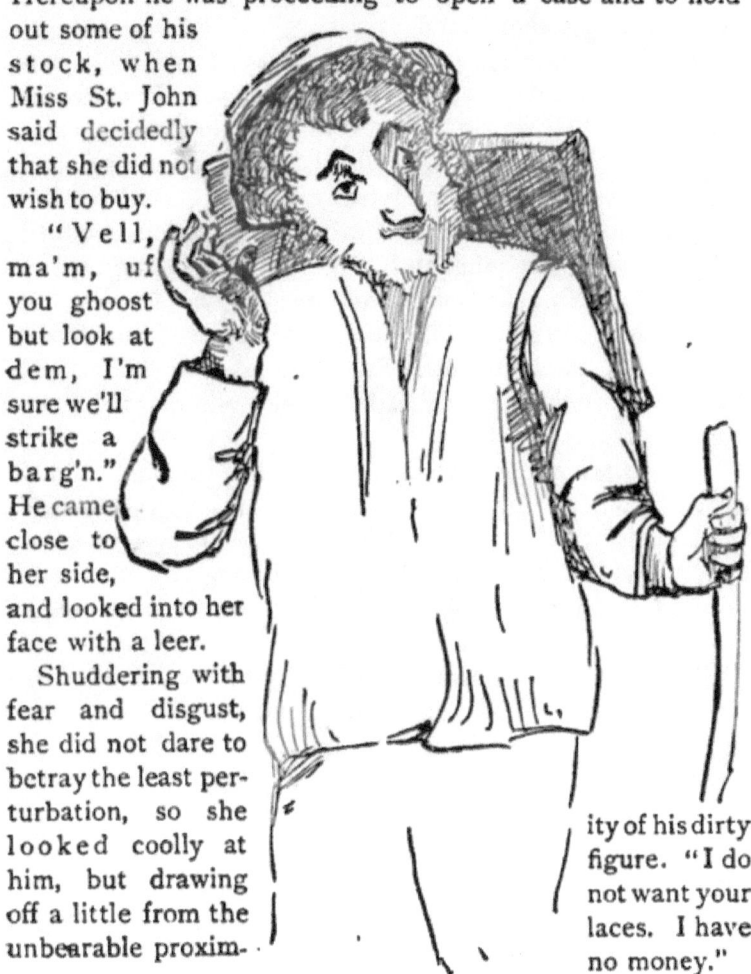

out some of his
stock, when
Miss St. John
said decidedly
that she did not
wish to buy.

"Vell,
ma'm, uf
you ghoost
but look at
dem, I'm
sure we'll
strike a
barg'n."
He came
close to
her side,
and looked into her
face with a leer.

Shuddering with
fear and disgust,
she did not dare to
betray the least per-
turbation, so she
looked coolly at
him, but drawing
off a little from the
unbearable proxim-

ity of his dirty
figure. "I do
not want your
laces. I have
no money."

The man jeered as he glanced at her white hands and at her earrings. "I nefer gif up a lufly ladee like you, vithout making some kind uf a barg'n. Really, now, uf you hav n't no money, you might like to trade those earrings or that ring for something. I am sure I could persuade you—" he was insisting with one hand raised, palm upward, to his ear as he held his shaggy head on one side.

"I tell you I do not wish for any of your goods!" Miss St. John hoped to get rid of him without serious trouble. But now he took a quick step towards her, saying, with a hard look: "You shall buy sometings. The old man has insulted me, und now I vill have some money from you!"

Quick as thought, Miss St. John started back, and drawing a pistol from her little pocket, she pointed down the road.

"If you are going down the road, sir," she said, calmly as she could, "and should see a blue-jay, I wish you would just whistle a bit. I want another specimen for mounting. I'm doing a little sharpshooting this morning; brought down two little fellows just now and would n't mind doing it again before dinner."

She was able to speak quite easily before she had finished this sentence, and as she did so she turned the pistol in a careless manner toward the impudent peddler.

He gave a quick, sharp look at her impassable countenance, and shut his box together in trembling haste. He closely watched her as he drew the straps and threw the huge burden to his shoulder.

"I'll whistle, yes, when I get down the road. I'll hurry, yes; I'll see a blue-bird for you."

Miss St. John saw that she had made the desired impression, and that the man was thoroughly alarmed.

"P-please, ma'm, wait till I get out of the line, ladies don't always aim straight. Goot-by. Don't shoot till I get away, quite."

The pack was on his back, and he was out of sight before the artist had fully convinced herself of the success of her ruse.

Replacing the toy pistol in her pocket, she blew three shrill notes upon her whistle. This soon recalled her three companions, who were tired of their trampings, and came briskly back at her call

"Really, I do believe Aunt Dude is scared. How pale she looks!"

"What is it?"

"I don't see anything to be afraid of."

"What is the matter, Dude?"

"I am afraid we shall be late for dinner," answered the artist.

"Is that all?"

They went back to the Widow Ryerson's, down by the post-office, to dinner.

CHAPTER XIV.

They go Chestnutting.

THE next stopping-place on the pleasant journey down the river was at the house of an uncle of Mrs. Mather's. Mr. Stearns had been many times pleasantly entertained at the cosy home of his niece in the city. He was a widower, without children, dependent upon a house-keeper for society, and was greatly delighted to welcome the party of high-spirited young women, feeling that their liveliness waked up his youthful spirits, and cleared away the cobwebs of old fogyism which a life of loneliness and inaction had fostered. So he made it very pleasant for the travelers, only sorry to hear them say that they would stay but a day or two under his hospitable roof.

Thursday morning, two weeks from the day of their departure from home, the four gleesome friends, with bounding blood and an exhilaration induced by healthful exercise in the open air, long hours of refreshing sleep, and appetites which astonished and flattered their caterers, started out in quest of chestnuts.

"There's plenty of them down on the edge of Farnham's woods," said their good host, "and as the frost was

(154)

sharp last night, I reckon they'll come down lively this morning," and he directed them to the woods a mile away.

"Good-by, Mr. Stearns," called Mahala, as they started their wheels. "Remember and have plenty of dinner for for us at noon, for we shall be hungry as four bears when we get back with our bags full of chestnuts."

"Good," responded their genial host, to whom Mahala's merry quips and gibes were welcome as sunshine. "We'll try and roast beef enough to satisfy you!"

"Who are the young ladies who seem to be enjoying an ideal pleasure-trip?" said a young man in hunting-jacket and knickerbockers, who had come around the house with his gun and dog, just in time to see the tricycles glide swiftly away.

"Morning, Philip," said Mr. Stearns, without taking his eyes from the departing quartette. "Isn't it a queer sight? They came here last night, from Hartford. I don't mean to say they came direct from there, because they have been two weeks on the road. One of them is my niece. She's married—"

"Which one?"

"Well, the little plump one; she's riding behind now. Her husband is F. W. Mather, of Wright, Mather & Company."

Mahala was now looking around and pointing at something by the wayside. She was laughing as usual, and showing her pretty teeth. Her mouth was a generous one, as her brothers often told her in moments of unpleasantness. Her piquant profile came into view as she threw back some laughing words at her aunt.

"Ah, who is the one turning around now?" asked the hunter carelessly.

"Oh, that's Miss Wright," responded the older man, heartily, "and she is the life of the party, though none of them get left very often. Four fresher and brighter girls I never saw before," he added.

"Oh!" said the young man. As he went off in the opposite direction, he smiled—he laughed outright. Something in his thoughts was very amusing. Soon he stopped; then, as he came to a set of bars in the stone wall, he entered the fields, making a slight detour back of the house. He came out into the road and tramped away in the direction our party had taken.

The first severe frost of the season lay upon the fields, as the tricycle party trundled along. The fences were white with its glistening rime, and the leaves of plants and tender shrubs hung limp and blackened by its nipping breath; but every blade of grass, every spike of dried golden-rod, and every fallen twig were as sparkling crystals, along the shaded places. The clear and bracing air lent a new color to the faces of the travelers, and they ran rapidly over the smooth road to keep their blood in quick circulation. They all wore perforated chamois jackets under their dresses, and in vigorous exercise defied Jack Frost.

As the sun rose higher, the myriad of tiny ice crystals which earlier gemmed everything out of doors, wasted away. The air was softened under its warm rays, and a saucy squirrel ran along the wall, now in, now out, up and down the fence-posts, with a flick of his brown tail and a little chatter at these new intruders upon his highway. A covey of quail started up at their approach, but at a signal from the anxious mother they scattered in all directions and lay motionless beneath the brown leaves until the strangers had passed. It was a worrisome time for poor Mrs. Bob White with her family of eight heedless young ones, who, although nearly grown, were not at all able to care for themselves, and she really believed they would stand staring at a man with a gun until they were all killed, if she did not insist on their swift retirement in some friendly nook. You are in no danger now, little mother, but hie away quickly under the wall, for there may be a hunter on the road.

"There are the woods, I am sure," said Mahala, as they pushed their machines up a short, steep hill.

"Yes, this must be the place," agreed Margery, and they chained and locked their wheels in a protected corner of the lot and trudged off over the undulating ground.

"O, what a splendid great tree!—there must be bushels on this," said Margery, who, with Mrs. Mather, had gone ahead. They seized some gnarled and crooked sticks which were lying on the ground, and began to poke and brush the brown leaves which thickly strewed the turf; but they searched in vain.

"There dosn't seem to be any burrs on it, either," said the disappointed young lady, looking upward.

"Why should Mr. Stearns send us so far, for nothing?"

"He probably did not refer to this tree, Margie, as it is an oak," said Miss St. John, coming up; and Mahala laughed in a most provoking manner as they passed by on their way towards the woods.

"Ah! Here are the chestnut trees," exclaimed Mrs.
Mather, in a few minutes, "with burrs by scores, too.
There must be plenty of nuts on the ground. See! The
wide-open burrs with their golden plush linings are many
of them empty."

They all went speedily to work, picking up the shining
brown nuts, which were lying by twos and threes upon the
faded grass, resting upon the dried leaves, or almost hidden
on a mat of green moss at the roots of the trees. They
brushed away the crackling leaves and picked up the fascinating harvest until they had perhaps a couple of quarts,
when Margery said, "We certainly have more than we can
use already. Why take any more? Some boys will
doubtless be woefully disappointed to find them all gone,
for I fancy we are the first in the field, and anxious young-
sters will be here to-day."

"All right, Margery, you are a dear to think of others
in such an exciting moment; but let's get a few more
for Mr. Stearns," said Mahala, and as she kept on picking
up nuts, eagerly flying here and there, and rapidly filling
her bag, the others returned to the captivating pursuit and
were all as busy as could be, when Miss St. John ejaculated faintly:

"Horror! Here comes a man with a bull-dog. And he
means trouble! See how red his face is!"

Striding across the field in his rough boots came a man
that one would dislike to meet anywhere. The alarm
of the almost defenseless women was not without
cause. A brutal face he had, with coarse overhanging
brows, and he showed rows of irregular and monstrous

teeth, as he came cursing, and leading a fierce bull-dog by a chain.

Mrs. Mather instantly laid her hand on her hip. She had never let her good pistol go out of her possession since the morning when they had the false alarm, when she had loaned it to Margery to practice shooting at a mark. Mahala's suppositious danger from tramps had served this purpose, to make her, as the guardian of the safety of the party, more careful to keep her weapon always on her side.

Miss St. John, made more timid by her encounter with the peddler, a few days previous, now began to feel that ill-fortune was attending the latter part of this journey so pleasantly begun, and continued so successfully, almost to its end.

"What are yez doin' here!" shouted the ruffian, as he came nearer. "Stalin' chestnuts, oi suppose!"

"Have you any right to inquire, sir?" said Mrs. Mather, stepping towards him, white but calm, with a proud pose of the head and a glitter in her eye that somewhat cooled the man's temper.

"In coorse I have, or I wouldn't be here. I tell ye, ye must lave them nuts on the ground or pay me for 'em. Oi s'pose ye know thim is worth two dollars a bushel. It's stalin' ye are, however foine ladies ye be."

"We care nothing for your chestnuts, sir. You can gather them for yourself," and taking her bag by the closed end, the lady with a quick gesture scattered the nuts far over the field. "Only relieve us of your insulting presence."

This act of defiance, and the stinging contempt in the
last remark, was enough to thoroughly enrage the man.
He had expected to bully the unprotected girls into paying
him for the nuts, or by forcing them to give up the contents of their bags, to reap the benefit of their toil.   But
now, frantic with rage, he sprang after Mahala, who alone
still held on to her harvest, and with a frightful oath was
about to lay a hand upon her arm, when like a log he fell
to the earth.

His dog sprang upon him, whining and licking his face.
In a second or two he moved, and turning upon his elbow
to get up he met the eyes of a young man in hunting-
jacket and knickerbockers, who stood with his gun in his
left hand looking down at him.   The fist that dealt the
stunning blow behind the ear was still clenched and ready
to repeat the dose if necessary.

Miss St. John had seen the stranger running towards
them almost simultaneously with the advent of the fero-
cious man and dog, and like Sister Ann, in story, she had
waved and beckoned with energy and hope to the rescuer.

"Now, Finnegan, tell me what you purposed to do!
Insulting and terrifying ladies like this!" said the
stranger, with fire in his brown eyes, his nostrils distending with his quick breath and his breast heaving with indignation.

"They was stalin' the nuts, and I won't have it," muttered the fallen man, sullenly, and he glared at the frightened party like a caged hyena.

"Stealing is a poor word for you to use, who are only
cutting my father's wood on shares!   I have heard of your

villainous robbing of boys at this place, and when I heard
these ladies were coming here, I took pains to be in the
vicinity. Now, take your miserable carcass off the land
and I will see to it that your contract on these premises

ends to-day. Leave! I will stay here to see you go.
Ladies, perhaps you had better return to your wheels,"
he said, politely addressing them.

The discomfited scoundrel had risen to his feet and

stood stealthily glowering around, under pretence of ad-
justing his clothing. As he stooped to recover his hat, he
hissed "S-st! boy!" and pointed towards the ladies, who
were starting away to their wheels. The beast sprang
forward with a low growl. Instantly, the gentleman
brought his piece to shoulder and the bull-dog rolled over
with a deadly wound in his side.

"You were foolish, Finnegan, to do that," said the
young man, coolly, as he turned to the revengeful brute,
"there's another barrel ready for you, if you get too
wild. I fortunately had just loaded, as I came upon the
scene of your brilliant exploits. Now, leave, will you?"

More than ever baffled, and grinding his teeth in futile
rage, the man stopped for a minute to bend over the
defunct dog, and seeing that he was dead, gave his lifeless
body a kick, and walked sullenly away.

Their protector watched the furious Irishman well out
of the field, saw him disappear far up a lane, and then
walked over to the spot at a little distance from the disagreeable encounter, where the group was waiting to
express their appreciation of his prompt services in their
behalf.

"Ladies," he said, addressing them as he drew near and
lifted his hat, "I hope you will suffer no ill effects from
the outrageous conduct of that brute." He turned and
looked again in the direction the man had taken. "I regret, exceedingly, that I have not insisted upon his discharge before. But my father, considering only that he
was a good worker, would not listen to the tales of his ras-
cality which have come to my ears since I came home.
Is there anything more I can do for you?"

"You will certainly let us thank you for your assistance in this very unpleasant situation," said Mrs. Mather, warmly, giving him her hand.   He accepted the friendly grasp with perfect ease, again lifting his hat from his fine head.   The lady continued, "It was perhaps foolhardy in ladies to come into the woods alone, but we have never before been troubled." (Miss St. John had said nothing of her small unpleasantness with the peddler.)   "We should be glad to know to whom we are indebted for this timely aid," she added, giving him a look of frank gratitude.

"My name is Philip Farnham," was the simple and direct reply.   "I have been in business in New York for seven years, but return to my home here, every fall, in time for duck-shooting," and he gave a little deprecatory glance and slight shrug at his worn costume.   "So far from receiving thanks for this trifle, I acknowledge that I am glad to have had the opportunity to put a quietus upon that wretch, no less than to be of service to you."

"Sir," said the chaperone, "we can never forget this experience, and my husband, Mr. Frederick W. Mather, will send you hearty thanks."   She turned to the group behind her.   "My friends are Miss St. John, Miss Margery Prescott, and Miss Mahala Wright, of Hartford."

The artist cordially extended her hand, Miss Prescott made a graceful inclination of her tall figure and expressed her obligation in a few well-chosen sentences; but Mahala, blushing furiously for some unknown cause, said, irrelevantly, and with an air of great unconcern, which was intended to convey the idea that she had not been frightened at all, "I am glad I did not give up my chestnuts," with a little hitch of her dimpled chin.

"So am I, Miss Wright," responded the new acquaintance, with great heartiness, and he stood and looked after with a curious smile as she skipped lightly away to the corner where the tricycles were. Then, after making a few polite remarks concerning the machines and their utility, and casting another look about him to assure himself that the furious and reckless Irishman was at a safe distance in the opposite direction, Philip Farnham bade the party good morning and proceeded down the road, thinking that the mounting of the tricycles might be an awkward thing for be-skirted femininity, and he would not be near to embarrass them. But he quickly turned about after striking into the brush, and from this coign of vantage saw that his fears were entirely uncalled for, as the gray forms stepped inside the wheels and resting lightly on the two handles, put their feet upon the bars in front and rose gracefully to the saddles. They gave quick impetus to the wheels with their hands and were away. Only the tips of their toes were seen beneath the heavy folds of their skirts as the treadles rose and fell. Certainly it was an ideal locomotion. The young man now stepped out of the brush to get a better view of the swiftly-receding riders, and at that instant Miss Mahala gave a look to the rear. He quickly raised his hat, and she, red as a rose, impatiently turned her eyes.

Margery, who had been severely shaken by the fright, was still tremulous and pale. "Oh, girls!" she said, earnestly, "what a fortunate deliverance out of the clutches of that horrible man! I could not have run a step, I trembled so. I was so thankful when I saw this gentleman coming. His eyes fairly flashed fire as he struck the man! How terrible it was to see him fall so like a clod to the earth!"

"But what an admirable person Mr. Farnham seems to be," said Miss St. John; "he is doubtless of a good family. You could see that in his well-shaped hand. It was brown, to be sure," she added, "but that was from hunting, of course. I like side-whiskers, too; yes, he is my idea of a man."

"Why, Aunt Dude!" exclaimed Mahala, laughing nervously, "you would not fall in love with a stranger, and one with red hair, too!"

"He has not red hair," spoke up Mrs. Mather, defensively; "it is just a lovely auburn, and if I had not an old fellow somewhere," she added, with a little yearning in the merry tones, "I am not sure what might not happen to me. Well," she continued, more soberly, "It certainly was a boon to us that such a muscular cavalier was around."

"Yes," grumbled Mahala, under her breath. "He is always *around*, I believe."

A light broke upon Mrs. Mather.

"Some people are always happening about, and intruding themselves," said the perverse girl, with surprising unreasonableness.

"Why, Mike," exclaimed Margery, in astonishment, "I never saw you so contrary. What ails the girl?"

"She is tired and cross, I suppose," was Miss St. John's opinion; but Julie Mather had her own ideas about it.

"There's nothing the matter," asserted the girl, with some petulance, "except that I don't agree with you in admiring this young man. Of course, it was very obliging in him to knock the man down and kill the dog; though it is nothing more than he would have done for a lot of factory girls; but as for thinking him at all nice, I don't! I can't bear the sight of him!"

Mrs. Mather gently shook her head at Miss St. John, who was about to argue with her pettish niece, and changed the subject by pointing out a mendicant robin, now sadly wandering about in his old dilapidated clothes, and as Mahala's ready sympathy with all living creatures in feathers and fur went out at once to him, good humor was once more restored.

"Poor fellow!" said Mahala, in humorous pity, "he is not such a dandy, now, as when he came out in the spring! What a handsome swell he was then, in his jet black cap and red vest! and now how shabby he is, to be sure! You had better get into the thicket and out of sight as soon as you can, young fellow! You are *passé* for this year."

Mr. Stearns was much disturbed to hear of the perilous adventure which had befallen his guests, and blamed himself, over and over again, for allowing them to go into the fields alone. He was saying this for the twentieth time as they sat at the dinner-table.

"Oh, we should probably have come out all right, uncle, if I had not lost my temper and scattered the nuts around," said Julie.

"Temper!" roared Uncle Stearns, bringing down his fist upon the table so that all the glasses jingled. "Great Scott! who could keep his temper under such an insult? I wish I had the villain here," said the wrathful old gentleman, tightening his fingers. "I'd wring his neck for him!"

"Well," said Miss St. John, giving her head a satisfied little shake, "young Mr. Farnham fixed his ear for him. That's one sure thing!"

"So the fiend was reaching for Mahala, was he, when Farnham knocked him down! Well, well, that would annoy a handsome young fellow like Phil."

Mahala winced under the old man's harmless joke, and found no pert answer like those which usually came to her lips.

"Uncle," said Julie, as their plates were changed for pie, "you are probably well acquainted with Mr. Farnham. He seems to be a well-bred person."

"Well-bred? Why, certainly. The Farnhams are one of the oldest and most respectable families in Essex, and Philip, personally, is fully up to the standard. He is the youngest partner of Estey, Brown & Company, wool brokers in New York, and is rich, they say. That is of no consequence, however, as he is an energetic worker and a real gentleman."

"Mrs. Bronson," Mahala whispered to the housekeeper at the beginning of this eulogy, "I do not care for dessert; may I be excused?" and had quietly left the room. But astute Mrs. Mather noticed that she lingered in the hall long enough to hear it through, and was inwardly amused, for she knew that if there was anything Mahala doted upon it was squash-pie and new cheese.

CHAPTER XV.

The Farnhams call upon the Tricycle Tourists.

AT evening, Mr. Stearns's rather bare and uninteresting sitting-room had taken an unusually bright and
cosy appearance.

Her uncle, who had been looking through the telegraph
columns of the paper, turned to the cheery group around
the center-table and said, "Julie, I hope you and your
friends will come here soon again." He took off his
glasses and sat regarding the young ladies, who were
gracing his home, with unalloyed pleasure as he wiped and
polished his spectacles. "I never realized how dreary
the house was until you came. Somehow, you seem to
furnish it with life and color."

Mahala was curled up in the corner of the wide lounge,
reading an old-fashioned love-story which she had found in
the top of the "secretary" and drawn forth from its
uncongenial companionship with a concordance, a dic-
tionary, Young's "Night Thoughts," Pope's "Essay on
Man," Watts' "On the Mind," some almanacs, and other
miscellany.

(168)

She wore a tea-gown of light blue, with dainty ruffles at the throat and wrists. One slender foot, clad in black silk hose and pointed slipper showed underneath the graceful folds of the soft cashmere robe, and her deep blue eyes with fringed dark lashes ran back and forth along the quaint lines of the book she read.

Plump Mrs. Mather, who knew her possibilities and did not tamper with esthetic styles in clothing, wore a perfectly-fitting dress of dark maroon velvet. She was busily engaged in making a napkin-holder for her uncle. She had seen that the dear old man was in continual trouble with this convenient article at table. He would drop it to the floor, recover it, and tuck it into his bosom or into his coat-tail pocket, and when it was needed was surprised and annoyed at its unaccountable absence from his knees, and would hunt for it, slapping his sides and looking under his chair in vain search. So, with a pair of clasps which she had found at the store, and a bit of ribbon, she was working on some "stitches" in silk floss, and deftly fashioned the useful little article as she chatted of pleasant things.

"Be sure you wear it, won't you, uncle?" she said; "for if you use it once you will never be without one. Fred finds his invaluable. I will keep you supplied as they get worn."

Miss St. John, always in subdued colors, had exchanged her gray wheel-dress for a genteel black silk, which was soft and lusterless, and was mechanically knitting on some scarlet wools. She was discussing charitable societies, and the results of their work, with Mr. Stearns. He was

disposed to think that the ponderous machinery of some
of these institutions absorbed much of the money donated
by a trusting public. "It seems all out of proportion to
the meager results," he was saying. "In a town of say
fifty thousand inhabitants, which are largely counted
among the upper class, with small and easily get-at-able poor
districts, with the town alms-house, Widows' Home, Church
Home, Woman's Aid Society, Woman's Christian Association, Young Men's Christian Association, and half a dozen
other associations, it would seem impossible for any pauper
to escape, and as if the tone of morals must be well-nigh perfect. Is such the result of your evangelical guild, your
combination for city charity, and your free kindergartens,
sewing-schools, and reading-rooms? It is the impression
among us country people, that it is a lot of fuss and
feathers, without any adequate result from the thousands
of dollars which are poured out every year for the poor."

The lady raised her bright gray eyes to his honest face.
"That there is considerable machinery about the system of
organized· charity there is no doubt, and probably full as
much in our city as in larger places, because it has become
the fashionable thing to do. You see, we ladies of the
inner circles do no work. We attend the meetings and
see that no outsiders come in to vote different methods
from those we consider to be proper. Money we collect
from the lay members each year, to be sure, but there
their usefulness ends, with the exception, perhaps, of half
a dozen devoted women, who sit and cut out garments;
manage the different departments; and report to us once
a year. We vote to accept their work. Most of us are

too toney to know how to sew, and are too delicate to make personal visits to our protegées, and so we hire an almoner to do it for us."

" Ha! ha!" laughed the amused listener.

"Now, Dude, you stop such sarcasm," interposed Mrs. Mather, who was smiling in spite of herself, while her cheeks were hot with vexation. " You know it is far better to give the dispensation of alms to a competent person than to work individually, oftentimes at cross purposes, repeating assistance to some families and neglecting others who are worthy."

" Yes, that is true, Julie, if the whole idea of these institutions, publicly organized to support the thriftless portion of the community, who are too lazy, or too abandoned to all responsibility in their own or in their children's welfare to work for themselves, is not fundamentally erroneous."

" These are certainly vexed questions," said Miss. St. John, fairly, "and felt to be so by many members of charitable societies. The fact is, certain men will waste their money, whether their families are helped or not. The question then, is, will you let their wives and babies freeze and starve because you cannot convert them from their worthlessness ?"

"You must look at the effect of your work in the aggregate," insisted Uncle Stearns.

"We know it is a thankless, discouraging, and heart-weary task," said Mrs. Mather, troubled with the recollection of her trials in the work, "and none realize it so well as those who come into direct contact with the poor. But shall we stop work because we do not see direct results for our pains ?"

"Perhaps not," answered Mr. Stearns, who was a trifle hard-headed, although notoriously soft-hearted; but the head held control, as a man's always should. "But should we not look to the showing of ten years, in order to judge fairly of the result of the instinctive sympathy which you philanthropic souls have extended to these suffering classes, without considering whether you were not indirectly working harm to humanity in general? Now, is the amount of pauperism in your city less in proportion to the population than it was a decade ago? If not, your institutions are falling far short of their object. While in town the other day, I was in Judge Green's office, and the subject was under discussion. He, and other practical men who were there, claimed that poverty is steadily increasing in Hartford, in spite of the astoundingly large sum which statistics show has been devoted to bettering the condition of ignorant and helpless humanity. Facts, Julie, are—"

"Stubborn things. Yes, I know," said Mrs. Mather, with her own inimitable faculty of playful abuse, which was generally rather flattering to the recipient, "and so are hard-hearted old uncles, who talk very severely and yet would stop to kick a caterpillar out of their path rather than tread upon it! I saw you do it this morning! Now, permit me to say that these same facts which are ever referred to as incontrovertible, can be arranged or selected so as to prove almost anything. Your crushing reference to statistics only implies, to me, that whereas ten years ago we passed by on the other side, unconscious of or indifferent to the sufferings of our fellow creatures, we now seek them out, and bring to light an alarming number of cases of degradation and suffering. I have no doubt it existed in the same degree ten years ago. Do you imagine that the abject misery of thousands of poor people in London is any worse than it was before Dickens wrote of it and opened its gaping squalor to the world ? "

"Mrs. Mather," said her uncle, not ill-pleased, "allow me to protest against any personalities in a discussion. It is extremely poor taste. You will not for an instant hear me advocate any neglect of this great problem which is forcing its ugly form into view with startling prominence in the present day. My idea simply is that instead of throttling the monster of shameless pauperism, we are now fostering it with a system of coddling, until it will gain such strength that it will turn and rend us. Now, braving your wrath that any one should be so cruelly calculating, I must tell you that Judge Green said that he figured that with the money that has actually been given to charity, during these years, he could have boarded every deserving pauper at the Alden House, and given them rides in carriages every day."

Miss St. John laughed delightedly.

"Dude," said Mrs. Mather, somewhat annoyed at this presentation of a conclusion against a work in which she was much interested, "I believe that your heart is lost in your pursuit of art, which is cold and unsympathetic. It demands the admiration of the world, and gives nothing but the privilege of gazing upon its perfections in return. It is a cold, unresponsive mirror, and tends to chill its votaries to human joy or woe, except as they are interested to reproduce it. Who was it—Giotto ?—that tortured a poor old man to death so that he might paint his dying agonies ? "

To this feminine retort Miss St. John answered, smiling, " It was Parrhasius, dear. But, Julie, do not bring art into disfavor, because I smiled at an amusing statement, and because Parrhasius was cruel."

The perfect equanimity with which the artist regarded her friend's rather illogical retort in favor of her charitable schemes, no less than the spirited rejoinders of the warm-hearted little chaperone of the visiting party, was a great diversion to Mr. Stearns. He had not been so entertained for a long time. He softly rubbed his hands together and waited for the little woman to finish.

"And, uncle," she flashed, turning upon him, "I must beg you and the astute lawyers who thus summarily closed a question which few feel competent to answer, to consider, that mere physical relief is only one of the objects of an enlightened charity. It costs more to send a boy to school than it does to give him a dinner, and the educational schemes now in practical working in sewing, training, and cooking schools, in mothers' meetings and reading-rooms, as well as in constant advice and counsel, are far more expensive in time and money than an occasional turkey or a basket of cold pieces."

" My dear niece," said her uncle, with affectionate regard, " I am sure that the work that you and others do in this field is a power for good to your souls. The admiration I feel for a generous, warm-hearted little woman who forgets her own fatigue for the sake of the Lord's unfortunates, makes me feel that I would not have the work

given up, or differently managed ; but," and he smiled in
a teasing way, "is it fair to the paupers?   If it is a fact
that they increase under this petting, which is such a rare
discipline to you, should you not magnanimously refrain
from it, and let some clear-headed, hard-fisted, Christian
man take the management of your half-dozen societies con-
solidated into one, and care gently for the innocent and
disabled, while dealing decisively with laziness and
crime?"

Miss St. John leaned eagerly forward to catch Mrs.
Mather's reply to a proposition which instantly offended
her as a champion of the dignity and executive powers of
her sex.

Mrs. Mather smiled across the table at her friend, and
then turned again to the old man, who sat intensely enjoying the discussion he had brought about by a few remarks
calculated to stir up the ire of these wide-awake ladies.

"To your idea of consolidation," answered Mrs. Mather,
"I say yes.   A thousand times, yes.   To your declaration
that charitable societies tend to foster laziness and crimi-
nal neglect of opportunities for self-help, by their proffered
aid, I say, its truth has yet to be proven.   To your last
proposition for a masculine manager of all charities, imply-
ing that women are actuated rather by their quick sympa-
thies than by good judgment, I say, that in common
with many other men, you are condemning our methods
without that understanding of them which would qualify
you to an unbiased conclusion.   You jump at once
to the conclusion that, being women, we have not
progressed with the rest of the world beyond the old

and injudicious practice of giving money or provisions to any worthless individual who makes a demand for it. I wish to call your attention to the fact, that one of our women, who is a prominent dispenser of funds trusted to her for the purpose, was among the first in the country to think out the problem for herself and advocate the lending of assistance with the direct purpose of inducing indigent ones to help themselves. She has even made it a point not to give anything to those who are able to work for it. She works with this idea constantly in view. Earnestly urging upon her backers the folly of indiscriminate charity, as doing more harm than good, she endeavors to open the chances for discouraged humanity. If she could bring all of the society which supports her to her own practical views there would be less heard about 'fuss and feathers,' less gush and fashionable display, and less wide-spread mischievous effects from a palpable loss of the main idea, under a mass of circumlocution and absurd mismanagement But, taking the running of any of these societies, which are managed by ladies, I am confident they will compare favorably with any which are under the charge of 'hard-fisted men.'"

Miss St. John clapped her hands softly. "Why, Julie Mather, do you know that you are almost advocating woman's rights? I am surprised at you." As indeed she was.

Julie threw her a little smile, and continued, "Well, I let all these knotty points go, unless I am disturbed by some obstinate old uncle, whom it is necessary to set right. I am convinced that the educational schemes are of deepest importance. There is certainly no danger of making children too kind or polite. No fear that in teaching them to do honest work, they can be injured. This work is large enough to occupy many efficient helpers. When you commence with a child and make him clean, you have taken the first step towards leading him out of pauperism. When you teach them to read, to use their brains and hands, you have given them that which no drunken father can take away. When you have convinced a poor boy or girl that it is brighter, happier, better to be moral, you have cured crime, or rather prevented it. It is enough for me," she said, kindling, "to see the children coming out of filth and ignorance under our ministrations. This work takes all my leisure time. Let those who are disposed quarrel over office-holding, or pine for recognition by the figureheads of societies. Uncle, there are some things not reducible to statistics."

"Bravo, little woman! I am proud to acknowledge that you have a wider comprehension of the subject than I had given you tender-hearted women credit for. What we need everywhere is a clearer understanding of the principles of this subject. We are not justified in closing our eyes to the needs of our fellows, but he or she that brings into exercise an intelligent caution against injurious alms-giving is a veritable philanthropist, in having worked towards the permanently beneficent ends. But," he said, returning to his first idea, "an awful sight of money goes somewhere, with no very encouraging results. However, if they enjoy it (I mean the ladies; of course their pensioners do), I am not sure that it does any harm!"

"Uncle, you are incorrigible! We get you all convinced, and then you fly back to your original statement. That is supposed to be exclusively a woman's prerogative," answered his niece, regarding him somewhat reproachfully.

"Yes, sir," said the artist, "if you could hear our managers talk you would not dare to offer such faint praise. Why, they consider they are bringing about the millennium."

"Well, I suppose they see results that others cannot. It's probably all right, if they like it."

The old man did not come down very gracefully from his high ground, but Mrs. Mather realized that she had made some effect upon his mind in favor of her favorite branches of charitable work, and said no more.

"Certainly these societies work for good. Whether they achieve the greatest possibilities, or not, it is hard to say. And," she pursued, shaking her head at him, "while I cannot help seeing the ludicrous side of many of their procedures, I decidedly object to your insinuation that they make mistakes because they are women. Men have yet to be proven infallible, and I think all organizations, whether masculine, feminine, political, social, or charitable, have such features, and such is life."

"There now, it is all settled," said Mahala, from the lounge. She now arose and clasping her hand behind her head, stood for a moment looking at Mrs. Mather with quizzical affection. "There's no use trying to read here," she said, as she came and placed her hands beside her friend's face as she stood behind her chair, "your conversation is so much more interesting than—"

Here the door-bell rang vigorously, and Mr. Stearns proceeded to the door. Mahala flew back to the lounge in the corner, and Miss St. John sat unwinding a line of scarlet zephyr, while Mrs. Mather looked expectantly towards the door.

"Ah! Good evening, sir, good evening," the voice of Mr. Stearns was heard to say. "Madam, I am very glad to see you. Come right into the sitting-room. I must introduce to you my young ladies," he said, proudly.

"Thank you," rejoined a pleasant voice, "it was to see them that we called this evening."

Mr. Stearns came into the room and stood on one side to allow a beautiful lady with soft gray hair to enter.

"Mrs. Farnham, this is Mrs. Mather, my niece," and Miss St. John and Miss Wright were in turn presented to the graceful lady, who wore a dress of heavy satin, an India shawl of exquisite fineness, and an unmistakably aristocratic bonnet with rich plumes

Mrs. Mather's quick eye took this all in at a glance, and she was not surprised to see the tall figure and strong face of Mr. Philip Farnham, now in exceptionally neat and elegant attire, following the lovely old lady into the room.

She quickly went to greet him in her own cordial manner, and while expressing her pleasure at meeting him again, she heard Mrs. Farnham saying: "I made haste to call upon you, ladies, and say how much I regret your unpleasant encounter with Patrick Finnegan in our woods. I really hope the fright has not made you ill, nor disheartened you from pursuing your very interesting journey, of which I have heard."

"Oh, no," answered Miss St. John, "only Miss Prescott has felt the shock somewhat, and as her ankle is still a little lame from a slight sprain, she has gone to bed. She will be very sorry not to meet you."

"And I am very sorry not to see her," the lady graciously replied. "Miss St. John," she said, suddenly, "I am sure that I have heard of you before, through my friend, Mrs. Trowbridge. Is she not also a friend of yours?"

"Why, yes, indeed," said Miss St. John, with great enthusiasm, and their conversation was at once launched upon a sea of pleasant reminiscences and flowing interchange of ideas.

Mahala, who had seen the entrance of Philip Farnham with dismay, had sunk again into the comfortable lounge. There she sat, fingering the long ends of blue satin bow at her neck, with eyes cast down and toes demurely crossed. She made an extremely pretty picture, but, as Mrs. Mather well knew, was feeling terribly embarrassed and uncomfortable. Seeing that Mr. Farnham had cast many glances towards that corner, and by several remarks thrown in Mahala's direction (which, however, elicited no reply from her) had shown a desire to draw out the shy girl, Mrs. Mather turned her conversation to her uncle for a moment.

Then Philip rose and crossed the room, and taking a seat on the lounge beside her, in the easiest manner possible commenced a talk of polite nothings and agreeable remarks upon things in general, so that before long Mahala had somewhat forgotten her unnatural reticence and was

telling him about her brother's furore for "specimens."
She descanted wittily upon the annoyance of the family
when some of the beetles refused to die under chloroform,
and went crawling about the house with long pins through
their horny bodies.   "But that was before he knew anything about cyanide of potash," she continued, raising the
long lashes as she gave him an artless glance and rolled
the blue ribbon over her taper forefingers.   "Now, he just
puts them into a wide-nosed bottle with this poison in the
bottom, and they crawl about perfectly happy for a while,
until the first thing they know they are dead."

Philip laughed, and told her of some gorgeous beetles
he had brought from the South, and said he would like to
send them to her brother, feeling sure that so enthusiastic
a naturalist as she described him to be would take far
better care of them than he might if he kept them in his
possession.   Mahala could not refuse such an acquisition
for Joe, and thanked him prettily for her brother.

Soon, again, Julie caught fragments of their chat.   Mr.
Farnham, who evidently considered the frank and unassuming style of the sprightly girl very charming, was getting personal.   "I am sure, Miss Wright," said he, "that I
heard your friends call you Mike.   How did you come by
such a cognomen?"

Mahala then told him how "the boys" disliked her old-
fashioned name, and said she was such a good fellow that
she should have a boy's name.   So, as Mike was Frank's
name for every one, and he did not know what else to call
her, she was dubbed by his favorite appellation.

"I feel that it is hardly appropriate, and not very attract-

ive," she said, opening and shutting her book with a
pensive air, "but if the boys like it, that is enough," and
she looked at her listener with her eyebrows raised, while
she showed the tips of her white teeth.

"Yes, indeed.   So it is, Miss Wright," assented the
young man, with a warmth which seemed a little in excess
considering the triviality of the subject.   "Your devotion
to the boys must be very pleasant to them; and, you
know, all names are not appropriate."

"No," she said, with a quick impulse, and a wicked
smile, "I think yours should be Rufus," and then, frightened at her temerity, she colored a little and looked away,
and then at him askance to see the effect of her saucy
words.

"Certainly, I see,—'The Red,' " answered the gentleman, passing his hand over his crisp hair which was clip-
ped rather closely to his fine head, not in the least disturbed.   Then he said slowly, and looking intently at her
with a meaning smile, "And when I can recall a name for
a fire-hang-bird, I will suggest it to you.   How would
Oriola suit you?"

Mahala was crushed.' She threw him one piteous glance,
in which shame, conviction, and dread were mingled.
The worst had happened—she was disgraced, ridiculed.

"Oh, Mr. Farnham," she cried, crimson with mortification, "were you—did you—"

"Yes," he answered, laughing at her mercilessly, "I
was, and I did."

"Oh," she exclaimed, in low but indignant tones, "how
could you do such a thing?   How came you to be away

up in Haddam, anyway? I think it was horrid in you!" and she turned away her coquettish head and bit her lips.

Philip seeing her unfeigned distress, hastened to say most earnestly, "Miss Wright, I assure you there was no intent on my part to distress any one, when I went up the river that morning hunting. Hearing cries as of some one in need of help, I ran through the woods and jumped the fence, to see a young lady in a rather unhappy situation." He suppressed a smile in a most exasperating manner. "But as your friends arrived just at that moment, and you dropped from the birch, I jumped back again, so as not to embarrass you, when I could be of no assistance. I could see from the cover of the woods that no one was seriously hurt, so I went on my way."

Mahala was twisting her fingers and winking very fast.

"Am I to blame for this, Miss Wright?" asked Philip, leaning towards her kindly.

"No; you were only doing the kind and chivalrous thing," she answered bravely, at last, "but I — I am being justly punished for my hideous rudeness."

"I protest that it struck me as the most natural and unavoidable accident in the world," declared Philip. Mahala smiled in spite of her vexation.

"Do you forgive me, then, for being near? It was impossible that I should have foreseen such a *contre temps*. Please tell me that you will not dislike me for it."

"Come, Philip," said the gentle voice of his mother, "we are making a shockingly unfashionable call; it is time to go. My dear," she said to Mahala, as she took her hand, "I wish to know you better, and also to see you on your tricycles, so I have invited your friends to come and dine with us at four to-morrow afternoon. I hope you will certainly come. Mrs. Mather thinks that Miss Prescott will be hardly able to use her wheels, so I shall send the carriage for her."

An eloquent glance from the red-brown eyes of Philip (burnt sienna, Miss St. John called them) seconded this kind invitation so persuasively that Mahala stammered her thanks and professed herself under the leading of her aunt and chaperone, and **Mr.** Farnham and his mother took their leave.

CHAPTER XVI.

Dinner at the Farnhams.

"I THOUGHT we were going on our journey to-day," said Mahala the next morning, and as she had completed her toilet she sat down sideways upon a chair, and resting her arm upon its back, clasped her hands and pouted a little.

Miss St. John, who was fastening her collar at the glass, turned upon her with considerable asperity.

"Mahala Wright," she said, "you are developing an amount of perversity of late which is astonishing. Ordinarily, you would be charmed to visit such an old manse as Mr. Stearns tells us the Farnham house is, to say nothing of the pleasure of knowing such delightful people. Really, you are trying to one's disposition."

"Well, well, auntie, I do not mean to vex you, and certainly have no objections to going to Mrs. Farnham's if you all wish it. Don't be angry, dear, I only—"

"She only put in her disclaimer, to be consistent," lightly added Mrs. Mather, who had just come into the room.

"Consistent!—in what?" demanded Mahala, turning

(185)

swiftly upon her friend; but her eyes, which she tried to make unconscious, fell beneath the quizzical gaze of that lady, who merely said, "Oh, nothing."

"Well, I think you are all getting enigmatical," sniffed Miss St. John, "and I move that we go down to breakfast."

At precisely three o'clock in the afternoon, the carriage, drawn by a pair of fat bay horses, driven by black Robert, who had grown gray in the Farnhams' service, arrived at Mr. Stearns's door to convey Margery and himself to Squire Farnham's house.

The old gentleman protested that he could carry Margery over in his buggy, but Mrs. Farnham had insisted that the horses needed exercise, and it would please Robert so much to drive a beautiful young lady in his carriage once more; so he reluctantly consented to be waited upon. The trio, on tricycles, followed the carriage, and soon the party arrived at the Farnhams' place, where Philip stood on the stone steps at the entrance to greet them. He carefully assisted Margery up the flight to the door, where she was met and kissed on her presentation to the sweet mother. Then he turned again to welcome the gray-suited ladies, who now came smoothly up the circular driveway. Mrs. Farnham, having thrown a light shawl over her head, now came briskly out of the house.

"Oh, here you are at last, my dears," she cried. "Don't alight! I do want to see those machines work. Are you too tired to run around the circle just once for me? Oh, how perfectly fascinating that must be!" she said to Philip, as they ran so rapidly and noiselessly over the smooth drive. "It is only when I see the freedom and out-of-door sports of young girls in this age, that I wish I had been born fifty years later."

"Ah, Mrs. Farnham," said Julie, as she stepped from her wheels, "one must feel, in knowing you, that there are compensations in having been brought up in the old school, though we do enjoy our strength and the robust health which this exercise in pure air brings us."

"Miss St. John," said their hostess, as she led her into the house, "how independent you are enabled to be of cars and carriages, on your sketching tours, by your tricycle!"

"Yes," answered the artist, "it is a great convenience to me.   In fact, I wonder how I ever got along without it."

"Miss Wright," said Philip, with a vivid color in his bronzed cheek, as he took her neatly-gloved hand, "I am very glad to welcome you to my home.   You have done us all a great kindness in coming.   My father, who is quite feeble, has been anxiously waiting your arrival."

Mahala looked up, following his slight gesture in the direction of one of the windows, and saw an old man watching them from the library, into which they were soon shown.

A wood fire was burning in the capacious chimney. Book-cases lined the walls, and contained a valuable law library, as well as standard works in theology, science, philosophy, and fiction.   The ancient, hard-wood wainscoting and mantel had been preserved.   A few choice pictures and some pieces of bric-a-brac filled various niches and lightened the dark walls.   An air of cultivation and luxury pervaded the room.

Squire Farnham turned from his conversation with Mr. Stearns to receive the visitors as they entered, and expressed his pleasure at their visit and great admiration of their tricycle costumes.

"We had to wear them, sir," apologized Mrs. Mather, "as Mrs. Farnham particularly requested to see us in traveling garb."

"Why, certainly," said the gratified squire, beaming upon one and another, "I should have been much chagrined to miss seeing these unique dresses.   You look like female hussars, with your buttons and braid.   Come here, my dear," said the old gentleman to Mahala, "you are like a peach; so sweet and fresh! Don't mind an old man's compliment," for Mahala blushed as he took her hand, "I am sure you are willing to entertain me for a little while."

"Oh, yes, sir," answered the kind little maid, "I am very fond of elderly people. It will be a pleasure to me. Some of the happiest hours of my life have been spent at my grandfather's knee. We lost him only a year ago," she continued, softly.

"Young people do not always count it a loss when old ones are removed. But go now, Miss Wright, with Philip and mother, who are going to show your friends some of our antiquities. They are not much, but Philip values them very highly, since such things have become fashionable."

"Father," said Philip, remonstrating, "you know I always prized family relics, and I repudiate the charge of following a popular craze."

In the square hall near a window which was draped with a sash-curtain stood a high and massive clock.

"This," said Philip, "is one of the first of Harrison's gridiron pendulum-clocks. It is number five, I believe, and therefore must have been made soon after 1726. It was brought to New York by an ancestor of my mother's, a Philip Lindsay, who was a younger son of an English earl."

"Never mind the genealogy, my son," said Mrs. Farnham, smiling.

"This clock kept perfect time," the young man continued, "until about ten years ago, when some wheel was worn out and the old time-piece was still. But, within a few weeks, I have had an expert in horology examine it, and by the substitution of one new cog it is now running perfectly once more."

The case was of the richest mahogany, which was beautifully carved in symbolical and grotesque figures.

"I *am* proud of it," acknowledged the young man, "and—"

Just then the silvery cadence as of tinkling bells struck quickly upon the ear.

"Ten, eleven, twelve, thirteen, fourteen,—" Mahala counted, and turned in amazement to Mrs. Farnham, who was laughing with her son to see the surprised looks of their visitors as the bell struck on to forty-four. "That is only our Anne Boleyn," said she, as all joined in the laugh.

"Well," said Miss St. John, looking around the hall, "if the Queen reiterated her remarks as many times as that I do not wonder that Henry cut her head off. He probably did it in self-defense."

"Here it is," said Mr. Farnham, leading the way to the first landing of the oaken staircase. "It is one of Tompkin's clocks, and was made in the seventeenth century. It is a fac-simile of one which was presented to poor Anne Boleyn by Henry the Eighth. They seem to have had an unaccountable penchant at that period for striking clocks. This one formerly struck forty-four at twelve o'clock, and between twelve and one o'clock no less than one hundred and thirteen times. It not only struck the quarter hours on eight bells but also the hour, after each quarter. However, the mechanism is long ago worn out and we seldom wind it. I did so, in an idle moment yesterday, and your presence seems to have given it new life."

It had been presented to Squire Farnham in England as the souvenir of a dear friend, some twenty-five years be-fore, and was of satin-wood inlaid with brass filigree-work in gothic form, and surmounted by a lion rampant on a shield.

The delighted girls were shown a great-grandmother's wedding-set of china, with her monogram in gilt upon each piece. A massive silver salver, wrought into pictures of the chase, in matchless *repoussé* work, upon which the valiant henchman had proudly borne the boar's head into the feudal dining-room of a Farnham great, great, great, great, great grandsire.

In a case of inlaid wood, which Philip took from a drawer in the desk, was a sort of picture-book of some forty or fifty pages.

"This book," said he, "was picked up by my father, at an old book-stall in Wirtemburg, twenty-five years ago. While glancing over the stock of aged and yellow manu-scripts and folios, as he often did, being something of a biblio-maniac, he was thrilled with joy and surprise to rec-ognize in it a genuine and unmistakable *Biblia Pau-perum.*"

Here, Mahala, who had been not a little discomfited at her own ignorance of things which seemed so familiar to these Farnhams, said with a little chagrin in her tones: "But, Mr. Farnham, common people do not even know what a *Biblia Pauperum* is," and she made a comical little mouth at the name. "Of course the words seem to imply 'poor man s Bible,' but I never heard of such a one as this." She saw cuts in the quaint style of the middle ages, giving the leading events of Christ's saving work.

"It is not at all strange that you are not acquainted with this book," said Philip, smiling, and carefully turning the leaves, "as it was used as a text-book before the Reformation, by monks, in preaching, and took the place of the more expensive and unattainable Bible among the poor laity. As these lower orders of the clergy took the title of *Paupers Christi*, 'Christ's poor,' the book was so called. It is in Latin, you see." As he replaced the book in its case, he said : "I am sure you must be tired with musty old relics, now, and I hope I have not bored you too long with my showman's harangue. How would you like to go out and see the cattle, and horses, and dogs ? "

"Oh, one could never tire of this beautiful old house," said Mrs. Mather, enthusiastically looking around. "It is ancient enough to be modern! How fortunate for its possessors."

"Oh, yes," joyfully assented Mahala to their entertainer's proposition. "Do let us see the stables. I can always make friends with animals."

"Do you have any particular difficulty in that respect with human beings ? " said Philip, giving her a humorous glance, which Mahala answered with a bright flash from her eyes.

"Certainly," said Mrs. Mather, "we should enjoy it much to see the horses. We will get our hats and—"

"Mr. Farnham," said Miss St. John, coming out of the library, where she had been gloating over some art magazines, "Your father is very anxious to hear some music before dinner, and your mother says if you will tune your violin she will soon be here to play the accompaniment. After which, some of us will play," she continued, as she saw a slight intention to demur upon his face.

"Very well," he said, resignedly, "so be it, if it is my father's wish. Mr. Stearns," he said, looking in at the library-door, "if you will give father your arm into the drawing-room, I will do my twisting and scratching as soon as may be."

While the old man and his friend and the ladies were coming into the room, the amateur violinist began the excruciating process which always precedes string playing.

"Miss Wright," said he, "will you be kind enough to strike A, on the piano? Now—now—thank you. That will do, I think."

He did not make a long affair of it, and when his mother came smiling into the room from a secret consultation with old Viney in the kitchen, and sat down to the piano, he began to play. His bowing was easy and graceful, his inflections in thorough good taste, and the tones which he brought from his cherished Straduarius were round and full.

After playing several sweet selections from Beethoven, a Larghetto from the Second Symphony, and an Adagio from the Fifth Sonata, Philip set upon the rack the "Lost Chord."

"It is by Sullivan, you know," he said, turning to Mrs. Mather, "not strictly a violin piece, but one of my favorites. I do not attempt concert pieces, realizing that they are beyond my power. I think it is better to play such things as these well, than to haggle at music which would tax the skill of Wilhelmj;" and as the strong pure harmony of the composition rose and fell, finely modulated, and carefully finished, Miss St. John nodded to Margery. "Always in good taste," she murmured.

The young lady, scarcely knowing whether the ambiguous remark referred to the selection, its rendering, or the modest repression of the performer—which, more's the pity, all amateurs do not exercise—bowed impressively in return.

"Mr. Farnham," exclaimed Miss St. John, as he laid down his violin, "I am ashamed to confess that before you began to play, I trembled, for I have so suffered from bad violin-playing that I feel like running away when I see a non-professional take one in hand. I congratulate you upon your touch. Your violin sings; nearly all amateurs' squeak."

"You need never tremble for anything Philip does," said his father, speaking from his easy-chair near the window. "It is not his way to fumble at anything."

"Tut, tut, father," said Philip, looking at him with an affectionate smile, "you mean to say that, knowing myself, I do not undertake great things."

"Now, Miss Wright," said Mrs. Farnham, as she rose from the piano, "having shown the clumsiness of my old hands without apology, I trust you will put more life into the instrument with your light fingers."

Mahala, who had been well trained on this point, and realized that one object of her expensive musical education was to give pleasure to friends, quietly arose and gave her hand to Philip, who approached her bowing and led her to the piano.

"Shall I play that little valse and pizzicati, by Delibes, Aunt Dude?" she said, turning to Miss St. John.

. "Certainly," answered her aunt, "it follows naturally after the violin."

"But it is rather a poor imitation, as I shall give it, I fear," said pretty Mahala, looking with a little timidity at the violinist, as she commenced the piquant staccato movement. She played without affectation and with a crispness and delicacy which was born of her own nerve and a perfect technique.

"Ah!" sighed Squire Farnham, as she rippled out the last chord, "that is inspiriting. I could almost lock my fingers at arms' length and dance, *à la ballet*, myself, to such music."

This ambitious expression of the dignified old man raised a general laugh at his expense. Mahala was leaving the piano, but he would not have it so.

"No, no," he cried, "something more. I shall not have you here often to play to me!"

As the old man said the last words, Mahala turned smiling to him and met such a burning glance from the brown eyes of his son who stood back of his chair, that her heart gave a quick bound, and something in her throat was like to suffocate her, but she managed to say, "I will play you the March of the Marionettes, if you like a burlesque in music."

"Oh, anything you choose will be charming, I am sure," said Mrs. Farnham.

"Well," said Mahala, showing her dimples, "you must know that this is the funeral march of a broken doll. It is by Gounod, and pleases every one who is not too severely classic to enjoy fun."

"A kind fate forbid that we should ever get to that!" said Mrs. Mather, who was delighted to see her pet showing to such advantage.

"The first discordant sounds are the wails of the bereaved companion marionettes, and you must interpret the rest for yourselves," said Mahala, and she struck the harsh notes with an evident sense of the humor of the piece and fell into the ludicrous measured monotones of the march. Every listener was fain to smile as she cleverly brought out the sudden and exaggerated grief of an explosive chord, which was immediately followed by the hushed tread of the successive measures. Louder and nearer came the manikin procession, until on the return the minor and jerky movement was again taken up and finally died away in the distance.

"Good! good!" cried the amused listeners, laughing, and falling into an animated chattering over the inimitable bit of humor in music, when Robert appeared at the door. "Mrs. Farnham," he announced, with much dignity, "de dinner is served."

Mr. Philip Farnham had offered his arm to Mrs. Mather in going out to dinner, and it so happened that Mahala, who had been pleased to take the seat beside the old squire, found herself also beside the son at the table. If Mrs. Mather had anything to do with this arrangement, which seemed so intensely satisfactory to the tall young gentleman, she must answer for it to her own conscience. It was really remarkable how much these two people had to say to each other, and how absorbingly interesting their exchange of ideas upon the most trivial topics.

"I understand that Hartford society has quite a literary tone," observed Philip across the table to Miss St. John, during a lull in the hum of conversation. "With the resident coterie of brilliant writers who have gathered in your beautiful little city, and the distinguished visitors whom they draw into their circle, it must naturally be so."

"Yes, doubtless," responded the lady, raising her brows with a wicked twinkle in her bright eyes. "Any one can walk or ride without extra charge by Mark Twain's or Charles Dudley Warner's house, and I, myself, have a speaking acquaintance with the Misses Stowe's pug dog. To be sure, he is hardly as select in his tastes as one might expect, and often follows after the grocery wagon or any child he may happen to fancy, and is returned, after some days, and ransomed by his mistress. Still, I feel a sort of prestige in being recognized by him."

A generel laugh followed this sally, and as it subsided Mrs. Farnham said, "Surely, Miss St. John, you do not depreciate the elevating effect that must be felt, from even the sight about the streets, of those who have accomplished so much in literature."

"No, Mrs. Farnham, she cannot," quickly interposed Mrs. Mather, "but Miss St. John cannot resist a little sarcasm because we are all so proud of our literati."

"And because writing does not happen to be in her line," added Mahala, with some indignation ; "but I have known auntie to walk five miles to see a celebrated artist!"

"Ha, ha! There, Miss St. John, now you are certainly silenced!" exclaimed Squire Farnham. "By the way," he continued, turning to the artist, "have you seen C. D. Weldon's last etching? I am told it is excellent. I used to have a taste for pictures;" and they began to talk of celebrated proofs and remarques, and after-the-letters, and discussions of the scarcity and rising value of certain engravings, and a general interest was excited in the listeners, so that Philip said quietly to Mahala: "I judge you incline to literature more than to art?"

"Yes, I confess I do," she replied, modestly, "one cannot help but feel the mental impetus which the familiar presence of successful authors does lend to society. But while encouraged by their example to attempt some things, we always feel it is like holding a penny dip to an electric light."

"Fie, fie, dear. It is well to maintain self-respect in this, as in other matters," said Mrs. Mather, who had been keeping up the picture discussion by an occasional pertinent question, when conversation seemed likely to flag, but who now showed she had two ears.

"Miss Wright has written some very pretty things, Mr. Farnham ; and, what is more, sold them, too."

"Ah, Julie, please!" cried Mahala; but Mrs. Mather now returned to art.

"Do you know, Squire Farnham," she said, with great interest, "what has finally become of the few last copies of Folo's line engraving of the *Madonna dei Candelabri?*

There is one in the possession of a friend of mine, and he would not part with it for— "

" Miss Wright," said Philip, with admiration in his face, " I am daily surprised at the versatility of American girls. It is a charming fact that many of our modern journalists are beautiful ladies.   I would so like to know what you have done."

"Oh, it is really nothing at all, to speak of, and except for the possible innuendo in your word *versatility*," she answered, archly, " I would not tell you anything about it.   Do you think it likely that any editor would accept an article from a girl who could be capable of swinging on birches?" she inquired, as she dipped a piece of celery in the salt by her plate.

" Oh, Miss Wright, that is unkind !   I never thought of such a thing.   I was considering only your bright and winning ways, which are the antipodes of what we used to expect in a literary woman ; your musical accomplishments, your love of nature and out-of-door life on your wheels, and— "

" Well, that will do," Mahala interrupted, putting out her hand and dimpling a little.   " Pray do not feel obliged to farther perjure yourself to be polite," and she laughed merrily at his indignant attempt at a protest.

"Surely, Miss Wright is holding her own, again," said Julie to herself, dishonorably listening.

"But, tell me about your writings," entreated Philip again.

" They are really nothing," reiterated Mahala, toying with her napkin, " except a few little chatty sketches of no depth or importance, which an editor has been kind enough to publish. When I first got out of school I had the usual graduate's idea of a career, and of course was much gratified when my little sketches were accepted."

"I wish I might see your articles," said Philip, eagerly, "I am sure they are full of sunshine and kindness."

"But," continued the youthful author of the sketches, "I must tell you that what little confidence I had gained from the publication of the poor little compositions was taken out of me when I wrote a story. I suppose the good editor, who had become my friend, would have taken it from pity, but as that was just what I did not want, I sent it where no one knew me, to ascertain if there was any merit in it. As it soon came back to me with a polite printed slip declining it, I began to see the truth."

"Which is—" said Philip, interested.

"That it requires something more than a small gift of light talk on places and persons to write a novel. Brains are necessary, I begin to believe," she finished, sagely.

"What was your story about?" inquired Philip, curiously.

"Oh, a simple tale of a poor city seamstress and a young farmer whom she met in the country. It dealt with very unassuming characters, you see. I thought I would not begin with foreign nobility," she smiled at him.

"Of course there was something of love in it?" he said, softly, bending his head nearer.

"Of course," she said shortly, becoming much interested in the figures in the frieze. "Have you had good success in hunting, this year, Mr. Farnham," she offered, as the beginning of a new subject.

"Thank you!" answered the young man, with a business air, "I have had very good success, so far," and he began to laugh.

Mahala flushed.

Then, in a lower tone, he continued, "If I meet with no disappointment in the next few days, I shall count this the most enjoyable season of my life. But please tell me if your story was accepted at some other place."

" How very persistent you are, sir," said the little maid, looking at him in a manner which was meant to be saucy but which softened into a blush, as she looked away, anywhere to escape his disconcerting eyes. "Well, then," she said, dashing into the narrative to hide her unaccountable confusion, " I tried another magazine with the same result. Then I placed the manuscript in a pigeon-hole in my desk and let it lie six months. Then I took it out, and read it, calmly and judicially. It still seemed to me to be rather a good story—up to the average in respectable magazines, I think. So I made another offer of it, and it was again rejected. The boys, of course, knew about it," she went on, smiling at the recollection, "and, from at first confidently expecting to see it in one of the leading magazines, they began to make fun as it returned, and they now speak of it as 'the great American traveler.'" Here she fell into such a laugh at her own expense, that Philip, who had been indignant for her sake, could not resist the infectious ripple of merriment, and joined at first apologetically and then heartily, so that every one stopped talking to look at them, and Mrs. Mather cried, with a great show of inquisitiveness, "What *are* you laughing at?"

"I am laughing at a little story of Miss Wright's," answered Mr. Farnham.

"Which is too worn to bear repeating," added Mahala; and Robert came with the dessert.

"Where is 'the great American traveler' at present, Miss Wright?" said Philip, half an hour later, amidst the noise of leaving the table.

"It is in Boston, just now," she answered, good humoredly, "and has been gone so long that I almost begin to think it will make its debut there."

"Oh, I think I know what is the matter with my story," said Mahala, as she sat down on the window-seat in the hall with her attendant, "it is not in the fashionable style. It is a straight-forward narrative, with no psychology, and no impression effects. It is necessary just now, you know," she said, with her bird-like turn of the head and look askance, "to convey a world of meaning in one broad touch, just as artists daub on half a dozen blotches in a mist and call it Venice, or a Gypsy Camp. It is not now in good form to work out details, in anything. It is exceedingly unflattering to the reader's or critic's perceptions. Perceptions must be taken into account and respected. It is because I have not done so, that my story will probably have to go to a dime publication."

Philip was greatly amused as well as somewhat surprised to hear the prattle of his charming new acquaintance, which, delivered in the most inconsequential and girlish manner, yet possessed an intelligence which showed that she was using her mind to evolve original conclusions. He had been getting rather *blasé* in New York, and had almost forgotten that there might be an attractive medium between the traditional young woman of literary tastes, who is always decorated with a green veil, blue glasses, and a copy of Emerson,—whose ideas of style are null, and whose information of the world's work and culture is bounded by the narrow horizon around "the Hub," and the stylish New York girl, self-possessed and worldly-wise at eighteen, but with so little unengaged time at her command as to be unable to think of anything long enough to digest it and have opinions concerning it. Unfair as this idea of the distinguishing characteristics of girls in the two cities, which are often thus compared, may be, Philip entertained it, as many another man has done, judging the whole from types he had known. But in the actions and conversation of this alternately merry, harum-scarum, and wise and philosophical Miss Wright, he told himself he had discovered a very interesting phase of girlish character. There are many such in the several cities, mid-way between the centre of worldliness and the acme of self-complacent culture.

Mr. P. L. Farnham was much interested, "merely in a new style of girl," he said to himself, and he continued to think of her long after the visitors had made their departure, and Robert had returned and reported their safe arrival at Mr. Stearns's. He had taken the "Times," which he had not found time to look at, or indeed thought of, since the mail came, and had been reading an occasional paragraph to his father. The Squire, who was somewhat fatigued by the unusual excitement attendant upon a spirited political discussion with Mr. Stearns (Stearns was

terribly obstinate, he said), lay back in his easy-chair, listening with closed eyes; but somehow Philip found less
interesting matter than usual. "It must be an awful
grind to get up a paper every day," he said, "It's no
wonder they are stupid occasionally."

He had sat silent during fifteen minutes, reading over
one line a score of times, while his mind's eye saw only
flitting glimpses of a pair of dark-blue eyes fringed with
long lashes, the toe of a neat and practical boot, a gray
dress closely fitting the lithe, graceful figure, and the
quaint silver chatelaine she had worn at her waist. Then
came a vision of a blue gown with satin ribbons, tiny slippers, and a book in hand, curled upon a lounge in Farmer
Stearns's sitting-room. Then, a struggling figure hanging
by the arms from a nodding birch tree, cries of distress,
and an ignominious fall to the earth.

He smiled behind the paper. Every little gesture, every
smallest change in the bewitching dimples around the
frank mouth, came ever and again into his strangely-wan-
dering thoughts; and always a bewildering maze of curling
hair, clustering in soft curves about the intelligent forehead, and growing so prettily about the neck. He arose
at last and walked out into the hall, and stood looking
over the sash-curtain, out into the night, and began hum-
ming "Little ringlets round her ears." He had considered the hero of "Shandon Bells" a weakly, love-sick fellow. Why should this line come to his mind? But it
seemed very pretty now, and so descriptive of certain little
whorls which he had lately seen.

> "You hear the secrets that she hears,
> Little ringlets round her ears."

Hum,—he wished he knew what the rest of the verses were.

He thought he would ride over to the post-office in the morning and just look in at Mr. Stearns's, to see if he could be of any service during the day.

How kind they were to remain over for the party.

Twenty-eight to-morrow!

His mother always insisted upon making a birth-day party for him. It had bored him somewhat, in times past, to do the agreeable to a horde of distant feminine cousins, and the young men in town, with whom he had so little in common.

But this, this would be so different. He would ride over to town in the morning. In fact, Mrs. Mather had invited him to do so.

What a charming lady she was; and so fond of M–Miss Wright.

What a vile name to call her by!—"Mike!" how perfectly rude and horribly inappropriate! It should be Psyche. No, that were an omen of unhappiness. Sprite would do better, or—

He thought he would go to the barn to see if his saddle and things were in order. He had tramped so much of late, that poor old Prince had been neglected.

"I think I'll ride him to-morrow morning," he said to the old colored servant. "You may have him ready for me at seven o'clock—no! Hang it! That won't do—you may saddle him at half-past eight, Robert."

"I'm mighty glad to hear ye say that, Mister Philip, for he has n't had a gentleman on his back but two or th'ee

times since he come from de boat.   He tried his bes' to
th'ow me, the fust time I mounted him, but he found an
old nigger kin stick on, ef he can't look so terrible got up
as his master kin.   H'yah! yah! but aint he a reglar
steeple-picker, though, when he's out on show!"

His young master smiled, and saying good-night, walked
to the barn-door.   He turned.   "Robert."

"Yes, sir."

"I don't mind if you have him at the door a little past
eight.   I have several places to go to."

"All right, sir.   I guess I'll jes' put a little extra shine
on that silver.   It looks mighty purty nex' to the russet
leather," said Robert, as he got out his chamois-skin and
powder, and took down the bridle from its place in a
closet.

CHAPTER XVII.

———

Philip's Day.

"HAVE you any commissions for me, mother? I am going to ride over to town," said Philip, the next morning, as he drew on his gloves in the hall. They were drab, to compare with his neck-tie, which scarcely showed above the close buttoning of the high-collared coat, and with his pantaloons, which were of the same soft tint and were tucked into high boots.

"No, I think not," the lady replied, laughing a little, "you could not bring over one letter without distending the pockets of that perfect coat in a shocking manner. No, dear; Robert will attend to everything. Be a good boy," she added, half in jest and yet in tender maternal pride, that, strong man as he was, in the prime of his strength and self-reliance, he was still "her boy." He lifted his hat from his red-brown locks, and looked back with an affectionate smile as Prince sprang blithely away.

"He is a handsome fellow, if he is my son, Robert," said the loving mother, as she turned after watching him out of sight.

"'Deed he is, missus," answered old Robert, rubbing his

(207)

hands together, "and I'm bleeged ter say some younger ladies may think so, too."

"Yes, yes, I know," said the lady, who was accustomed to remarks from Robert which might have seemed unpleasantly familiar in a whiter skin or less aged retainer. "They must, you know, if they have eyes in their heads."

Mothers are so singularly warped in their judgment of these matters.

"Ah, good morning, Mr. Farnham," called a voice from the side of the road where it crossed a bridge.

He drew up his horse and saw Miss St. John by the way with her sketching apparatus arranged for use. Philip dismounted at once.

"Oh, pray do not dismount," cried the lady, who held a palette in her left hand, while she poked among the tubes in her lap, and squeezed one after another, leaving a line of colors around the board.   She had a thick rug under her feet and her hands were protected, if not adorned, with gloves with the finger-ends cut off.

"I thought, as we were to be here another day, I might as well get a sketch of this bridge and old mill," she said, in her quick manner, raising her gray eyes from her work. "It would be a pity to lose so picturesque a point.   Don't you think so?"

"Really, Miss St. John," said Philip, "I had never thought of it in that light; but you are getting a pretty picture out of it," said he looking over her canvas.

"No, you are wrong.   The picture is there," said the artist, extending her hand and giving it a little sweep across the view, "and I can only feebly reproduce it.

'Art may err, but nature cannot miss,'" and she made hooks by the sides of her head with her fingers to signify quotation marks. Then she exclaimed, "Do you know, it seems to me that most people go about this beautiful world with their eyes shut!"

"Possibly," said the gentleman, somewhat absently, and looking around as if in search of something.

"Probably!" insisted the lady. "Look at this scene. Could anything be more perfect in coloring than the grays of that old wood, and the deep maroons and browns of those blackberry-vines? Then see the little clouds of the feathery clematis on the rails of that fence. And all against the green of the sward, and the blue of the sky and the varying tones in the rippling water! What is wanting to make it perfect?"

"I would suggest a bit of life," said the business man, with a critical coolness, which was in strong contrast to the enthusiastic enjoyment of the artist.

"Well, there you have it, exacting man! Oh, is n't he too cunning? Let me get that!" ejaculated the lady, pointing to a lusty squirrel, who suddenly jumped up from the side of the bridge, and with an intensely hurried and business-like air, sat quickly with his umbrageous tail curved above his head, and raising his handy paws to his mouth, commenced to gnaw a hole in a large walnut which he had brought with him.

The artist made some rapid touches upon her canvas, and an impression was added to the picture. Although indistinct, it was a gray squirrel.

Mr. Farnham raised his riding cane to his eye. "What a shot!" he cried.

"Oh, you vandal!" said the lady, with indignation. "To think of killing him! Masculine nature is certainly cruel. I am disappointed in you, Mr. Farnham," she added, severely.

"Pray do not be, Miss St. John," rejoined Philip, calmly, "because we do not shoot squirrels when there is any other game."

"But murder defenseless birds," she answered, quickly. "I do not see how you have bettered your position."

"Ah, well, Miss St. John, you must remember we are not all artists, nor women. No one can have a higher appreciation of the natural loveliness of the one, nor of the qualities of mind and heart which permit the other, than I; but you must admit that practical pursuits and harder nerves are necessary to us who are knocking about the work-a-day world."

The artist shook her head at him. "Ah, now you think you have disarmed me, with your flattering speech. Where are you going?" she asked, with the good-humored brusquerie which was one of her characteristics.

"To—to the post-office," Philip replied, not quite at ease. "And possibly to call upon your friends, at Mr. Stearns's, to see if I can be of any service to them."

"Oh, they sent their telegrams the minute they got back last evening, and I suppose will be looking for replies by this time. Still,"—she continued, looking at the mill with her head a little on one side, and giving some imperceptible wipes to her canvas, "that's better isn't it?" she said, lost in contemplation of her work. "Still—what was I saying? Oh! You might call, though Margie (Miss

Prescott) was going up to Deep River with Mr. Stearns, now I think of it. Mrs. Mather, I think, will be in—as sh゛ is always writing to her husband, I believe."

Not a word of *her*, thought Philip. "I hope to have the pleasure of seeing you this evening," politely said he, as he took hold of the reins at Prince's shoulder and quickly rose to the saddle.

"We shall certainly be there if all is well. Good morning," answered the artist, bowing as he raised his hat, and returning instantly to her beloved work.

"Mike," suddenly exclaimed Mrs. Mather, who sat at the window of the "spare room," which was, according to country custom, in the front of the house, "here comes Mr. Farnham on horseback! See how beautifully he rides. His is a figure for Fifth avenue and the park, rather than this sedate street. Perhaps he is coming here."

"I hope not," said Mahala. "It is really enough to make one dislike him to hear you and Aunt Dude cite his perfections;" but she came to the window with a very rosy face and peeped through the muslin curtains.

"He seemed very much smitten with Margery yesterday," continued the fathomless deceiver, in an exceedingly careless tone. "His attitude of devotion, as he assisted her to and from the carriage, was very affecting. Perhaps these two matchless beings may majestically decide to love each other. It would seem most appropriate, now she is off with poor Felix," and she went back to her little chair by the side window with a glove in her hand which she was mending, and sitting down in quite a heat, com-

menced to sew on a button, with some jerking of the
knotting silk.

"How do you know she is 'off with Felix,' as you call
it ;" said Mrs. Mather. The young girl made no reply except to cover one eye with her hand and wink with intense
meaning with the other.

"He is coming here," said Mrs. Mather, looking out of
the window and bowing cordially to some one below.

"I think I will go down to the door," she said, rising,
"for Mrs. Bronson is intent upon cooking this morning.
Of course you will come down as soon as you can, dear,"
she said, pausing at the door and looking back at Mahala.

"I don't know whether I shall get down before he goes,
or not," indifferently replied Miss Wright. "I have one
or two buttons to sew on, and they all need tightening,"
she said, critically examining the glove.

"Pshaw!" and Mrs. Mather ran down stairs laughing.

The instant she had left the doorway, Miss Wright's dignity vanished, and rising she sped softly to the window
and stood with flushing cheeks and quick breath, peeping
through the thin curtain, as the horseman sprang from the
saddle and came up the walk with a glow of expectant
pleasure in his fine face.

Then Mahala took two handfuls of her dark curls and
wrenched them fiercely as she turned to her chair. "Oh,
why! Why, do I care about this man who never does
anything that is inelegant—who is so sure of his ability to
please and always seems to be laughing at my poor despi-
cable, hoydenish mishap? But I do, I do," she whispered,
buttoning her boots with eager haste.

As she arose from her seat upon the floor, which is the customary girlish attitude in dressing the feet, she saw her agitated face in the mirror. "You are a little fool! Yes, a perfect fool!" she said to it; which expression seemed to relieve her mind, and she sat down by the window to get cool.

"Ah, good morning, Mr. Farnham," cried the young matron, who opened the door without waiting for Philip to ring, saluting him with the friendly freedom and charming bonhommie which married women who are perfectly secure in their husbands' love, and are free from all fear of imputations of undue regard for other men, can exercise so pleasantly; "come in. We thought perhaps you might ride over, this delightful morning."

"We," whispered Mahala, who was listening at the head of the stairs. "Julie Mather, who gave you leave to say that?" She bit her lip. "I shall take care to contradict that, in *my* first remark."

"Yes, Mrs. Mather," said the deep voice of the visitor below stairs, "it was so extremely bright this morning that I thought I would give Prince a little exercise. The old fellow has suffered from disuse since I brought him on from New York, and as I had some errands to do in town, and you so kindly asked me to call—"

"Oh! Indeed! She asked him to come, did she?" said the listener at the head of the stairs, straightening up her slender figure with a quick suspicion. "Mrs. F. W. Mather, what does that mean? Can Julie so demean herself as to turn one of these detestable married flirts? New York men are terribly fast, I understand, under all their

polish.   Heigh—" but she held her breath, stopping the
sigh in the middle, for *he* was speaking again.

"I had a spicy little interview with Miss St. John, who
was sketching at the bridge as I came by.   She is certainly
a most entertaining and attractive lady, with her love for
art and her strong common-sense and quick retorts."   He
laughed enjoyably.   "She called me a vandal and told me
she was disappointed in me, in less than five minutes after
my arrival."

"Good gracious!   Has Aunt Dude begun it, too?"
gasped Mahala, as a flush rose to her face.   "Auntie *is*
very attractive, and not more than five years older than he;
but I will never call him uncle!" she exclaimed decisively,
and then as the idea struck her more forcibly, she sped on
tip-toe into the chamber and laughed in smothered cachin-
nations until the tears stood in her eyes and the changeful
face became rueful.   But how fast they were talking down
there in the sitting-room.   She stepped noiselessly to the
balustrade again.

"I hardly understood what she meant by saying you had
sent telegrams and were expecting replies this morning,
and was about to ask, fearing that something might have
occurred to prevent your coming to our house to-night, to
call you home perhaps, when she dismissed me by becoming absorbed in her work; and now I recall it, said you expected to attend the party."

"Oh, dear," said Mrs. Mather, who was laughing heartily, "how like Dude that is!   She has so little regard for
the concealment of the harmless subterfuges by which we
women strive to be appropriately dressed without apparent

effort at all times.   But in this instance, as no one who
gave us credit for good sense would imagine that we
should come on a jaunt of this kind prepared for a party,
I do not mind admitting that Margery and Mahala have
sent to Hartford for some evening dresses.   Miss St. John
and I will do very well in spare dresses which we brought
along, but you could not expect the girls to place themselves in juxtaposition to the resident belles without an
appropriate costume.   No young lady who respected herself would do it.   But for goodness sake don't say I told
you!"

"Certainly not," answered the gallant visitor.   "I have
a great respect for ladies' judgment on anything pertain-
ing to matters of this kind, and should not have presumed
to inquire into this secret had I known it to be such."

"Well, that is rather nice of you, at all events," said the
dishonorable listener at the head of the stairs.   "I will
not go down unless he asks for me.   I am determined in
that!" she said to herself.

"Miss—"

Hark Mahala!

"Miss Prescott is not in this morning, Miss St. John
told me.   I am sorry not to see her.   Is her sprained ankle
getting strong once more?"

"Entirely well, I think," answered Mrs. Mather.   "A
few days' rest was all that was needed to set it right."

"I am very glad," said the manly voice again.   "I
judge she must be a very graceful dancer, and I have promised myself the pleasure of a waltz with her this evening
and—"

Mahala choked.

"I won't go to that detestable old party! Yes I will, for fear they will think strange. But how stupid it will be! I—I have dreaded it all the time! I wish I had never come on this rowdyish trip, anyway. Ah!"

"Miss Wright is well, I trust, this morning? Is she in?"

"She is," responded Julie. "She was very busy when you came, but I think her sewing must be nearly finished by this time." She stepped to the stairs. "Mahala!"

No answer.

"Excuse me, I will speak to her," and the demure matron looked a little out of patience as she mounted the stairs, but this gave way to amusement when she found the chamber-door tightly closed.

"Come, dear," she said, in loving tones, intended to be heard down stairs, as she opened it, "Mr. Farnham is getting tired of my conversation; can you not leave your work and come down now?" In a whisper: 'Really, Mike, your caprices are almost too much for my good temper! You should never allow yourself to be rude to any one."

"Yes, Julie," answered Mahala, with a preoccupied tone. "I was going right away. I am taking the last stitch now," and she grinned composedly at the look of wrath with which Mrs. Mather regarded her empty hands, and ejaculated in low but stern tones, "Oh, you consummate fraud!" and they both went down stairs.

"I was so surprised to see you this morning, Mr. Farnham. I did not know, until just now, that Mrs. Mather knew you were coming, or I might have done my mending earlier."

Here Julie started visibly, and gave her a look showing that she had betrayed the fact of her listening at the stairs ; but, confident of the tact of her chaperone, she looked collectedly into Philip's face as she greeted him, and glancing out of the window as she took a seat by it, she remarked that it was a beautiful day to ride.

Her nonchalance completely disarmed her friend, who was justly vexed at this new whim, but as usual ended by being greatly amused at the assurance of the young offender, in taking it for granted that her friend would not betray her double-dealing.

"If you are surprised, I hope you are not displeased, to find so recent an acquaintance calling so soon again."

Mahala vouchsafed no reply, except that her cheeks grew a little pinker.

"It is a boon to me, no less than to others here," said Philip, addressing both, "to be allowed to meet you ladies, when we expected nothing more than the usual monotony of country living this season."

"Oh, how can you consider the country monotonous ?" airily rejoined Miss Wright, having waived the first deprecating remark. "There is such endless variety in nature's moods. The trees, and flowers, and ferns, and mosses are an ever-fascinating study ; and sweet-singing birds, and jolly little squirrels, innocent little deer-eyed calves, and timid sheep are so much better company than most human beings. Even an occasional snake prevents one from getting dull," she added, thoughtfully.

" Not every one is given an eye to see the beauties of
nature as you seem to, Miss Wright," Philip answered.
"It is indeed an enviable faculty," he said, regarding her
with admiring eyes, "and must fill many a lonely hour
with exquisite pleasure. I confess to have my enthusiasm
for a country home somewhat dulled by a busy life which
I so much enjoy in the city. Of course, nothing can
shake my attachment for the old house, but it seems that
nearly all the interesting people round about the town are
gone with my childhood." And so they fell to discussing
matters in general, which have no particular bearing upon
this story.

At last Philip turned to Mahala: " Since you are so fond
of beautiful scenes in the open air, Miss Wright, I regret
that I did not harness Prince to a buggy and ask you to
ride to Red Hill. The vista down the river is something
to be remembered. I think you would enjoy a view of it,
and if Mrs. Mather will go, I will go home and return with
the carriage in half an hour." He had suddenly recol-
lected himself and included the chaperone in the invitation.

"Oh, please, do nothing of the kind," said Mahala, with
much animation, "you see I so much prefer my wheels,
and I intended to get away somewhere this morning.
Shall we go, Julie?"

"Certainly, dear. You will doubtless enjoy it im-
mensely," answered the inefficient chaperone, leaving herself out of the question with culpable disregard of her
bounden duty.

"But you will go, too?" quickly asked Mahala.

" Willingly, rather than hinder a pleasant ride. But if you would be kind enough to excuse me," said the lady, looking from Mahala to Philip pleadingly, "I could take this quiet time to write to my husband. I should consider it as a favor, still if you insist—"

" Why, surely not, if you really prefer to remain here," said Philip, courteously, "although we should be glad of your company." (Julie knew it was a fib.) "I trust to Miss Wright's appreciation of the lovely ride to compensate her for a dull companion. She likes calves and squirrels better than people, anyway, so that one does not feel that much is required of him, which is a consolation."

Mahala forgot herself and flashed him a pouting, merry glance, as she bounded up the stairs after her hat and gloves.

Philip looked gratefully at the faithless Julie. " Mrs. Mather, would there be anything to offend your chaperonish sense of propriety if we should not return in time for lunch ? It is now nearly eleven o'clock," he said, consulting his watch, "and the middle of the day is the pleasantest, out of doors, at this season and—"

Mrs. Mather smiled. " Mahala needs no chaperone, Mr. Farnham," she replied. " Her pure heart and native sense of propriety are always a sufficient guide to her in gentlemen's society."

" I am proud to hear you vindicate the reliability of a representative American girl," answered the young man, warmly.

" I had a real time, oiling my tricycle this morning," said the young lady, as she came pushing her machine out

of the driveway at the side gate.   "So it will run well, I
hope." Philip sprang to meet her, but she said, "Please
allow me to manage it.   You might break it, you know, or
something." She showed her white teeth while she pretended to frown.

"Is it not a greasy business to care for a tricycle
properly?" asked the fastidious cavalier.   "Should you
not leave that to—"

"To whom?" she said, saucily elevating her chin and
gazing at him through her dark lashes.

"To—to a servant, or to some one who has already black
and oily hands," Philip answered desperately.

"No," Mahala answered, shaking her head, "it is no
worse to clean than a sewing-machine, or only a little, and
I could not trust to strangers, certainly.   Well, sir," she
continued, as she quickly rose to her saddle, "I am ready.
Perhaps you had better mount your steed, if you are coming," and the saucy minx started off at a great pace.

Now, Prince, being an experienced New York horse,
possessed such an imperturbability to new and unfamiliar
objects as is only gained through much worldly knowledge and many and various vicissitudes on the road.   He
was stylish, self-possessed, and elegant from the tips of his
small black ears to the end of his banged tail.   He was
cool in the close vicinity of steam-cars, whether crashing
along at grade before his high-bred nose, or flying above
his intelligent head with a deep roar and terrific speed
upon the elevated railways.   He had stood patient and
philosophical in a Fulton street pack for an hour, and had
been inured to the sight of every known vehicle, from the

immense mail-wagons and steam fire-engines that wait for
nothing, to the tiny jerking dog-cart carrying a dude. He
had locked wheels with the landau of Madame Millione,
and grazed a swill-cart by the way. He had been entan-
gled in the inconsequential and exasperating toils of an
undisciplined goat-team in the park, and had a bicycler
take "a header" into his very face, while the machine fell
clattering against his sinewy legs. He rose superior to all
such accidents (which the carelessness and unskilled driving
of other teams inevitably bring upon the horse who most
thoroughly understands himself), realizing that to lose his
temper or betray fear or surprise, were inexcusable in an
animal of his breeding. His business was to shine, to
arch his neck at telling moments, to curvet gracefully
about the carriages of his master's acquaintances, to amble
easily, to trot gently or to run like mad, as his rider indi-
cated, and he meant to do it, undisturbed or distracted by
little episodes along the way. Therefore he looked know-
ingly towards Mahala as she mounted her saddle and heard
her sweet voice as she spun away, and fell at once into a
quick trot as his master sprang to his back.

"Do not go so fast, I beg of you, Miss Wright! You
will certainly be fatigued before we return, if you use your
strength so at first," Philip remonstrated, reining close beside the delicate machine which Mahala sent so swiftly
along. The street was shaded by elms and ran in single
and now double roads through the wide space between the
straight and massive trees. She instinctively chose her
way, now in the drive and now to one side or the other on
the firm, smooth sward. Her lissome girlish form sat

easily between the wheels, her gauntleted hands resting
lightly on the handles at her side, and her heavy, gray
skirts fell in clinging folds about her energetic feet, which
showed just a heel or toe below the graceful draperies. A
brilliant color was in her cheeks as she turned her animated face towards Philip, who rode in a little anxiety by
her side.

How jauntily she wore her hat!   No one else wore a
hat like that !   How prettily it sat upon her small head.
And what a turn to the plump shoulders and round arm !
(Fie, man ! The dressmaker does all that.) "Really, Miss
Mahala," (there ! So much for allowing yourself to call
her so to yourself !) "Miss Wright," he interjected,
quickly, "you must know that it is five miles or more to
Red Hill and back.   I very much fear you will be too
tired."

Mahala slowed up to a walking pace, to which Prince
immediately accommodated himself, as she said, "Thank
you, Mr. Farnham, but I am not likely to get fatigued with
a five-mile run in this exhilarating atmosphere; but perhaps it may be as well to go slow until we are beyond the
center of the village a little.   I have caught a glance of
several shocked faces at the windows as we came along.
Is the spectacle of a lady riding a tricycle shocking? We
are so used to it that we forget that strangers may not
approve."

"Shocking !" said Philip, in earnest admiration, "far
from it.   It is charming.   It is thoroughly ladylike, and
at the same time has a flavor of independence and life and
healthful pleasure about it, that could but be captivating
to all who possess health and good spirits."

"But I thought the lady we just met, with the thin light hair and the puppy on a string, looked displeased. She bowed to you, but stared at me in maidenly horror."

"Ah, ha, ha!" laughed Philip, in deep enjoyment of Mahala's quickness to catch the disapproval in the lady's eye. "That was my cousin," he said.

"Oh!" exclaimed Mahala, a little frightened.

"Yes," he continued, "she spends her time in watching her neighbors; making slippers, and other things he doesn't want, for the minister; has compiled a book of hymns, browbeats her dressmaker, and looks after the morals of the town. She thinks it rude in a young lady to laugh aloud, detests children and men, and loves no one but herself and that dog, who is never out of her sight. She will be at our house to-night."

"Dear me," said Mahala, doubtfully, "is she—is she nice to know?" she stammered, at a loss what to say. How could his cousin be so disagreeable! Must resemble some ancestor of a remote branch of the family, she mentally decided. "I think I never met just such a person; you must exaggerate her peculiarities."

"Perhaps,"· smilingly assented Philip. "You would scarcely meet just such a type in town. It is remarkable as a product of country places. An old maid, city born and bred, is not such a formidable creature. She has opportunities to see the world as it is, can but feel the beneficial effects of an enlarged mental horizon, and has a chance for culture and an enforced self-discipline which rounds the corners and dulls the edges of selfishness. Lizzie might be a person of influence and worth in society,

in a city where outer influences would dispel her egotism
and positive assurance of her own infallibility. But here
her active mind, otherwise unemployed, turns upon small
gossip and an utter condemnation of any luckless wight
who dares to differ from her fixed ideas of religion or social proprieties. I am acquainted with my cousin. She
has followed me with a sharp criticism since my boyhood.
I do not love her, I fear, as a cousin should."

Mahala laughed merrily at the serio-comic air with
which his last sentences were delivered.

"Excuse me one instant," suddenly exclaimed Philip, as
they rode along the street, "I would like to stop a moment
at the store."

"Certainly ; I will ride on slowly," nodded Mahala.

As she quietly ran along the road near the sidewalk, a
jolly old man, of rosy face and rotund form, came trudging
to the post-office. When he caught sight of the sweet
young lady riding the unheard-of vehicle, clad so daintily
and in quiet style, looking up at the graceful trees and
gazing about at the comfortable homes that ranged on
either side, he stopped. He planted his stout stick firmly
upon the ground, and said audibly, "Hevins an' airth!"

Mahala turned quickly, and looked into the jocund vis-
age, now sobered with surprise. His whole appearance
was at once so droll, friendly, yet with a consuming curiosity in his wide-open eyes, that Mahala smiled in spite of
herself. Whereupon the old fellow's face expanded into a
pleased look, and he said: "Now, Miss, really, if you
won't take it unkindly, will you tell me what that thing is
that you are a-ridin' on?"

"Yes, I will," said Mahala, good-humoredly. "It is a tricycle. Did you never see one before?"

"No, I never did," answered the old man. "I've seen the bicycles, of course; but it beats me! Where did you come from? I know you don't belong around here; that is, I judge you don't," he added as Mahala quizzically said "Why?"

"Oh, I don't know, unless by the general cut of your jib. Where be you from? I would like to know, if it don't make no odds to you."

"I am from Hartford, sir," politely responded Mahala, who rightly inferred that this was a kindly old soul unrestrained by polite reticence in his questions.

"Hevins an' airth!" he ejaculated again. "But you haven't ridden from there, to-day?" he pursued, evidently attributing marvelous possibilities to the machine.

"Not to-day." answered Mahala, as she heard Prince's quick steps behind her.

"Ah, how do you do this morning, Captain Amos?" said the genial voice of Philip as he rode up. "I am glad your rheumatism lets you out once more. I am coming in to settle with you for that boat very soon."

"All right—there ain't no hurry—any time," answered the old man, to whom the arrival of Philip, as escort to this charming girl and her wonderful machine, was an added shock of surprise and wonderment, and subsequently furnished a topic for gossip at the store for an hour.

As Mahala, bowing pleasantly, said "Good morning, Captain Amos," and started her wheels, he stood and watched them far down the street, and as he trudged onward he remarked "Hevins an' airth!" He turned once more, but they were out of sight. "And now," he said, with a curious shake of the head, "how did she know my name? That's what I want to know!"

On they rode, now slowly, enjoying the pure air, the blue sky, and the glimpses of homes, and trees, and river, chatting freely upon all they saw and thought, living in the passing hour, which was so full of a nameless charm and golden light.

Philip was only solicitous, fearing that she would become fatigued. "I am ashamed," he said, "to sit here on Prince's back and see you propelling your own vehicle."

Mahala instantly assured him that she enjoyed the exercise above all things. "It is merely a walk for me," she explained, "with no more exertion, except when by transmitting more force to these wheels they lend me far greater speed. I think these cycles must be a realization of the seven-league boots," she added, with animation, and shot ahead, so that Prince, pointing his small ears forward in surprise at this unexpected action of the queer machine which he was escorting, struck instantly into a quick canter and was soon by Mahala's side.

"Oh! here we are at the top of a little hill!" exclaimed the bright-eyed girl. "Now you shall see where I have the advantage of you, Mr. Farnham," and resting her feet on the bars in front, she laid her hand on the brake and went flying down the hill in what seemed to Philip a most reckless manner.

"Beware the water bar! You may get upset!" he cried, hastening after her. She was waiting for him at the foot of the hill.

"Well," he said, in some dismay, "you certainly were the victor that time, but—"

"Beg pardon," she said, bowing, "not I, but my machine, is 'The Victor.' You see, I can slow up instantly," she said, touching the brake, and glowing with enthusiastic pleasure in the sport.

"It is coasting, you know, without winter frost and snow."

"It certainly seems very exhilarating," assented the

gentleman, looking at her bright red cheeks. "I have never tried a wheel, Prince supplying all the exercise I have time to take. Still, you feel when riding horseback that you are, after all, doing a sort of lazy thing. But you are perfectly independent of any volition but your own muscles on a wheel. One has a sense of pride in a vigorous tramp. Riding a tricycle must give something of this inspiriting feeling."

"Exactly!" answered Mahala. "There is an unaccountable fascination about it. I think you have explained it. Still," she continued, glancing up at him with a mischievous twinkle in her eye, "it is not *au fait* for women to be independent in New York, is it? I think the wheels may be more generally used in Massachusetts."

"Independent? Yes. We want them to be independent in health and joyous love of life, in stanch principles and a high culture, as well as in a practical education, by which they could care for themselves if no stronger arm were near to fight the world for them. But we would each like to have some lovely woman dependent on him for love and protection, giving him in return the advantage of her quick intuition and pure counsels. There need be no question—"

"So I think!" quickly interposed Mahala. "Wouldn't you like to try the wheels for a little while, Mr, Farnham?"

Philip came down from his pedestal so suddenly, that for an instant he scarcely realized his position. But casting a searching glance at Mahala's innocent face he said, with a short laugh, which was a curious mixture of surprise, chagrin, and amusement in one exclamation, "I don't mind. Probably you will like to see me tip over!"

"Oh! no indeed! It is impossible to do so!" protested Miss Wright, as she took out her little wrench and busily proceeded to raise the saddle.

Philip had also dismounted.

"There!" she said, with a business face, "I think that will be about right for you. I will lead Prince. You will need both hands."

So he followed her directions, and starting off with some success he became bolder and put on more speed, and at once turned right about and ran promptly into a fence.

"I told you the least turn of the handle would change your course," said Mahala, coming up with Prince's nose near her shoulder. "Whoa, Prince! I—"

She was shaking with laughter to see the comical expression of doubt with which he was regarding the machine, showing at the same time a determination to conquer next time or perish in the attempt. "Oh, I give you leave to laugh," he said lugubriously, and they both laughed loud and long at his expense. "But I am going to try it again, just the same," he declared, as he pulled the wheels back into the road.

The next trial was eminently successful, and at the young lady's request he gave her his hand, and, placing her foot in it, she sprang to Prince's back.

"I shall hardly try fast riding on this saddle," she said, as they proceeded at a walk, "but I think that Prince knows that I am at a disadvantage without a pommel, and will be good.　I can keep up with you on the wheels, I think."

So they rode for a mile.

"You are not a novice on horseback, I see," said Philip, who, while earnestly engaged in managing the tricycle, still kept a close watch on Prince's behavior until he saw that Mahala was used to managing a horse.

"Not exactly," she smilingly answered, "but since I have had my wheels I have not cared so much for riding as formerly."

"Do you then prefer the tricycle?" asked Philip, as he assisted her to dismount.

"Yes, very much," Mahala answered, as, after lowering the saddle, she took her seat once more.

They met a farmer and his wife, driving to town.　A large basket of eggs, a covered wooden pail, evidently containing butter, and several bags of potatoes, were in the wagon.

The friends tried not to smile or look conscious as this team met them; and they saw the astonishment depicted upon the countenance of its occupants.　As they passed, the man turned in his seat and was heard to exclaim, "Wal, I vum!" but the woman never looked behind.

Soon, a clattering grocery wagon overtook them, and went rattling by at such a pace that pails, baskets, boxes, and small parcels, with which it was loaded, knocked about in great hazard.　And as the impudent young blade who drove went by, with a pencil stuck under his hat, he gave Philip a very knowing grin, and lowered one eyelid in an intensely mysterious manner.

Mahala caught the look, and glancing quickly to Philip, was surprised to see him biting his lips, with amusement in his eyes; but she wisely made no comment.

"Here we are at the foot of Red Hill," said Philip. "Now, you cannot ride your wheels up so steep an incline."

"I can put it up quite a steep hill," responded Mahala, "but it is often pleasanter to walk for a little distance."

"This is quite a long hill," said Philip. "Now, shall I walk with you, or will you ride Prince again? Here!" he exclaimed, without waiting for an answer, "why cannot I hitch this strap to one of your cross-bars and draw you up the hill?" And with an access of buoyant spirit which sat not illy upon the whilom dignified young man, he hastily unrolled a long leather thong which was coiled at his saddle, and with much laughing and exclaiming, with alternate confidence and dismay in contemplation of the novel scheme, from Mahala, he fastened the strap back of her small wheel, sprang again to his saddle and started Prince with caution.

That sagacious animal, perceiving that this was an unique excursion in all its features, slowly felt for the additional weight behind him, and soon gauging it, walked soberly up the hill, just as if he had not a young gentleman on his back who, half turned in the saddle, was laughing and slapping his knees in high glee, as he regarded the joyous and sweetly dimpling face of the young lady who sat uttering little exclamations of triumph and clapping her hands on the curious vehicle in the rear.

Undignified? Very. Hoydenish, perhaps. But, ladies

of uncharitable hearts and vinegarish remarks, it was pure and unadulterated fun. Would there were more of it in this sober, prosaic world!

"Dear me," said Mahala, looking at her watch as they stood together on the brow of the hill, "how the morning has flown! It is after twelve. I shall be late to lunch. What will Julie think?"

"I told her that we might not be able to return by twelve, so she will not be wondering at all about us," said Philip, who was tying Prince to a sapling. "You know it was nearly eleven when we started," he added.

"Just half-past ten, I believe, Mr. Farnham," said Mahala, looking at him with a wicked smile. "But as Julie does not expect me I do not mind. It has been such a delightful ride, and I am not hungry; that is, not very hungry." Then, apologetically, "Isn't it dreadful to have such an appetite?"

"Yes, it is—awful!" said Philip, with an upward glance of the eye and an exaggerated sigh. "However," he continued, "I don't mind telling you in confidence, that I am ravenously hungry—famished. My craving for food is something alarming. I believe I could eat a raw turnip if I had one." He looked around.

"A turnip *is* pretty good," said Mahala. "Is there no field near, I wonder?"

"Are you really hungry?" inquired Philip, rising from the stump of a tree on which he had rested.

"Awfully!" replied Mahala.

"Good!" said Philip. "I see a basket behind that rock. I will investigate its contents."

And to Mahala's surprise he brought up a covered basket and proceeded to open it.

"But, Mr. Farnham," she remonstrated, objecting to such a confiscation of the find, "it is not ours. We must not take—"

"It is no one else's," replied Philip, stoutly, as he drew forth a large bottle of milk with a glass on the head of it. Next came a paper of butter crackers. Then came a box of guava jelly, two lemons and a box of sardines, and at last some rosy-cheeked apples.

Mahala was astounded. "I will not touch one morsel," she declared, "until you tell me where this all came from. Are you a fairy to summon such a feast with your wand? No, these things are too material. How did they come here? Please tell me, so I can eat something."

Philip had opened the box of sardines, and, carefully wiping his knife upon a fresh green leaf, which he plucked from a bough overhead, he dexterously placed one of the small fish upon a cracker. Then cutting a lemon in half, he tore a small bit of paper for a plate, and placing the viands upon it he extended them to her with great ceremony. Without seeming to hear her entreaty, he uncorked the bottle and poured out a glassful of rich foaming milk.

"Please tell me where these goodies came from," pleaded Mahala, again. "I am nearly starved!"

"You should not have questioned my honesty, Miss Wright," said Philip, with great dignity.

"Well, I never will, again," said she, penitently; "I did not mean to, only I was so surprised."

"Well then, eat, fair maid! Did you not see the gro-cery boy, who passed us at the foot of the hill, and the im-pudent wink he gave me as he went by?" said Philip, in-tent upon fishing out another sardine.

"Yes, I did," answered Mahala, "and thought him ex-ceedingly facetious, not to say familiar. But what of that? I am very obtuse."

"What of that? Why, I ordered these things when I went into the store. I often order a sausage and a loaf of brown bread left here when I am out gunning. There's nothing like that to tramp upon. I mean, to stand by a man. But on account of the expected presence of a lady at the feast, I ordered a more delicate *menu*. Now, what have you to say?" cried Philip, as he squeezed the lemon over his fish.

"I say, this is one of the most delightful surprises of my life," answered Mahala, looking at him in undisguised enjoyment. "Nothing could be more appropriate and thoughtful. I should have been a little unhappy in half an hour more." "But," she stopped drinking her milk, "How shockingly prosaic!" She took another sip, and looked askance over the edge of the glass. Then, as she looked around, "In full view, too, of this perfect landscape! With the lovely river and the green fields beyond, the deepening tinge of the dying foliage, through the whole gamut of color, from bright crimson to the brown, sere leaf. The blue water to the south, the sunlight on the winding roads by forest, and stream, and—"

"If you don't need that tumbler to gesticulate with,

Miss Wright," said Philip, with an injured air, " I would like some milk.   I have not had a drop !"

"Why, that is too bad.   You shall have some at once," and Mahala, discontinuing her eloquence, poured out a brimming glass.

"This guava jelly is delicious for dessert," she said, opening the paper box.   "No, that knife will taste fishy." She shook her head as he gave it an additional rub, and extended it to her.

"You may wipe, you may polish the knife if you will, but the scent of the sardines will hang 'round it still. My fruit-knife is clean," and she took a small silver knife from her pocket, looking demurely at Mr. Farnham, who leaned faintly against a tree, but failed to excite remorse for her shocking parody, as his mouth was full, and his facial expression consequently not a success.

And so they chatted, and laughed, and gibed, for half an hour.   The only shocking thing about this picnic, to us veracious chroniclers, is the fact that they had known each other less than a week.   But the truth must be told at all hazards.

"Poor old Prince must have some lunch," said Mahala (when they had eaten an amount which would not be specified here for anything), dividing some apples into small pieces with her knife.

Philip sat idly watching her as she fed his horse with the fruit.   How deftly she used her hands.   It was one of Philip's theories that the use and action of the hands was a clear index to one's capabilities, mental as well as mechanical.   How Prince enjoyed the touch of the caressing fingers, as they gently smoothed over his eyes, and picked out his forelock.

"There, old boy," she said, patting his neck hard, under his mane. "They're all gone! Aren't you much obliged, eh?" And she took his soft nose into both hands as she looked into his handsome face. "All right! I know you are!" and she returned to the flat rock and began to pick up things.

Crumpling up the paper wrappers, she said, "It is one of the beauties of dining like this, that washing dishes is so very easy."

"Yes," answered Philip, "I will help you clear off the table;" saying which he seized the empty tin, and threw it far away into the woods. "The silver, I see, you have taken care of. The cut-glass I will return to the basket" Putting the empty bottle into the basket, he placed it in its niche in the rock. "Sykes will take it on his return," he said, wiping his hands on his handkerchief. "And now, as I don't see but our housework is all done up, we can enjoy the scenery before we return. I want you to notice that line of elms," said he, standing by her side, and pointing up the river. "See how their interlacing branches form a perfect gothic arch over the street they border. Nothing more beautiful than natural forms has ever been introduced into architecture. Every effort of man, in this as in every other branch of art, is but an imitation of, or design formed upon, nature's original plan."

"Yes, I remember," said Mahala, "that the capital of the Corinthian column is only the working out of an idea drawn by a monk from a large flower-pot, with a square board lying on top. It had been set upon a plant whose leaves, struggling out from under its almost crushing weight, grew up against its side, much as we see them in the conventionalized form."

" Some one has compared architecture to petrified music. I never could quite see the force of the comparison. Can you ?" said Philip, anxious to bring out her girlish thoughts upon any subject.

" Oh, yes, I see what he meant," Mahala replied, ("if it was a ' he.' I never spoil a bright idea by looking up its author.) I have seen churches that were as grand anthems with the theme ever repeated, coming again and again, in modified or more ornate form, rising from the heavy chords of the massive pillars at the base, to the lighter and sweeter thoughts as the creation progressed. These solemn old-fashioned dwelling-houses, with a row of columns across the front, look to me like a poor attempt at a funeral march, by an incompetent composer. An imposing idea, thinly carried out. Don't you think so ?" she asked, turning to him with a smile.

" Oh, if you say so," cried Philip ; " I have seen cosy houses which in their very air were a perfect embodiment of ' Home, Sweet Home.' But in that one thinks more of the words than the music."

"Yes," said Mahala, drawing up her forehead, in a little thoughtful frown, "but I think that was hardly the idea we commenced upon. It is form, rather than sentiment, that makes architecture and music comparable."

" Oh, I see it now," said Philip, who had seen it all the time ; "you would consider that little three-pointed house over there as the first bar of a waltz."

" Perhaps," she answered, laughing, " and some of those modern houses which are a confusion of dormers and steep roofs, inexplicable windows and inexcusable juts, like one of Chopin's intensest emotions, or a jig played out of time." Then, with one of her swiftly-changing expressions which were such a fascination to him, " Is not all purely æsthetic architectural construction symbolical of moods based on nature's forms ? " said Mahala, with introspective vision, as her dilated eye rested on the ether of distant hills. " Now, surely we have exhausted this subject ; had we not better start for home ? " said Miss Wright, as she drew on her gloves, and, taking out a little hook, proceeded to button them.

" A sensible suggestion," said Philip, " but one I have no particular sympathy with. Oh, if these pleasant hours would not pass ! Can't we make the sun stand still, yet a few hours ? "

" I am afraid not," Mahala rejoined, practically ; " there is but one instance on record, I believe, where it has stopped its course at the command of a mortal. And, although Joshua flattered himself that he had done it, I hear that skeptical scientists now question the fact, deciding that his quadrant may have been at fault."

" It has been such a happy day, to me, though," said Philip, as he started for his horse and Mahala took her seat on the tricycle. " I almost dislike to return to common living. I begin to have a strange reluctance, too, to go to New York next week," admitted the young man, as they rode slowly down the hill.

" Of course you will dread the parting with your parents

more each year as they grow older, and your father not
strong, too," said Mahala, in sympathetic tones.

"Yes, that must be it," said Philip. "Of course that is
it, though I never thought of it before."

The October sun grew almost unpleasantly warm for
Mahala, as they rode along the homeward way. They
were nearing the town, when Philip said, almost with a
sigh: "But my rooms in New York will seem so lonely
now. I have rather a nice place, too. But to eat at a club
with a dozen fellows you may like or not; to return to
lonely rooms at night, and sit reading or cogitating, still
alone, unless some acquaintance drops in, or I go out to a
fashionable, joyless crush, called a reception; or perchance
to the theatre, then to return, still alone—you see I don't
smoke; somehow, I never could adopt the 'filthy weed,'
however consoling it may be. Still, I have always been
content with my bachelor way of living, until now."

Mahala, who had listened so attentively as to encourage
his confidences, now looked up with an idea for his relief.
"Why don't you buy a dog?" she said. "We have a friend
who has a beautiful Gordon setter, that is a perfect treas-
ure to him. He calls her 'Lady.' She—"

Philip recoiled, as from a blow in the face, uttered a
quick word, which surely the recording angel mercifully
feigned not to hear. He gave Prince a stinging cut and
dashed ahead so fiercely, as to frighten Mahala out of her
further remarks. The incomprehensible girl looked confused, entreating, as she came up to where he waited in
cold politeness for her.

No more laughing now. No merry gibes or innocent
mirth.

They were not far from home when Mahala made her
unfortunate remark, and Mr. Farnham, dismounting with
severe courtesy, stood hat in hand, to assist her from her
wheels at the gate.   But now, burning with mortification
and unhappiness, knowing that he was angry, and she had
made him so, she commanded her face with difficulty, and
saying, " Good day," she pedalled swiftly in at the double
gate, and he rode away, without a word or a look at the
house.

How changed was the face of all nature !   Where all
had been bright and joyous, with the clearness and sparkling stimulus of delicious champagne, it was now cold,
drear, in spite of the sunshine.   He was benumbed,—
wounded to the heart.   He felt a dull indignation that she
should be so unkind,—yes, frivolous.   It was hard and insulting !   No woman worthy of a thought would so disregard respectful sentiment !   Gad !   He had been sold
out,—margin gone, investment a failure !   And at his age !
A fine birthday, this !

To confess to a girl that he was lonely, in his privileged
situation in the world, to expose the throbbings of his
proud heart, when just on the point of craving her dear
love, with reasonable confidence of success in winning it,
then, *then*, at this supreme moment of a wildly joyous day,
to be advised to buy a d—   Hell and furies !   He would
not, he could not think of it !   He was never so insulted !

He gave Prince a cut with his cane, and tore along the
way in a frantic desire to get away from it—from himself.
Scowling, with grinding teeth and a dark flush which

mounted to his hair and extended to his neck, he rode up hill and down.

Philip Farnham was in a passion. Who can blame him?

At last, finding himself some miles from home, up the river, he drew the rein and slowly turned about. How could she have done it!—she, so loving and merciful, even to beasts and insects. Could she have intended to treat him so badly? There was no provocation for a deliberate insult. Was it merely a girlish misapprehension of his feelings? Perhaps a feminine defense against what she felt might follow! Or perhaps she, so fancy free, so artless in her frank friendship, had not dreamed of such possibilities for herself. She was such a child, no thought of love had come over her innocent heart. It was; yes, he knew it was merely a piquant retort! Or she was so fond of animals, she might have been sincere in suggesting a canine companion for his lonely hours. Here he laughed aloud. What a farce! Then, how rude he must have seemed. Why, what a hot-headed fool he was to leave her so! She must be puzzled, perhaps hurt, by his hasty actions. He could judge of that at the party, at any rate. Only three o'clock. Five hours to wait!

Prince was walking quietly along. Philip took his handkerchief from his pocket and wiped his perspiring forehead.

"Too, toot."

He turned quickly around.

"Hullo! Kupfer, old boy, how are you? Don't you know me, Kupfer?"

" Und Gold !" Philip cried, with pleasure and astonishment in his face.

The young man on the bicycle which had overtaken
him jumped nimbly to the ground, and came wheeling his
machine with hand extended to Philip, who sprang from
his horse's back to meet him.

"Where did you come from ? Did you drop from the
skies ?" exclaimed Philip, in wonderment, as they clasped
hands, with great heartiness and unalloyed pleasure at the
meeting. ·

" Well," answered the other, " I did not exactly drop,
though I got it on you, as I knew your back.   The fact
is," he said, looking down and kicking a stone out of the
road, " I got a little down in the mouth, and the doctor
sent me away from the bank for a few weeks.   As he insisted upon out-of-door exercise, I decided I would take a
run on my wheel.   I thought of you, when I was up the
river a ways, and was going to inquire for your place,
thinking you might possibly be home for the shooting.
And so, here we are."

"And I am delighted to see you, chum," said Philip.
" Now, you will come right home with me, and stay over
Sunday."

" All right, if it is convenient for you.   I must warn
you I am getting to be a tremendous feeder since I quit
home and live out of doors.   Nothing like it, is there ? "

So, taking to horse and wheel, they rode along the se-
questered roads.

Pretty soon Philip remarked, " Plummer, have n't you
grown thin ? Not in love, I hope. By the way, I met one

of those Weaver girls who used to be so fond of us at New Haven, in at the Windsor, the other day. Lord, how old she looked! I knew they had taken several classes along, before we came upon the stage, but I had no idea they were so antiquated. Great business, is n't it, these girls petting the students? Fun for the boys, but death to them, socially."

"Phil, do you know, I feel old! Out of college seven years, and tired of germans, yet without a wife, and living in rooms. Heigh-ho! Well, what 's the news?"

"I heard you were engaged to a beautiful girl, Felix. Your prospects, then, are promising."

"Y-yes, I am, or rather, I was. Kupfer, old chap, I am in trouble." He then told his tried friend of the circumstances which opened this narrative, but did not mention the name of his *fiancée*. "And so, she disappeared from town, leaving no clue. Knowing her pride as I do, I fear I shall never regain my old place in her affections. I flew around several days, making such inquiries as I could without giving my own desertion away to a set of curious friends. After a week of misery and unavailing search, I met a boy, Harry Dwinell, who told me he saw a party of ladies on tricycles—"

"The devil!"

"What 's the matter?"

"Nothing, go on."

"Who were on the road to the colleges. I blessed him and continued inquiries, out in that section. No one had seen them. Harry came to me the next day, and told me they had gone down the river, on a sketching tour, chaperoned by Mrs. F. W. Mather. I rushed for Mather, to see if she was among them, but he was off hunting. So I have followed them, sometimes losing the trail and going miles out of the way (they don't seem to keep to the main road), and at Haddam I lost them. I cannot get the slightest trace of the party anywhere. And if I should it is doubtful if she is one of them, anyway. I am about discouraged." He looked mournful, and pulled his blonde mustache in despair.

Philip drew a long breath.

" Felix," he said, " they are here."

" Here? Where?" The warm blood rushed over the lover's face.

"In Essex. I have met them."

" You have met them," echoed Felix, looking at his friend with a queer expression in his face. " How should you meet them? Was one of them," he asked eagerly, "a lovely girl with dark hair and beautiful eyes?"

" Yes," said Philip Farnham, with a sinking heart.

" Has she a slender, graceful figure?"

" Yes," said Philip, again.

"Has she the most refined face, the most delicate hands, the most queenly carriage and the sweetest voice in the world?"

"Yes." Philip forgot Mahala's irregular nose, which would be better termed cunning than elegant.

" Then I have found her, at last!" exclaimed Felix, in boundless joy.

Philip was overpowered with a jealousy which he tried manfully to smother, but failed. He almost hated his

friend.   Plummer had won a prize away from him at
Yale, and now—

"Can you tell me where to find her?" the impetuous
lover exclaimed. "If I can once get a look into Margery's
eyes—" he began to say.

"Margery! Miss Prescott?"

"Why, certainly. Who else?" demanded Felix, regarding his friend with surprise.

Philip reached over and seized his hand, shaking it
warmly, to the imminent danger of throwing the bicyclist
off his balance.

"Why, yes, indeed, who else?   I congratulate you, old
chum!   I am delighted to hear you say so!   I am sure
you will be able to make it up with her.   She is a beautiful girl, and every way worthy of you!"

Felix looked at Philip in some wonderment at his sudden access of enthusiasm, but, blinded by his own eagerness to see his lost love, soon forgot a glimmering suspicion
that Farnham might be in love with her himself, and was
feigning this effusive gladness.   He thought at first that
Kupfer was probably smitten with Margery and trying to
supplant him in her affections.

Then Philip told him who the party were; how he had
happened to meet them; that his mother had called upon
them, and that they were coming to the Farnham house
that evening to a small party.

It was with difficulty that Philip could restrain Felix
from immediately turning about then and there and flying
to Mr. Stearns's house.   But his friend reminded him that
he was not sure of a cordial reception, and that a surprise

which he would manage for him would throw Miss Prescott off her proud reserve, and prove at once to her lover whether she had forgiven him in her heart.

She might take a whim to uphold her outraged dignity before the others, he was warned, so Felix held his panting impatience in check and was kindly welcomed to dinner by Mrs. Farnham.

As for Philip, a complete revulsion of feeling had come over him and he wished the time away until the guests should arrive, and he have an opportunity to tell her— should he tell it all?   If he could only find her in one of her less mischievous moods!   One might as well try to force a kitten to pose for a picture, as to make her listen to love when she was in one of her merry trains.

CHAPTER XVIII.

Coming to the Party.

"NOT coming!" repeated Philip, as with bare head he stepped down to the carriage to hand out the ladies who had just arrived from Mr. Stearns's. "Not coming!" again said he, as Miss St. John assured him it was no mistake, and that her niece was not feeling well.

His heart fell within him. He had come forth with such abounding joy at the thought of touching her hand again, that the disappointment was all the more intense. He saw Miss St. John did not think it of much importance, and had already passed within, greeting the old gentleman, his father.

Margery was gathering up her flowing skirts and mounting to receive the warm welcome.

Seeing a look of sympathy in Mrs. Mather's sweet face, "What is it?" he asked, in under breath, as she gave him her hand and they went together up the stone steps to the door.

"Well, if it is not the capriciousness of feminine instinct in general, in this instance it is, that she is quite ashamed of herself and mortified at the effect of her conduct this morning. She gave me an account of your ride, said you left her offended, but professed she did not understand why. I never inquire closely into another's affairs, and therefore fail to understand why she would listen to no reason about it. She determined from the outset not to be present here this evening, nor to appear again to you. At this moment, I dare say, she is packing the trunk with her things, so there may be no excuse for detention as soon as the hour for departure arrives."

"Departure! Oh, don't speak of it, Mrs. Mather. How can I bear this!" As he detained her and hurried off his words, he passed his hand nervously across his face.

"Is it so?" she said gently, with a comprehensive look, which brought a low exclamation from him.

"I must, I shall see her again! Pardon me, I will go for her! I shall not be missed. Say not a word. I will make an excuse, and—" Mrs. Mather passed on to the dressing-room, glad to find her detention had not been noticed.

Margery was putting the little finishing touches to her incomparable toilet. Miss St. John was giving her energies to a pair of lovely, tinted kids, which were all but too snug.

Philip strode to his mother's side, who was smiling sweetly as their minister, who had arrived among the first (a clergyman of some years' residence among the people of Essex), was presenting his young half-sister, who had come to pass the winter at the parsonage, and whom he now introduced for the first time to the society of the place. He was assuring his hostess that he was rejoiced to accept so pleasant an opportunity to present his young relative to his friends.

"We are happy indeed, Mr. Butterfield, in this acquisition to our company. You are truly welcome, my dear," she said, turning to the young stranger, whose sparkling eye gave double value to the quiet "Thank you."

Then turning to the clergyman, Mrs. Farnham said, cordially, "I am more than glad to see you here to-night, sir, because—"

"You thought, being Saturday, that a minister might not care to be out, but," he said, smiling genially, "birth-days must be attended to, and we shall close our festivities at an early hour. I would not miss welcoming in Philip's next year, for a great deal."

"I must present my son to you, Miss Butterfield; and father, where is he?" she added, casting her eyes about the rooms.

"I spoke with him, in the hall, just now," answered the minister. "He said he would return here in a moment."

Philip entered with such rapid movement, and his hasty words were so quickly spoken that his mother found no time to detain him for an introduction to the stranger.

"I shall be back in a moment, mother. Something requires my attention outside." He whirled away and was at the stable before his mother could arrange her sentence of inquiry. It was so seldom that her son was disturbed from his deliberate composure, and so rarely excited to any hasty action, that she presumed some stupidity on the part of those preparing the entertainment had come to his knowledge and he was of necessity called to correct it.

Philip was shortly at the gate of Mr. Stearns's house. He dropped the lines, and sprang from the buggy. "How fortunate Tom's team was there ready! I shall make it right with him," said he, as he fastened the horse.

After the friends had gone from the house, and left Mahala alone, the house-keeper concluded to visit a sick neighbor, whom she frequently waited upon. She asked Miss Wright to excuse her for half an hour. The front door she left unlocked, for as she stepped out she said, " I will be back in a few minutes, Miss Wright. You need not fear anyone's coming. No one is apt to come in of an evening here, unless to borrow the paper or to see Mr. Stearns on business, and it is too late for that now."

As Mahala sat by the open fireplace, where a bright burning log lay, now smoking, now blazing, for want of something to do she had turned it over two or three times. She felt such perfect wretchedness at being left alone, and an utter despair of bettering the situation by going over and over it in her mind. As she sat, bending towards the fire, with the old-fashioned brass-headed tongs in her hand, half admiring their glitter, half watching the blaze, but under all, depressed and miserable, she heard the quick roll of the carriage, the step of the horse. She dropped the tongs. She started to her feet. She felt unprotected. She clasped her hands together tightly. Standing midway between the fire and door, she listened. She could hear her own heart-beats. Steps she heard—quick steps. What should she do? Turn out the lights? Oh, that those shades were down! How foolish!—perhaps the man had returned for something the girls had forgotten.

Yes, what a silly thing she was! Goodness, how her heart beat! Since that horrid Irishman attacked them in the woods she trembled at every sound.

There was a knock. She must go, then. She had sat there regardless of the undrawn curtain. Philip had seen her as he stepped quickly along the piazza. He saw she was alone. Before she had reached the door, his hand was on the knob. Without thinking he might alarm her, he opened the door. She started back in fear. Then, as he came apologetically forward, she gave a little nervous laugh. "O-ho," she said, and burying her face in her hands, she turned half around and dropped into a chair by the door.

He saw he had frightened her. Full of deep feeling himself, he stopped a moment, to gain self-possession. He laid off his great coat, and came forward rubbing his hands, for, with the cool of the evening, and the burning of his brain and heart, they were chilled. He walked into the parlor, closed the door, stood a moment in silence before the fire, acting mechanically, thinking only of her.

This had given time for Mahala to collect herself. Leaving her place she came forward and settled negligently into the easy rocker, where she had previously been sitting.

Each felt they had a part to play. Each meant to play it well. Philip turned a glowing face to her. "I have come for you," he said, in deep undertone.

Mahala forgot the party, forgot her friends, forgot the whole world.

Philip stood before her. He had come for her!

She gave a little gasp. " Come for me ? " she repeated, and then it burst upon her. Why, he means to the party !

" Oh, but I am not ready," she said.

" No ? But you will get ready, will you not ? "

What pleading in the voice and eye ! Could she resist ? It was not authoritative either; if it had been, she would have said " No " at once. " It is impossible."

He quietly stepped towards her. She arose looking full into his magnetic eye. He reached out his hand. Hers met it. For a second they stood. There was no premeditation, it was all spontaneous, involuntary. The peace was made.

He laid his other hand on hers.

" Miss Wright, we all want you there. Will you not return with me ? I will wait as long as is necessary, but I am sure you will come."

Mahala dropped her eyes under his burning gaze. He seemed to be reading her through and through.

What—what did this manner mean ?

" I will," she said, with a new submissiveness.

A wave of triumphant feeling rushed over Philip's senses. He threw it off as ungenerous. Deep love was yearning in his breast.

" Then, get ready," he said, quietly. " You are beautiful, now. You cannot array yourself more, in my eyes ; but for others, perhaps—yes, for others, perhaps," he murmured as he bit his nether lip. Still holding her little hand, he touched his lips to it, and put her from him. Then, opening the door to let her pass out : " Go, now. I will wait."

" I will not be long," she sang out joyously, as she tripped up the stairs, her face all dimpled with smiles.

" So the pink silk is not all for naught," she said in girlish ecstacy, as she drew forth the lovely dress and shook out its sheeny folds and tossed it on the bed. "And all I planned has come to naught. *Mais dieu dispose*,—is it not always so? I meant to be so cold and indifferent. I meant—oh, my hair will do!" and she turned about and looked in the glass.

" I won't have a flower, even. I will just button up this," she said, as she put on her waist. "I won't stop to dress my feet; I'll slip these under my cloak. I can put them on when I get there." She went to the closet and took down her aunt's warm sketching-cloak.

" Heavens, what will they think of me! How could he leave? I will not keep him waiting a minute longer! Gloves! Oh, dear! where's my fan, and handkerchief?"

Her eyes fell on them the next instant, and she caught at some violet perfume, gave the bottle a little shake over her handkerchief, and touched it to her eyes and lips before hastily gathering up her voluminous draperies under the friendly cloak.

Philip still stood, his elbow resting on the mantel, staring into the smouldering fire, the sputtering log every now and then giving a turn to his vision. How differently it had come out!

" I thought to appeal, to humble myself, to meet her irony— her banter,—to contend, to be baffled, perhaps, and return discomfited. No, I did not intend to allow myself to be overcome. I came to conquer."

A crowd of thoughts like these rushed through his brain. He seemed to have lived more in this day than in all his life before. Further he mused. "It has seemed a thing incredible to me, that in love a man will humiliate himself so before the woman he admires. But I could be content to sit at her feet all the day. How sweet she is! what music in her very step!

> "'She is coming, my own, my sweet.
> Were it ever so airy a tread,
> My heart would hear her and beat—'"

Mahala tripped down the stairway. The door opened, and, all muffled in cloak, not a vestige of the pink silk showing, she was there!

"Did I keep you long? Were you getting all tired out —worrying lest they should miss you from the house?"

"Oh, no; I was not thinking of them. I was recalling something from Tennyson."

"Do you like Tennyson?" she asked, as he opened and closed after her the street door. His reply did not reach her as she ran ahead in her excitement to jump into the buggy. She almost stumbled over the quiet house-keeper, who was feeling for the gate-latch.

"Oh," she said, "I have concluded to go to the party, Mrs. Bronson. Good-night."

"Did you say you liked Tennyson?" said she, as they were fairly tucked under the blanket, and the horse going at a rapid pace along the dim road. "He is the tonic that I take in regular doses at stated periods for the health of my soul," and she laughed, low and sweet.

"In the same way that I go to 'Sartor Resartus,' I pre-

sume, in moments of mental debility, and spasmodic dis-
taste for lighter food," answered Philip. " Yes, I am fond
of Tennyson, too. At one period of my callow youth, his
poems were my almost daily recreation, and I was particularly prone to reading them aloud to lady friends during
college vacations, under shady trees or by the seashore,
you know. Although now I am past those boyish enthusi-
asms, I still retain a sincere admiration for the poet, and
I find that many charming bits of his inimitable descrip-
tions and sentiments remain in my memory."

They were nearing Farnham House, when Philip said,
" By the way, Miss Wright, do you know Felix Plummer
of Hartford ?"

"Know Felix? Well, I should say I did! Felix, why
he is Margie's betrothed. One of the noblest fellows in
the world !"

" You may then, perhaps, be surprised to know that he
is here."

"Here?"

" Yes, in Essex ; at my house."

"Why, how came he there? Do you know him? How
delighted Margie will be to see him. I did not know that
she expected him."

Philip, perceiving that she had no knowledge of the
breach between the lovers, which Felix had confided to
him, merely spoke of their former friendship at college,
and told her that the meeting of the afternoon was totally
unexpected to both of them.

Mahala had an idea in her wise little head that Margie

would be also surprised to see Mr. Plummer, but kept her own counsel on the matter.

"Here we are. I will lead you by a side-way up stairs, so that no one will notice that we are late."

Robert stepped to the carriage to take the lines as it drew up to the house, and Philip led her in at the side-gate. To a maid who stood in the hall he said, "Conduct Miss Wright to the dressing-room."

CHAPTER XIX.

The Party.

TO return to Margery. A tremor had passed through her proud heart (now doubly wounded by the apparent indifference of her lover to her conciliating letter, which she had written to him with such reluctance to abase her pride, yet unwilling to do injustice to him) and had taken the nerve from her grasp as she opened the box containing her white pongee silk. A tide of recollections flooded her soul and caused her for an instant to become ghastly pale.

"Oh, if I had not sent for this one," she said, in pain; "I could have gone through·it, with almost resignation, in any other. But another party, and wearing this!"

She leaned on the foot of the bedstead and covered her face with her hands. "It will be the third time I have worn it. Oh, so happy the first evening. So wretchedly miserable the second! How can I put it on again!"

She dashed a tear from her eye, hearing the gay voice of Mrs. Mather, who ascended the stairs at that moment to robe herself for the evening. She turned from the dress on the bed, which seemed a ghost of dead hopes, and

was in the act of loosening her heavy hair before the mirror, when her friend entered. Her averted face was not
noticed, or at least not remarked on, as she uncoiled her
long tresses. Proceeding with her toilet, she said, "Do
help me, Julie! This maze of drapery, somehow, I cannot
manage."

"Well, I don't wonder, my love," said Julie, taking the
dress in hand. "You have it all twisted. The right
side of the overskirt on the wrong of the underskirt."

"Nothing is really easy to get into except our wheel-
suits and our wrappers," said Margery, trying to extricate
herself from the confusion. "I know this is to be fastened
up somewhere. Miss Fordyce said my maid would know,
but I am sure I do not. I always turn it the wrong way,
I think," she said, not sure of the fact, but trying to get
some idea into her mind except the one that would insist
on obtruding itself.

Once in the dressing-room at the Farnhams' she had
no time to think of herself. The straggling groups which
they met as they threaded their way there foretold them
of an interesting evening. Merry girls were already
giggling on one side, while young men were holding themselves aloof in doorways and along the hall.

Some audible whispers made the friends smile, as an excited curiosity could not be withheld.

"Tricyclers," said one little fellow, who had been asked
only as companion to his older sister.

Mrs. Mather smiled and nodded to him as she passed
along, recognizing the little fellow who had one day in
mischief tried to run a race with them on their wheels,

and who ended his burst of speed with a tumble in the
dust.

Margery and Miss St. John were at the dressing-room
door ready to descend to the reception below, loitering an
instant for their companion, when a maid stepped quickly
to Margery and laid in her hand a loosely-folded white
package. She said: "A friend asks if you will wear
these, miss," and was gone before Margery could ask a
question.

She turned to Mrs. Mather, asking, "What shall I do?
Would you wear these?"

"What?"

"Why, these," displaying some choice hot-house roses.

"Oh, how lovely! Wear them? Of course. Just
what you need to brighten up your dress, and your cheek,
too, my love," said Mrs. Mather, a little anxiously. "Where
did they come from?"

"Oh, I do not know. Mrs. Farnham, perhaps, sent
them. How very kind, was it not? Do help me put
them somewhere. Where shall it be? *Bouquet de cor-
sage?*" said Margery, laying them against her waist.

"No, they get so broken there." Here, let me," and
Julie shook them loosely in her hold. Catching at some
of the flowing lace around Margery's neck, and, entwining
a cluster, she fastened them with bewitching grace on the
left side.

"Just above your heart, my dear. How lovely and fragrant they are! Now your dress is perfect, and yourself—"

"Do let's go, Julie. Others want to come here," broke
in Margery, quickly, and turned away.

"Well, take these in your hand," said Mrs. Mather, gathering up the remaining roses. "Enfold the stems in your handkerchief."

Mr. Stearns awaited the trio at the hall-door and descended, leading Miss St. John, whose bright, happy face showed how much she was enjoying.

"Was it not too provoking in Mike," whispered Margery, "not to come?"

Mrs. Mather smiled with inward satisfaction.

They soon made their way to the hostess, and were so kindly greeted with warm reception and introduction upon all sides, that each was soon lost to the other, engrossed by the interest of new acquaintance. Margery alone fell into the background, and soon wandered listlessly into a little recessed flower-room, which adjoined the library. There she sat, alone and sad, in a low chair, with the flowing train of her creamy dress lying upon the floor at her side. She slowly opened and shut her fan, as she looked with dreaming eyes before her. She let her hands drop into her lap. It was too much. She could not bear it. If she could but get away. Somewhere. She looked around despairingly, and — "Felix!"

The color which had flickered in her pale cheeks on her first arrival, but which had faded and died out as she sat alone, thinking, always thinking, of him, now blazed in her radiant face as she held out her arms to him with this low cry, and half arose to her trembling feet.

"Margie! Darling! Oh, my love, why did you leave me without a word? How could you leave me so? I am not so bad as you thought. You have almost broken my

heart!" and Felix came and seized her gloved hands, covering them with kisses and kneeling before her, bowed his blonde head upon them.

"Felix!" she said, in a low voice. He looked up. "I am to blame; I was jealous, wounded," she said, very gently. "I am sure I have wronged you. Can you forgive me? Did you receive my letter? Were you too angry to answer it?"

Glance now a moment at that pink figure standing expectant, almost on tip-toe, at the door of the dressing-room. She had stepped out from her wraps, her cheek nigh matching the color of the silk she wore, which was of soft rose. The dainty little foot encased in black silk stocking and kid slipper, the black, undressed glove reaching above the rounded elbow, the vivacious turn of the jauntily set head with never a curl quite in place and not one out of place, tilting first on one side, then on the other, displaying to advantage the full, white throat, set off by a broad band of black velvet, she stood waiting for Philip.

Meanwhile the young host walked along the upper hall, looking for the little gray figure which had stood with him in the light of the fire but a space ago in Mr. Stearns's parlor. Where was she? He peered among the company below. He had ventured but a moment before as far as the door of the ladies' dressing-room, but, seeing only the back of a pink silk dress, had as cautiously retired as he had incautiously advanced, thinking to find only his sweet, gray girl. "Can she have gone down without me?" he murmured. "Perhaps mother met her, or the little chaperone. But no, surely she would wait for me."

The black fan was now raised in the air, and shut together with a little "crack" at him. The pink figure now
took on a look natural to another garb."

"Why, what a dolt! That I should fail to know her
under this guise," said Philip, as he hastened to meet her.

"Here I am," she laughed. "Don't you know me?"
perceiving his bewildered state. Her pearly teeth glistened
between her laughing lips. She placed her hand on his
arm, and he, half-dazed, regarded her with delight. He led
her to his mother.

"I persuaded Miss Wright to come," he said to her,
quietly, "you see, mother."

Miss St. John had scarcely recovered from the stunning
surprise of Felix Plummer in loving attendance upon Margery, attired in his bicycle costume, when her eyes fell
upon her niece in all her bravery of evening toilet talking
animatedly with young Peterson, who was looking an un-
told admiration. He was a young cousin of the Farnham's, and while not exactly Philip's prototype, was quite
of the family bearing, being a son of the sister of Philip's
mother.

Miss St. John advanced upon the unconventional girl,
with indignation in her eye, just in time to see her gracefully accept the arm of Tom Peterson and go to join the
frolicsome games in the other room.

As she passed her astonished relative, tossing her head
a little one side and looking back over Peterson's shoulder,
she said with smiling complacency, "Aren't we having a
lovely time, this evening, auntie?"

As Philip and Mahala stood together awaiting their turn

in the dance later in the evening, she said, archly, " What would your conservative English cousin of the 'Lindsay branch' say to such an escapade as ours this morning?" referring to a lady Philip had spoken of, as having given him the lovely intaglio which he wore.

"Oh, as to that talk of conservatism," replied Philip, smilingly, "it is held but a tame, light amusement, this gliding swiftly, quietly, modestly along on those wheels, compared with the exciting, wild delight of spurring a blooded steed over a six-foot rail; an amusement which has been a sport of English dames for centuries. But, perhaps," continued he, as together they glided across the floor, "that has helped to make the fine English physique."

With songs and dancing, with laughter and chatter, and flirting beyond conjecture, with piano-playing, with artistic and literary conversations in the library, quiet words in the flower-room between lovers, looking at pictures, promenading and sipping ices, the evening passed away.

The guests departed. Ladies in shawls and fleecy rigolets came muffled to the door, congratulations and best wishes were exchanged, carriages rolled up to and away from the porch, and the party was ended. Then, when the lights in the rest of the house were out, and everything so quiet after the pleasant din, Plummer and Farnham sat an hour in the library, before the open fire. As the old clock in the hall struck the hour of twelve, they bade "good night" in subdued tones, and went to rest.

CHAPTER XX.

—·—

The Finish.

DURING the Sunday that immediately followed the events of the last chapter, it was decided by the older tricycle tourists not to prolong their trip beyond the place which had proved so hospitable and interesting a resting-place.

It was evident, Miss St. John said, as she sat with Mrs. Mather in their chamber after church, and looked over and arranged a collection of sketches, that Margery now had no thought but of her regained happiness.

Mrs. Mather, who was jotting down some amusing notes for the delectation of her husband on her return, arrested her busy pen, and raising her face with pleasure shining in it, said with sympathetic warmth, how glad she was that the dear girl was reconciled to her lover again. She confessed that the sight of her ill-concealed sadness, during all their pleasant journey, had been a weight upon her mind. It was so delightful to see them happy together once more.'

"Yes," Miss St. John had answered, slowly, with her eyebrows raised, as she carelessly scratched the outline of a cat's head on the margin of Saturday's *Courant* which

(270)

lay upon the table, "but it made her rather indifferent to the continuance of the journey. Margery was living now in a supreme content, which showed in every action, was heard in her musical voice and shone in her soulful eyes. It was beautiful as a study; she would like to paint her face with that expression, as Hero, immediately after Leander crept ashore on the termination of one of his long swims, but her associates were for the nonce forgotten."

Mrs. Mather said she was sure, for her part, she was willing to be forgotten for a time in view of Margery's joy in the presence of her lover. A little red spot came into her cheeks, and she looked reproachfully at the artist.

Miss St. John said she believed that was not the point. She could also survive without Margery's constant companionship. The question was of the advisability of continuing a trip when at least one of the party had lost interest in it. It was not likely that Margery would be separated from Mr. Plummer, now. He had called to take her to church, was riding with her then, and probably would again make his appearance in the parlor in the evening.

" Why, Dude," said Mrs. Mather, opening her blue eyes, "surely you cannot begrudge Margie—"

"I do not begrudge anything to any one," Miss St. John replied, with emphasis upon the objectionable word, and making a shower of dots on the paper. "I merely say that we may as well end the trip here, because we cannot have Felix Plummer accompany us and enjoy the absolute freedom and unconventional pleasures which have distinguished this outing until we came to Essex."

Mrs. Mather saw that something more than was apparent upon the surface of her friend's remarks occasioned this acidity in the general tone of Miss St. John's demeanor. She felt guilty about something, and as if Dude was only waiting for a chance to make unpleasant accusations upon her. Much to her relief, Mahala here came into the room, with not a shadow of anything unusual in her merry face, and said she thought it was high time some one came and waked up Uncle Stearns, who had been snoring frightfully under his paper ever since dinner.

So they went down stairs, and the day passed away.

Mahala listened with a surging of blood at her ears, when the door-bell rang at evening. A great pang of disappointment smote her heart when, peeping over the balustrade, she saw Mr. Felix Plummer enter alone. But she had seen *him* at church, and the few casual words he had said to her, as they came down the steps, contained such a world of meaning, in *his* voice, with *his* eyes looking down at her so! Philip was doubtless bound by filial affection to remain with his parents this evening. He always did right and was so thoughtful and kind!

She stilled a faint sigh, and suddenly brightening as a mischievous idea came into her head, she ran down stairs in haste. She knew Margery was staying to add some imaginary adornments to her beautiful person before the mirror, so to meet with greater favor in her lover's eyes, and she flew noiselessly down, scarcely touching the steps with her slippered feet, with her blue gown floating behind, and entered the dim parlor where sat Felix before the fire, waiting. Stealing up behind him, the merry elf

placed her hands upon his shoulder and chanted with a
sob in her voice, into his ear :

> "Would you come back to me, Margie, Margie,
> In the old kindness that I knew,
> I would be so faithful, so loving, Margie,
> Margie, Margie, tender and true—"

"Mahala Wright! You little witch!" exclaimed Felix
with a joyous laugh, as he seized her hands and brought
her around to the front. "What are you talking about?"
Then he said, in a low tone, as a wave of tenderness swept
over his mobile features, "Tell me, Mike, did she confide
to you that she was unhappy before I came?" and he
looked up to the kittenish person before him, all eagerness
to hear of her—his love.

"Tell me? Not a word!" was the answer. "Girls, I
wish you to understand, sir, do not go about telling everything they know," and she gave her head a little toss as
she stood back and regarded him with considerable superi-
ority. "I'll guarantee, now," she said, "that you went
about confessing *your* bad feelings to half a dozen people."

He could not deny it.

"Poor dear Margie suffered in silence. Now, Felix
Plummer, I have been smothering my indignation ever
since I began to see that something was wrong with her,"
pursued Miss Wright, with a savage expression which was
scarcely imposing upon her dimpled face, "and now I
must say, that whether it was you or anyone else that has
made her sad for an hour, he deserves—"

"But tell me, Mahala," pleaded Felix, paying no heed
to her, only waiting to hear the assurance again that his

w. & w.—18

beloved had sighed for him. "Was she sad? Did the others suspect, too? Was she lovely and unselfish as ever? Did you perceive that it was I that she was sorrowing for?"

His blue eyes were moist with earnestness and loving regret, as he held a fold of her skirt when she would have turned away.

"Well, yes," said the girl, as she looked kindly at him, remembering that Margie was happy once more. "I did suspect it was you, Felix, who had grieved her, as she never mentioned your name, and seemed so *distrait* sometimes, in spite of her effort to be like herself."

"Ah, poor girl!" said the lover, bending his head for an instant and breathing hard. "But, Mahala," he said, looking up quickly again and reddening, "don't you really know what it—what our slight misunderstanding was about?" He watched her face closely.

"Not a word, I tell you, Felix," she answered, meeting his gaze fully. "But it does not need a very deep mind to guess," she thought, "when any one has seen you being led around by that Bangtry creature."

Felix rose to his feet and expanded his chest deeply. "Well," he said, looking towards the door, "then you never will."

"Well," mimicked Mahala, making him a sweeping courtesy, "I don't want to, Sir Orpheus." Then she came and gave him her hand with a friendly grasp. "I am only glad you have found your Eurydice. Good-bye! I'll skip now; Margery is coming," and with a bound she dashed out of the parlor and ran with considerable violence into the arms of Philip Farnham, who had just entered the hall.

"Oh! I beg pardon! I did not know that you—did I hurt you much?" said Mahala, blushing and breathless, as she made an effort to regain her composure.

"Well, not seriously, I think," said Philip, as he held the sweet confusion of curly hair, blue ribbons, white hands and fluttering form for an instant to his breast. "Did you not know I was coming?" he asked, as he let her go.

She stood by the newel in the hall, tracing the scroll-work with her forefinger as she looked down and smiled in trembling happiness. While he drew off his gloves and hung his overcoat upon the rack he said he had brought Plummer over, and had tried to be considerate and consume as much time as possible in tying and blanketing his horse.

"One should never intrude upon lovers' meetings. Do you not think so?" he said, in a low voice, as he returned to her.

Mahala did not speak.

"Solely on their account, Miss Wright," he said, as he stood so close beside her that her head was almost against his breast again, and looked down at her with a humorous expression around his mouth, which changed in the eyes to a deep tenderness, "so as not to disturb them, Mahala, don't you think we had better go into the sitting-room?" He laid his hand protectingly under her elbow as he spoke.

"Yes—that is, perhaps they would like it better," answered Mahala, raising her eyes bashfully, but ending the sentence with a low laugh.

Mr. Stearns looked up benignantly over his glasses as they entered the room, and, after making the caller welcome and asking a few polite questions concerning himself and parents, he took the *Independent* and retired to the kitchen, professing that he had a very profound article to read, and could not think in such a chatter.

Hearing subdued conversation below, Miss St. John had come out to the head of the stairs, just at the moment when Philip and Mahala were passing into the sitting-room. She took in the confiding attitude of the young girl, the blushing, artless look of trustfulness up into the warm, brown eyes of the tall man who bent so gracefully his fine head near to hers, at a glance. The air of guardianship with which Philip Farnham clasped Mahala's arm as they passed from view was a revelation, indeed ! ·

Miss St. John stood a picture of despair. What she had vaguely feared had come to pass. She clasped her hands in distress. Then she walked into the chamber and said, as she sat down with a hopeless sigh, "Well, I suppose the only thing to be done now, is to go home and give an account of ourselves."

"I am ready to turn about at any time, Dude, that you think best," said Mrs. Mather, who had been terribly homesick, if the truth must be known.

"Although we have not reached the salt water, where I expected to get some lovely marines," pursued the lady, as if not hearing Mrs. Mather's cautious answer, "it seems to me we had better return at once; I mean, to-morrow."

She sat making imaginary cross-hatching in a despondent manner, on the arm of the rocking-chair, with the end of her finger.

"Oh, how glad I am to hear you say that," said Julie, with a joyous light in her face. "I have a letter here telling me that Fred is home, and the poor fellow asks if we are not almost ready to come back." She would have taken the missive from her pocket if she had received the least encouragement from the other, but she did not: "I was going to be brave, and not speak of it," she continued, resting her hand upon the letter in her pocket. "I did not intend to be the one to beg off; but I am ready to go at any minute now." She arose with alacrity and began to pack up some stationery.

"Then, suppose we take the boat to-morrow night. You see as well as I do that Mr. Plummer will be an *attaché* ol the party henceforth."

"Yes, undoubtedly," answered Mrs. Mather.

"Dude," she said, after a pause, faltering a little, "how about Mahala?"

"What about Mahala?" said the aunt, dryly.

"Why—why, don't you think Philip Farnham is very much—attracted to her?"

"I am no judge in these things," the artist replied, shortly. She looked sharply at the little woman who sat folding and creasing the newspaper in an embarrassed manner upon her lap. "What do *you* think? You seem gifted with an understanding in these matters that surpasses—"

"What do you mean, Dude?" demanded Mrs. Mather, flushing hotly. "If you intend to insinuate—"

"I insinuate nothing," returned Miss St. John, smiling faintly. "There seems to be no call for an insinuation from me, as you seem already to defend yourself from something I should never have dared to suspect."

"Dude," said Mrs. Mather, piteously, wincing under the gaze of the sterner woman, "you cannot be sorry that Philip Farnham evidently loves your niece. He is one of a thousand. Of most desirable family connections, irreproachable in character and personal appearance, unquestionably generous and kind. What more would you have?"

"Really, you make out an attractive list of advantages in your"—she was about to say *protégé*, but perhaps recollecting her own predilection in his favor, and perhaps warned by an ominous look in Mrs. Mather's eye that it were prudent not to push her too far, she thought better of it, and said, "friend. Oh, Mr. Farnham is well enough, but I am so worried to have it happen to Mahala."

She spoke as if the girl had contracted scarlet fever or caught whooping-cough, and picked nervously at the bit of fine lace on her dress.

Seeing her so truly troubled about an affair which seemed in every way beautiful and interesting to her, Mrs. Mather recovered her composure somewhat, and asked: "Do you want her to remain unmarried?"

"I do not know that I wish to decide for her in any way. But, she is only nineteen! I want her to have her frolic out. The hard realities of life come all too soon.

She has only begun to live. With character and tastes unformed, it seems a pity to have her absorbed into the personality of a man."

Now, although Miss St. John seemed usually not to have acquired the fastidious objection to the male sex in general which most maiden ladies come to feel, it cropped out a little now that she was touched with the idea that her niece was giving her affections to "a man." She got along so very well without one, and saw so many things in other women's husbands that she knew she never could put up with.

"Well, Dude," said Julia, with a little softening in her tones, and a look of sincere pity for the joys unsealed to her, which scarcely put the spinster more at her ease, "from your stand-point I can see how you feel. But I was married at eighteen and have never for one moment in the ten years regretted it. Instead of the absorption, it was the rounding out of girlish character."

"Yes, yes. I suppose I am talking against human nature," said Miss St. John, sighing. "Listen, Julie: while I would not raise a finger to encourage, or prevent, this thing, I must say I regret exceedingly that this rapid fancy has sprung up while the girl is under my care."

She shook her head and sighed again. "I have wished a thousand times since the day of the encounter in Farnham's woods that there might be some excuse to go home; but I have not been able to find or invent a plausible one. Well, perhaps it is fate! But I shall not know how to face my sister when I tell her." She arose and walked around the room in a sort of desperation.

"Tell her nothing," Mrs. Mather quickly said. "There may be nothing to tell. If there is, let Mahala tell it. Perhaps Philip may. But, Dude," she said again, "I wish I knew you did not blame me in any way. I did not make them fall in love. I only—"

"You only smoothed the way. Do not imagine I have not seen your truly feminine maneuvers to make occasion for the two persons whom you admire to fall in love with each other. Well, Julie, I do not blame you. It was doubtless inevitable, without your gentle assistance. I know every happy wife will do all she can to help others into the same condition."

"Well, why not, Dude?"

The artist shook her head. "It is a grave responsibility to assume."

Mrs. Mather was miserable. How she wanted to get home and tell Fred! Dude almost made her feel as if she did not want to live. Would the Wrights blame her for anything? No, she would stand by her best judgment, which told her that Philip Farnham was a desirable connection for any family.

Miss St. John went on to say that if she should speak from her own feelings she would be glad to have Mahala forego the happiness, the companionship of married life, and so escape its wearing trials. She felt that the joys of maternity were ever overshadowed by a haunting care and recurring vicissitudes. The wifely love was often tinged with anxiety lest the other half of herself should fall short of noble manhood. But she supposed it was the intention of an inscrutable Providence for women to marry.

Mrs. Mather thanked heaven for the limitless joys of a natural, dual existence.

It was evident the next morning that the respectful attentions of a refined young gentleman to her niece did not seem such an irremediable calamity as when she first received the shock of conviction that Mahala had a lover. She was bright and good-natured as usual at breakfast, and chatted agreeably of the trip while they talked of going home. As they finished, she said, impressively, but with an ominous twinkle in her eye as she pulled a paper from her pocket, "Mr. Stearns and friends: I have here a document which I wish to read and comment upon, as showing conclusively the mutability of human plans in general and the unreliability of young femininity in particular."

"What is it, Dude?" said Mrs. Mather, folding her napkin.

"Read it, Miss St. John," said Mr. Stearns, moving his chair back from the table and taking a new position, with anticipation in his face.

"It will not reflect too severely upon me, I hope," said Margery, blushing in some perturbation.

"Oh, auntie!" screamed Mahala, as the lady unrolled it in another way and spread it out before her. "It is my list of Rules and Regulations! Where did you get it? Give it to me!" and she made a rush around the table for her aunt.

As she seized her arm, Miss St. John quickly transferred the folio to the other hand, and said: "Mr. Stearns, will you undertake to keep this young woman in order while I read?"

Mr. Stearns arose with mock solemnity, and taking Mahala by the arms held them behind her as he sat in his chair and bade Miss St. John to go on.

"Before proceeding, I wish to tell you, Mr. Stearns, and to remind these ladies," she said, looking severely upon them, "that these Rules and Regulations, intended to guide the conduct of these excursionists, were drafted by Miss Mahala Wright and sworn to by these other persons."

"So did you swear to them, Aunt Dude," interrupted Mahala, who was now sitting contentedly on the arm of Mr. Stearns's chair, while his broad hand rested affectionately on her shapely shoulder.

"I did," answered the artist, calmly, "and I defy any one to find an occasion where I have broken the faith. Listen, Mr. Stearns," and amid much laughter from the old gentleman, whose generous bulk shook with amusement, she read the "cast-iron rules," as she chose to term them.

"Now," laying down the paper, she looked fixedly in turn at her three companions, who already began to laugh confusedly with uneasy color in their faces in anticipation of her speech.

"I charge Julie Mather, matron and chaperone of this party, with perjury, in that she has shamelessly written to her husband on sundry and divers occasions, once or twice audaciously scribbling love-letters under my very nose, while under the pretense of learning to sketch."

"Oh, Dude, did you see that?" exclaimed Julie, with a peal of merry laughter, and the ceremony of the occasion was somewhat disturbed as Miss St. John retorted, "Of course I did! Do you think I am blind?" and Margery and Mahala joined in the accusations of fraud against their faithful friend.

Girls are often ungrateful.

Order was at last restored and Miss St. John continued, "Of course, when such duplicity as this becomes known of a person, little responsibility in the discharge of her duties of gorgon, duenna, chaperone is to be expected."

Mahala began to grow pink.

"I therefore make no comment upon the gross neglect of duty apparent to my grieved perceptions, but which has been accepted as a matter of course by these two young women."

Margery gave Mrs. Mather a little pat on the shoulder and smiled gratefully into her eyes.

Mahala turned very red in the face, but said intrepidly, "Margie, who was it auntie was worried about, the book agent (it cannot be she was jealous while receiving so large a share of his agreeable smiles herself), or was it Jerry Bodge?" Again her audacity saved her.

"I further complain, Mr. Stearns," continued Miss St. John, "that the murderous weapon of thirty-two-caliber, carried by Mrs. Mather, has never been of the slightest comfort on trying occasions, having doubtless been left with the toy-pistols in the trunk."

"Now, Dude!" exclaimed Mrs. Mather, "I protest. It has never been out of reach except one day, when Margery borrowed it for target practice. I say that I have been in constant readiness to use it in case of any emergency. Confine yourself to facts, please."

"The objection is noted; I will. And now, perhaps, you will be interested to know how my toy-pistol saved me from annoyance; to term it nothing more alarming." She told them about her interview with the pack-peddler.

"Oh, auntie!"

"Why, Dude!"

"You brave creature!" exclaimed her surprised companions, while Mr. Stearns said with some vehemence that it was not a safe thing for women to be out around so, alone.

"Oh, I don't know," the artist said, unconcernedly, "I suppose I was in the same danger that any slight young man would have been."

Mr. Stearns saw that she would not understand any perils which might deter her artistic wanderings afield.

"Well, to conclude my remarks, Mr. Stearns and young women, I will say that until women become more disciplined than this company has proved itself to be, they will scream rather than use whistles; they will exhibit an indiscreet resentment of the manners of an insulting brute, and then fall back upon the gallantry of a Quixotic young man to deliver them from the direct results of impru—"

"Quixotic!"

"Oh, my dear Miss St. John!"

"You were very glad to welcome Don Quixote with frantic gesticulations to make haste, I noticed, and first to sing his praises after the rescue, I believe," said Mahala, indignantly aroused.

"Well I will stop, for I perceive I am becoming unpopular, though there is much I could say just here," and Miss

St. John seemed in very good humor, now that she had freed her mind. "I claim, however, that I am the only one in this party who has followed the rules agreed to, and kept the main idea of the trip in view throughout all."

"You certainly, then, ought to be happy, in close harmony with an approving conscience, Miss St. John," said Mr. Stearns, as they left the table. "Now, suppose you bring your sketches down stairs and let us look them over this morning."

"With pleasure," was the response.

At this time, late in the story, when the reader may be half vexed at having followed so simple a tale thus far, it would be imposing upon time and patience to relate how before noon Messrs. Plummer and Farnham came into view down the street on horseback and bicycle, and announced their desire to escort Margery and Mahala to ride.

To describe their merry excursion by wheels and horse might seem to us a repetition of a former jaunt. To recite any portion of their absorbing conversations would be tautology to all who have known the sweet intercourse of plighted troth, felt the repressed excitement of growing passion, or imagined them in their hearts.

No. Let them go through by-ways and hedges, over brambly knolls and along smooth paths, under the almost denuded trees, crackling brown leaves and dried sticks under rubber tires and horse's hoofs; overhead the late October sky which is beginning to pale at the approach of sullen November, on the brink of the beautiful river, as it blithely nears the end of its long journey from the little lake up in the mountains four hundred miles away ; laughing, loving, sighing, hoping, let them go, while Mrs. Mather packs her trunk and Miss St. John has one good final argument with Mr. Stearns upon the equal rights of women to work and—never mind! She will talk it.

It was evening when they left the house which had so kindly sheltered them for a few days. But how replete with experiences had been that brief visit!

They stood upon the wharf in their gray dresses, their wheels in careful charge of the baggage-man, their trunk upon a truck, in pleasant desultory chat, as they waited for the boat.

The weird glare of the lights flaring in a gentle wind which moaned over the dark river, the low tones of the few town stragglers who had hung around to see the boat in, carried an undertone of indefinable sadness to the heart of Uncle Stearns, who shivered a little, and bade them come under the adjoining shed until the boat arrived.

Felix Plummer was going to Hartford with Margery. His *bicycle run* had cured his sickness and he returned a well and happy man, looking forward with intense longing to a day—(They are married now.)

Philip Farnham, too, was there. It was his last hour with *her* unless—

"Mr. Farnham," Mahala said, low, "you will—will you not come to Hartford? It has been such a pleasant thing to know you. I—I—perhaps you would like to see Joe's aquarium!"

The throbbing of the paddle-wheels, rush! rush! rush! rush! came on the breeze from a mile down river.

"She's a-comin'!" said the baggage-man as he jumped down from his roost upon one of the large posts, and brushed imperceptible chips from his nether garments. "Don't none of you touch them machines," he said to his assistants. "*You* can put aboard that grindstun, 'n' them cheeses, and that pile of stuff there. I'll see to the trunk"

"Mahala!" said Philip, seizing her hands, as they stood in the shadow, "I love you. You know I will follow you anywhere, everywhere, if you will but let me. But if I do, Mahala—you must understand me—I shall ask for you. Will you say I may? Tell me! Shall I come to see you Wednesday before I return to New York, and tell your parents that you love me? May I, dear?"

Just then Miss St. John grimly raised her umbrella with a snap, and turning around from where she stood with Mrs. Mather and Mr. Stearns, she took a few quick steps and silently handed it to Philip. He instantly relinquished Mahala's hands, said "Pardon!" glancing up at the sky; but then catching a gleam in the artist's gray eye that he began to understand, he took it, accepting it as her benediction, and sought Mahala's answer under its friendly umbrage.

That Mrs. Mather heard something resembling a favorable answer, under the silken canopy, there is no doubt, as she immediately became afflicted with a rasping cough and called Uncle Stearns and Miss St. John to the edge of the wharf to see the boat make a landing.

The line was thrown, the gangs shoved out and the baggage trucks began to race over the plank before it was hardly ashore.   Then came a cry of joy from Julie.

"Oh, Fred!   Here I am!   There's my husband!"   And genial Mr. Mather sprang ashore and into his wife's arms.

"Ah, Uncle!   You have taken right good care of the girls!   Much obliged, sir!   I went to New York Saturday and returned by the boat to surprise the little lady.   I was going to take her home anyhow."

He looked fondly at her as she clung to his arm.

"What in thunder is Plummer doing down here?   Who is that toney fellow with the little Wright?   Thought this was to be exclusively a woman party!"

The wheels were carefully trundled on board.   Uncle Stearns promised to come up and visit them soon, and Philip—he would go to Hartford Wednesday morning!

And then the party went on board the boat.

www.ingramcontent.com/pod-product-compliance
Lightning Source LLC
Chambersburg PA
CBHW030617030726
47497CB00006B/1534